i

THE HONORABLE TRAITOR

OWEN CONLON

If Germany loses, it'll be a catastrophe for Germany. But if Hitler wins, it will be a catastrophe for mankind.

Admiral Wilhelm Canaris

To my parents.

All that time in the front room reading the encyclopedia did not go entirely to waste.

CHARACTERS

Lieutenant Ako Wolff: an officer of the Abwehr and secretly a member of Der Widerstand.

Admiral Wilhelm Canaris: the commander of the Abwehr and one of the main leaders of Der Widerstand.

Colonel Hans Oster: Canaris's trusted deputy within the Abwehr and a very active figure within Der Widerstand.

SS General Reinhard Heydrich: head of the Reich Security Main Office and a former naval subordinate of Canaris.

SS Colonel Walter Schellenberg: Heydrich's trusted deputy within the SD.

TERMINOLOGY

Abwehr: The Third Reich's military intelligence organization. It nominally handled foreign intelligence-gathering, though many of its functions overlapped with its rival body, the SD.

Der Widerstand: Literally 'The Resistance', the secret anti-Nazi movement within the Third Reich.

Kriegsmarine: The Third Reich's navy.

Luftwaffe: The Third Reich's air force. The literal translation of the term saw it retained for use after 1945.

Schutzstaffel (SS): Originally a paramilitary organization which acted as security for the Nazi Party, it developed into a powerful state within a state under Heinrich Himmler.

Sicherheitsdienst (SD): The intelligence wing of the SS. Supposed to handle domestic intelligence-gathering, it developed a deadly rivalry with the Abwehr.

Reich Security Main Office (RSHA): an umbrella security organization comprising of the SD, the Gestapo secret police and the ordinary *Kriminalpolizei*, or Criminal Police.

Wehrmacht: The unified armed forces of the Third Reich, consisting of the *Heer* (army), the *Kriegsmarine* (navy) and the *Luftwaffe* (air force). However, the Wehrmacht was often used simply to refer to the army.

NKVD: Soviet intelligence. The precursor to the KGB.

PROLOGUE

Moscow,
July 25, 1941

"So, we're agreed then. You shall do us this favor?"

Ivan Stamenov hesitated. As ambassador of the Tsardom of Bulgaria, he had full diplomatic protection under international law.

Even so, such niceties could be conveniently ignored in wartime, especially with the Germans having surrounded Smolensk and no more than 10 days advance from Moscow.

He lifted the spoon, taking his time by blowing on the hot soup. Every extra second bought him time to consider his position. The *kharcho* was excellent, the spiced beef melting in his mouth and contrasting sharply with the sour cherry plum puree.

The seat under his backside in this private booth was soft black leather, and the starched white tablecloth was crisp and spotless. It was as luxurious as one might expect of a restaurant patronized by the elite of Soviet society.

There were other, cruder reasons for Stamenov to be careful of how he responded. Aragvi had opened just three years beforehand, just a few minutes' drive from the notorious headquarters of the NKVD secret police, the Lubyanka. It was rumored it had been designed personally by the equally notorious head of the NKVD, Lavrentiy Beria.

It was also rumored the tables were bugged, the better to catch small talk from the foreign dignitaries the NKVD wined and dined here. Furthermore, the man he was talking to, Beria's emissary Pavel Sudoplatov, was said to have personally organized the assassination of Leon Trotsky in Mexico.

"Explain to me again exactly what it is you require of me, comrade," Stamenov answered at last. "I'm having trouble grasping the nature of this request."

Sudoplatov grinned.

He understood Stamenov's hesitancy, and the ambassador's fears were not without foundation. But the tapes from these recordings would be delivered directly to Beria himself and, once listened to, would be destroyed.

Even if this scheme worked, the fact that the Soviet Union had originally proposed it would never be allowed to exist for prosperity.

However, Stamenov would comply with the NKVD request.

Everyone did, eventually.

1

One week later,
The border of Latvia and Estonia

Sergeant Ako Alfredo Wolff studied the map, spread out over a tree stump, which was rooted in a large clearing at the very edge of the German front lines. A forest separated his men from their objective.

The village was around two miles away and situated right on the main highway, if you could call it that, to Leningrad.

Riga had been taken the previous week, but there had been no time for him to visit the Latvian capital as he had desperately hoped.

Despite their exhaustion and their filthy uniforms and underwear, his requests for a few days' leave had been turned down. His unit was far too valuable to spare from the fighting.

The Brandenburger Regiment had become a victim of its own success. Technically under the command of the *Abwehr*, Germany's military intelligence, rather than the Army proper, the regiment went where it was needed most.

Two weeks ago, they had ensured the quick fall of Latvia's second-biggest city, Daugavpils, taking the main bridge leading to the town by driving up in two captured trucks while posing as Red Army troops fleeing the relentless German advance.

On that occasion, it had been 'half-camouflage' - enemy tunics pulled over their own - and the battle had begun earlier than planned when one of the Ivans spotted the arrivals' field gray trousers.

A two-hour fight had ensued, but the Brandenburgers had won the day, albeit with heavy losses. Which was why Wolff was standing here with a sergeant's epaulets on his shoulders, scrutinizing a map seized from a defeated Soviet. A position he neither sought nor wanted, but that was war.

"Well?"

The army major whose name Wolff had long forgotten stood looking at him impatiently. They were only a few hours from darkness, but the pressure from Berlin to drive for Leningrad was relentless.

Wolff stared back at him. At just short of six feet, he had several inches on the man. He was broadly muscled across the shoulders and, though just twenty two years old, had an air of natural authority conferred on him by coming through half a dozen infiltration missions.

Rank was theoretical here. It was clear who was really in charge. "I have the Ivan uniforms, Sergeant." Wolff turned at the interruption. Lenz had returned from the POW camp to which he had been sent a couple of hours earlier.

A good man, Lenz, who, more importantly, had been a tailor before the war and thus was a shrewd judge of size. If his men were to die in others' clothing, they at least deserved to wear those that fitted them.

"Enough for full camouflage?" Wolff asked, still ignoring the major.

"Yes, Sergeant. Even the helmets."

"You can't mean to put these Russian uniforms fully on over your own," the major spluttered beside him. "You are German soldiers, even if you're not actually from—"

"If it means my men have a better chance of survival," Wolff interrupted, "I will have them all grow mustaches like Stalin." Lenz sniggered. The major's cheeks colored, but he said nothing. Everybody knew how dangerous these infiltrations were and how many lives they had saved.

Still, as the battle in Daugavpils had proven, the Soviets were becoming wise to their tactics. To avoid instant identification as Germans, Brandenburger commandos were exempt from many Wehrmacht regulations.

They were not required to adopt the buzzcuts so beloved of Himmler, and the men wore collarless tunics to avoid being caught on the barbed wire under which they were frequently required to crawl.

However, a Red Army greatcoat thrown over Wehrmacht *feldgrau* was no longer enough to pass muster. In theory, Brandenburgers were supposed to remove enemy uniforms before launching their attack. But theory and the brutal, grinding reality of the war in the east had long ago taken separate directions.

"How old is this intelligence?" Wolff asked, returning to the task at hand.

"I don't know," the major sneered. "It came from your Abwehr superiors. Why don't you ask them?"

"Two days old," Lenz said. "I questioned the men at the POW camp myself when I was getting the uniforms. One of them told me the *Bolos* were getting ready to pull out when he was captured."

Wolff clucked his tongue. *Two days.* That was far too long in a conflict where the pace of the German advance meant information obtained in the morning was frequently out of date by the afternoon. The defenders could have retreated from the village some time ago and joined their comrades elsewhere. He made a decision.

"It will be dark soon. We'll wait until then and carry out some reconnaissance. If the intelligence is still correct, we'll go in dressed as Ivans in the morning."

"Impossible!" the major spluttered again. "Our orders are to take it today and continue the advance. Our timetable has us in Pskov next Tuesday."

"That's my assessment," Wolff replied calmly. "Of course, you're free to lead the mission yourself. How is your Russian anyway, Major?"

This time there was no response, the major simply turning on his heel and going off towards his own men, who had been observing the whole interaction from a distance.

Wolff watched as one of them mouthed the word *Beutegermanen* in their direction, Lenz responding with a smile and a raised middle finger. *Booty Germans.* They had all heard the term many times.

As *Volksdeutsche*, ethnic Germans raised abroad, they were supposed to be welcomed into the embrace of the Reich like long-lost cousins. Instead, they were derided as half-breeds and parasites, supposedly taking advantage of their long-lost Teutonic heritage to hitch a free ride.

It was why all of them had ended up in the 800th Special Purpose Instruction Regiment Brandenburg, referred to simply as the Brandenburgers after the town west of Berlin where its headquarters lay.

The regiment was the only one in the Wehrmacht where speaking a foreign language and being familiar with other cultures was seen as an advantage rather than something of which one should be ashamed.

Company I, to which Wolff belonged, consisted of Russian, Finnish and Baltic Germans, though as he had grown up in Brazil of Latvian-born parents, he could equally have belonged to the Romance language-speaking Company II.

His brown hair and eyes and easily-tanned skin meant he would have slotted imperceptibly into that outfit too. But Wolff had asked to be assigned to Company I in the hope of reaching Riga sooner.

There was another reason for the tension between his group and the infantry regulars. The latter was expected to obey orders without question, the former encouraged to be strong-willed individualists who thought on their feet.

As their old training sergeant major Horst Salomon had told them on their first day of special forces instruction: "I don't care if you're an *Arschloch* as long as you're a capable *Arschloch*."

The *Landser* who had been eyeballing Wolff and Lenz averted his eyes under the returned glares. The two Brandenburgers looked at each other and smirked. They had seen that before, too. The infantry might despise and resent them, but they knew Brandenburgers had been rigorously trained in unarmed combat.

Wolff and Lenz returned to their discussion about what form the reconnaissance would take. The conversation had moved on to what efforts Lenz had made to ensure the Soviet uniforms he had obtained were free of lice when they first heard the panzers approach. Sensed would be a better word.

There was something primeval about the way tanks shook the earth underneath their feet that made every soldier pause. The infantry stopped setting up the tents they had begun erecting once it became clear they would be spending the night here. They all stood and watched as the three tanks rumbled steadily closer.

"Here come the black pirates," Lenz muttered. It was not until the new arrivals halted at the edge of the clearing that Wolff could see that Lenz was correct. He had heard an SS armored division had been assigned to Army Group North after the fighting in France had finished, but had not yet seen any in action here in the Baltics.

Now here were three Panzers Mark III, a skull and crossbones painted on the turret beside each tank's identifying number. *SS Panzerdivision Totenkopf*. The Death's Head Division.

Like their army counterparts, these SS tankers wore black, but the contemptuous nickname used by Lenz referred to the dark ceremonial uniforms for which the Nazi Party's 'Protection Squads' were so famous.

The combat *Waffen* - or 'Armed' - SS had long ago switched to field gray, but the arrogance of men required to prove their Aryan ancestry back to 1800 still set them apart. Not least because their spotless 'racial hygiene' was the very antithesis of the Brandenburger ethos.

There was a subtle but detectable shift in atmosphere around the clearing.

The Brandenburgers and the infantry might normally be at each other's throats, but they would all close ranks in the face of these *Schutzstaffel* pricks. Wolff watched as the captain in charge of the newcomers climbed down from his tank hatch and went over to the major. Both men gave each other the Hitler salute.

Though outranked, Wolff could see by the captain's body language that he was immediately assuming command - and by the major's stance that he was ceding it to him. After a brief chat, the SS man turned and strode over to where Wolff and Lenz were still standing by the tree stump, the major trailing hastily in his wake.

"This won't be good," Lenz murmured. Wolff and Lenz both offered cursory regular salutes rather than the Nazi equivalent, and the captain's eyes narrowed. His glance flicked up and down, and Wolff watched the man's mouth tighten as he took in their shaggy hair and open-necked collarless shirts.

"Captain Stumpfegger agrees with my assessment that the infiltration should take place today," the major said. Wolff looked at him. He detested the man even more now.

"With respect, Captain, as I have explained to the major—"

"Nonsense, Sergeant. Berlin expects us in Leningrad by November. The *Führer* has ordered the city be razed to the ground. We have a schedule to keep to. You will carry out your mission at once. No delays."

Wolff bridled.

"Sir, the village is only a mile away." Out of the corner of his eye, he saw the cowardly major stiffen at the arbitrary reduction in distance, but plowed on. "The Russians will likely have heard the panzer engines and will be on their guard.

"If the infiltration attack is to succeed, it is much better to reconnoiter the village, then carry it out in the morning. If we go in now, the enemy could be fully alert and offer much greater resistance, which will only slow the advance on Leningrad further.

"You might also lose some of your panzers. A lot of the Ivans we've been coming up against recently have had that anti-tank rifle they use. The PTRD." Wolff cursed the man silently for forcing him to bring forward his plans.

The Brandenburgers were the tip of the spear, small groups designed to get in, cause chaos and disrupt enemy defenses until infantry weight of numbers arrived to seal victory. But Wolff did not like night-time operations. Too much could go wrong in the dark.

Stumpfegger's eyes moved up to the right as he calculated which outcome could potentially tarnish his reputation more, multiple casualties or delayed progression. After a moment, his gaze returned to Wolff, whom he addressed directly, the major forgotten.

"I think you might be correct, Sergeant." Wolff started in surprise. He had not expected such a response. Stumpfegger continued: "If you think they already suspect our tanks are there, then we shall confirm it for them." After noting the village coordinates from Wolff's map, he turned and shouted an order.

The two panzers which had been following Stumpfegger's lead armor began to form up alongside it. "Ako..." Lenz turned to him. Wolff nodded.

"Sir!"

Stumpfegger turned from where he was in the process of bellowing more instructions at his tankers.

"Sir, may I speak to you for a second?"

Stumpfegger looked at him, irritated. "What is it, Sergeant?"

"Well, sir, Corporal Lenz here heard from a POW that the enemy may have abandoned the village altogether," Wolff said. "I really think we should be allowed to carry out some reconnaissance before you begin shelling, sir. To save ammunition, I mean. Our supply lines are rather stretched at the moment."

But Stumpfegger saw through the ploy instantly and turned to face him.

"First you tell me that I risk losing tanks and now you tell me I might be wasting ammunition. You know, Sergeant, there are many in the Reich who question where the genuine loyalties of people like you and your unit actually lie. Obviously, the Führer, in his wisdom, has seen fit to bring you all back within a greater Germany, but still. As the ancient Romans had it, *qui cum canibus concumbunt cum pulicibus surgent.*"

Stumpfegger reeled off the complicated Latin phrase with a practiced air which suggested he was quite fond of quoting it. He smiled patronizingly at Wolff and offered the translation. "Those that lie with dogs, get up—"

"None of us have fleas, captain," Wolff cut him off sharply.

Stumpfegger's irritation at being interrupted mid-flow was outweighed by his surprise. "Well, well. An educated man. A relative rarity in the army, I must say." Stumpfegger looked at the major, who said nothing despite the insult to his troops and to himself. He turned back to Wolff.

"I'll take your word for it, Sergeant. Even though I hear you and your men have a habit of putting on these animals' uniforms." He waited another beat and smirked in satisfaction before turning back to where all three panzers had now lined up in a row.

Their turrets were already turned slightly in unison, the long barrels of their 50mm cannons pointing at the same angle. Wolff, Lenz and the major walked quickly to the side as the firing began, covering their ears against the cacophony.

If the ground had shaken from the clanking tank tracks earlier, it positively reverberated now as the panzers reared up slightly from shell recoil before slamming their 20 tons back down to earth. The two Brandenburgers were joined by the six other members of their small unit.

Four of them had been with Wolff and Lenz since the beginning of Operation Barbarossa, the invasion of the USSR. They had come through over a dozen of these missions together and knew instinctively they could rely on each other.

The two newcomers had joined them fresh from training following the last battle at the bridge in Daugavpils, in which their lieutenant had been killed. Wolff was still sizing the pair up. He had no fears over their competence.

Neither would be here unless they had made it through the same exacting drills dished out back at regimental headquarters on Lake Quenz. The doubts hung over their political leanings. He did not need any die-hard Nazis in his tight band. It was the one place in the Reich right now where he had successfully managed to stay free of them.

The eight men stood and watched the tanks recoil on their tracks as each high-explosive shell was launched. Wolff exchanged a glance with Lenz. Both had seen the aftermath of such bombardments.

"The Reds won't fancy that!" Scherwinsky shouted. Wolff looked expressionlessly at the man's ecstatic grin. Of the two newbies, it was Scherwinsky who concerned him most. The man had introduced himself as being from Danzig.

This had rung alarm bells.

Members of Brandenburger Company I were supposed to have grown up in locations outside the Reich with large ethnic Russian populations and to speak the language. It was said that a Brandenburger should not only know how to act like a Russian, he should know how to spit like one.

Danzig, in the former sliver of Polish territory between east and west Prussia, was a long way from any such spot.

When pressed, Scherwinsky had admitted he had been raised in Estonia but now considered himself a Danziger since his family had been resettled back in the Reich as part of the evacuation of Baltic Germans under Hitler and Stalin's doomed treaty in 1939. The lie was silly, but telling.

"That's if they're still actually there, Scherwinsky," Lenz answered after a moment. "Yes, you're right," Scherwinsky shouted back, clearly missing the point. "They'll probably already be fleeing, the cowards. Never mind, we'll catch up with them yet and get our crack at a Knight's Cross."

The eyes of Wolff and Lenz met again. Just what they needed. A bloody *Halsschmerz*, an 'itchy throat'. The lieutenant, along with all the other casualties from Daugavpils, had been awarded a posthumous Knight's Cross. This fool would have them in the grave too in an attempt to get his own tin necktie.

The bombardment continued for a while before Stumpfegger considered it enough and ordered the three tanks to move forward, followed by the regular infantry. Wolff and the seven other Brandenburgers brought up the rear. As they reached the edge of the woods, the major had his men fan out and flank each other as they sprinted, heads down, towards the outskirts of the village.

It was a textbook envelopment attack, with a full-frontal assault accompanied by troops spreading wide on either side. But there was no defensive fire.

Any Red Army forces in the village were either long gone or blown to smithereens. Heads low, Wolff and his men followed, though before they were even halfway across the open ground, the all-clear signal had been given.

Wolff, Lenz and the six others walked into the village and into the worst they had yet seen, even by the gruesome standards of the war they had been fighting so far. Several Wehrmacht regulars were being violently sick against the wall of the buildings which were still standing.

The carpet shelling with high explosive rounds had done its work, both to the small log *izbas* and the occupants sheltering within them. Body parts were everywhere, tossed around the single main street.

Clumps of flesh clung to hovel roofs. Wolff's eyes had searched desperately, willing there to be some feeble justification for what he was seeing. But not a single one of the dismembered bodies was clad in the drab olive green of a Red Army uniform.

Instead, they were those of women, children and old men. Lenz's intelligence had been correct, the defensive forces had withdrawn, leaving only those with nowhere to go and the hope that they would be treated fairly by the invaders.

In one house, Wolff found a pathetic-looking garland of flowers. It was something they had seen time and again since they first crossed into the Baltics. Locals coming out to greet them as they entered villages abandoned by the Soviets.

Some of his men took it as righteous justification for the war they were waging, as did the Nazi hierarchy, who gleefully printed pictures of the handovers in the newspapers back home. But Wolff recognized it for what it was.

People who understood their fates were out of their own hands and whose best hope of being left in peace involved currying favor with their new overlords. He felt his fingers clench tightly around his rifle. Only Stumpfegger was unaffected by it all, striding around inspecting the efficiency with which his orders had been executed.

The fury on Wolff's face must have been evident, for the SS captain had looked at him with the faintest trace of a smile, non-verbally challenging him to do something about it. It was then one of the infantrymen sent to check for concealed enemy returned, dragging a young, blonde girl who looked about nine years old.

Wolff had seen the expression on the child's face many times before on captured Russian POWs who had survived similar bombardments. Shell shock.

The girl was left in front of Stumpfegger, who leaned over and stroked her cheek, telling her in German how pretty she was. He received only a wide-eyed unseeing stare in return. Stumpfegger sighed and straightened up. "You and your men speak these people's language, don't you, Sergeant? Come here and translate for me."

Wolff stepped forward himself and kneeled beside the child. If nothing else, he could ensure any further trauma to her was minimized. After establishing she spoke Latvian, he spent a couple of minutes talking to the girl and learned her name was Lazda.

Lazda told him that the Red Army had left not two days beforehand, but three, taking all the food they could find and forcing her father and all the other able-bodied men to accompany the retreat. She had been on her way back from fetching water when the shelling had started and had arrived home to find the thatched roof of her house had collapsed. She thought her mother, grandparents and sisters were still inside.

Stumpfegger, who had been tapping his foot impatiently, interrupted, steering the conversation back towards the Soviet forces who had left. How many were they, what arms did they have? Did they have any artillery? The dazed child was unable to answer any of it.

After Stumpfegger finished, the army major belatedly posed a couple of entirely superfluous queries about how long the Russians had been there and where they were originally from before the questioning petered out. Stumpfegger made no attempt to hide his irritation. The matter of what to do with the girl hung unspoken in the air.

"So they left three days ago?" Stumpfegger said after a few minutes, looking at Wolff in amusement. "Congratulations, Sergeant. It seems you were right all along." Then, without another word, he unclipped his holster, pulled out his pistol and shot the child in the forehead.

For a split second, nobody moved.

They had all seen arbitrary executions of captured enemy. The notorious Commissar Order, issued just weeks beforehand, required Soviet political officers to be put to death on the spot and was invariably obeyed. But this was different. This was a terrified child.

Before he knew what he was doing, Wolff stepped forward.

2

Two weeks later.
Abwehr headquarters, Berlin

"You might have been shot, Wolff. Is that what you wanted? To be shot?"

Wolff looked down at Admiral Wilhelm Canaris from where he stood at attention and pondered how to answer such a ridiculous question. For a moment, he considered telling the truth. That he would have welcomed it. He had endured enough by then. Endless attempts to make a new life for himself in the Reich and rebuild things with father.

Even his vow to *Mammu* as she lay dying. All of it had come to nothing. But he refrained. He was already in enough trouble. He glanced to the left where Colonel Hans Oster, Canaris' balding second-in-command, sat staring back at him icily. He had the air of a typical Prussian. *Always be loyal and true* went their old code.

Only Wolff had been a little too honest and not very loyal. Well, not to Nazism anyway.

Wolff returned his gaze to Canaris, who was technically his regiment's commanding officer and who he was thus obliged to answer. "I accept responsibility for my actions and the consequences which follow it," he mumbled eventually.

"Do you?" Canaris replied softly. "Do you indeed?" When Wolff failed to respond, the admiral continued. "Well, we'll come back to that, and we might even see what we can do about it." Wolff stared at him, but Canaris had returned to reading the file on the desk, despite Wolff's sense that he already knew everything in it.

Rather than risk Oster's penetrating glare again, Wolff's eyes went to the bookshelf behind Canaris. There were tomes there in German, French, Spanish and even Russian. Wolff was surprised.

Not because Canaris was multilingual; many sailors were as a result of their travels and long periods at sea with nothing else to do but study. But because the admiral was a senior figure in a country which officially considered the latter language to be 'subhuman'.

Behind Canaris was a giant world map, again, not unexpected for a former seaman. To its right was the obligatory portrait of Hitler, albeit quite a small one. To the left of the map was a much larger framed photograph of a dachshund. Almost double the size, in fact.

Wolff did not know what to make of the juxtaposition. He had heard gossip that Canaris was not the most devoted National Socialist and there had been no Hitler salute when he was shown in. But perhaps he was overanalyzing matters.

"Are you a Nazi, Wolff?"

Alarmed, he returned his gaze to Canaris, who was looking at him with an expression that was hard to fathom. It was as if the old man was reading his mind. The question had thrown him completely. Its phraseology verged on disrespectful, especially amongst military men required to take a personal oath of loyalty to the Führer.

The preferred terms in Reich society were 'National Socialist' or simply 'a member of the Party'. 'Nazi' had originally been coined by the party's left-wing opponents, especially as the word was also a derogatory colloquialism for a hillbilly in Bavaria, scene of Hitler's original powerbase.

There was also the fact that Wolff was still entirely in the dark as to what he was doing here. If, as per his best guess, it was some sort of disciplinary hearing, it was a very strange one indeed. "Are you a Nazi?" Canaris repeated, his slightly more impatient tone making it clear that this query also warranted a response.

"Answer the admiral!" snapped Oster. Wolff suppressed his flinch. One did not cower in front of superiors. Even those whose role here seemed to be that of an attack dog.

"I used to be a member of the party," Wolff said, recognizing his own defensive tone. This was ludicrous. He was being made to feel ashamed of something most people in Germany wore lapel pins to brag about.

"Yes, in Brazil. Where you grew up and lived until you moved here in '38." Was he imagining it, or was there a mocking ring to Canaris' words?

"Indeed sir, my father founded the Porto Alegre branch after we settled there."

"Ako, though. Not a German name, is it?"

"No, sir. I was born in Riga in 1919. Both my parents were *Volksdeutsche* whose families had lived in Latvia for centuries, but my mother's people had, er, integrated a little more with the locals than my father's.

"We left when I was still very young. My father had been planning to move abroad for some time before I was born. He said that the Latvians had turned anti-German after the last war."

"But they still gave you a Latvian name?"

"My mother, sir. She wanted me to have a name which reflected my...birthplace. In case we never returned." *And my father refused to use it. Ever.*

Wolff had delivered the explanation dozens of times since his arrival in Germany with his father three years beforehand, but still occasionally stumbled. The Reich was no place to use the phrase 'Latvian heritage'.

"So she named you after a pagan chieftain who fought the German Christian crusaders?"

Wolff could not stop his mouth from dropping open a little in astonishment. The slightest flicker of a smile crossed Canaris' face, and he returned to his reading. Wolff stared at him a little while longer, but he was getting the distinct sense that Canaris was hopping from topic to topic to unsettle him.

He felt his irritation grow and allowed his eyes to take another tour of Canaris' office while he tried to calm himself. The room was largely in keeping with the rest of the Bendlerblock, as the H-shaped intelligence headquarters in Berlin's elegant Tiergarten district was known.

Despite its stately, neoclassical exterior and scenic setting on the banks of the Landwehr canal, the building's interior was gloomy and not at all lavishly decorated. *Der Fuchsbau*, they called it, appropriately enough. The Fox's Lair.

Apart from his desk, Canaris's personal quarters contained a threadbare carpet, separate chairs by the window and a low-slung sofa. There was a military-style camp bed in the corner and what looked like a dog basket underneath it. In fact, the entire office smelled of dog.

Wolff had never been to Army High Command in Zossen, around an hour south of Berlin, but some of the training officers from his unit had made the short trip over from their base at Brandenburg on the western outskirts. From their descriptions, he had expected the Bendlerblock to be much more lavishly decorated.

After all, as head of the Abwehr, Canaris was a top tier member of the Reich hierarchy. A golden pheasant, even if he eschewed the honey brown jacket which had earned the likes of Goebbels and other senior Nazis the nickname.

After being freed from *feldgendarmerie* custody, Wolff had been ordered to change into his parade uniform before reporting here, but he felt overdressed in such down-at-heel surroundings. Both officers in front of him were a far cry from the carefully tailored images he was used to seeing of senior Reich figures.

The admiral's navy Kriegsmarine tunic looked worn and crumpled. Beside him, Oster was in a civilian suit, despite his colonel rank. Neither man looked bothered by the August heat, which had emptied Berlin as the great and the good of Reich society fled to the Baltic coast or the Bavarian Alps to cool off.

Wolff tugged distractedly at the high-necked collar of his own jacket. He need not have bothered getting dressed up. His days of wearing the regimental mask and dagger insignia were almost certainly over. The SS captain Stumpfegger was connected, apparently.

The danger of the duties undertaken by the Brandenburgers had seen his regiment nicknamed the 'Ascension Day Commandos'. But Wolff had a feeling any penal unit he was assigned to would be given suicide sorties which would outweigh even those.

Full-frontal attacks against heavy machine guns, perhaps. Or charges through suspected minefields. Canaris looked up at him once more, this time with another unnerving intervention. "Why did you volunteer for the Brandenburgers, Wolff?"

It was another difficult question to answer. Why on earth would anyone willingly leave the rank-and-file infantry and sign up to a unit whose members were repeatedly sent off dressed in enemy uniforms, allowing them to be executed as spies if captured?

Why indeed?

To shake off the 'booty German' label? To prove himself after the incident in Hamburg?

Or because it seemed to offer the best chance of reaching Riga before it was too late?

But he stuck to the official version. "I felt my language skills might best serve the Führer in this way, Admiral." The merest trace of a smirk crossed Canaris's face before it returned to deadpan.

"I see. And exactly how good is your Russian?"

"Entirely fluent, I would say, sir. My mother spoke it to me along with Latvian at home when I was growing up in Brazil." *Once her husband had gone to work.*

Canaris and Oster exchanged a glance, before the admiral went on. "Fluent Portuguese and Spanish, some English... how good?" Wolff lifted his hand palm down and waggled it from side to side in the universal self-deprecating gesture.

Canaris smiled approvingly, before he turned grave once more. "So. The incident at the front. You attempted to strangle this..." He looked down at the file on his desk. "Captain Stumpfegger. Do you feel such behavior is acceptable?"

Wolff sighed. "Well sir, according to section 5.1 of the War Special Criminal Law Ordinance, no, I should not have..."

"Oh, forget about the regulations, Sergeant." Canaris sat back and folded his arms. The old bastard was enjoying this. "Do you feel you behaved in a way befitting a German officer?"

Wolff hesitated for a second. There was what he wanted to say and what he could say. "I feel what I objected to was behavior not befitting a German officer," he said eventually. Another slow smile spread across Canaris' face.

"Good answer, Wolff," he said. "Very good answer indeed. Don't you think so, Colonel Oster?" Oster gave the admiral a look that conveyed a familiarity beyond that of commander and subordinate, but said nothing.

Canaris turned back to the start of the file on his desk and began slowly turning the pages again. "You know, you didn't give me an answer earlier, Wolff. When I asked if you were a Nazi. Plenty of people are or were party members for all sorts of reasons, but not all of them are true believers." He looked up once more. "So?"

The old man was probing, looking for something. Wolff had difficulty believing what it was, but decided to give it to him nonetheless. At least partially. "My father is a Nazi, sir. More so than me." He stopped there. Even that sort of limited statement was enough to warrant a report to the Gestapo these days.

Canaris' smile broadened, and he looked at Oster almost triumphantly, as if he had won some secret bet between them. "Thank you, Wolff. We appreciate your candor." Canaris closed the file in front of him and pushed it away. "Have a seat, Sergeant." Wolff nodded his thanks and lowered himself into one of the leather wingbacks.

The admiral cleared his throat and leaned back in his chair. "You are with like-minded souls in this room, Wolff. Neither I nor Colonel Oster are Nazis. Quite the opposite, in fact." Wolff frowned slightly. What the hell was this?

"Both of us initially believed Adolf Hitler was the answer to this country's problems," Canaris continued. "But it soon became abundantly clear to us that he was leading us down the road to Germany's doom. Do you know why we lost the last war?"

Wolff opened his mouth to answer and then closed it again. The correct response in today's Germany was the *Dolchstosslegende* was to blame. The 'stab in the back' of the brave, undefeated German army by nebulous, largely Jewish forces. But he could sense that such rubbish was not necessary here.

"The British naval blockade of raw materials?" he guessed. Canaris nodded in agreement, as if he had passed another small test.

"Partly correct, Wolff. But mainly it was because the Kaiser became embroiled in a draining war on two fronts. We got a lucky break in 1917 when the Bolsheviks overthrew the Tsar and sued for peace in the east.

"The treaty we subsequently signed with them at Brest-Litovsk gave us control of Poland, the Baltic states and the Ukraine. All the *lebensraum* Hitler could ever dream of. We should have negotiated a peace in the west at that point, but Ludendorff pushed on Paris instead.

"That was a mistake. One we are repeating now on an even grander scale, even though Hitler himself specifically warned about the dangers of a two-front conflict in *Mein Kampf*." Canaris paused for a moment and leaned forward.

"But what if I told you there was a possibility of ending the war in the east right now in a similar fashion, allowing us room to negotiate a separate peace with the British? What would you think of that, Wolff?"

Wolff was not sure what to think of it at all. He had seen firsthand how many Soviets would desperately fight to the death rather than surrender, despite the endless string of crushing German victories.

"I would say that would put the Reich in a very strong position, sir," he said cautiously at last. "But even if it were possible, I'm not sure the Führer would be interested in it." Canaris inclined his head, conceding the obvious point. He paused again and looked at Oster, who gave the barest of nods.

Canaris turned back to Wolff. "And what if it were no longer up to the Führer?" he said softly.

Wolff remained still for a moment and observed the two men in front of him while he played for time. He felt his spirits soar, but everything he had learned since arriving in Germany three years beforehand was telling him not to react overtly. There was no doubt about what Canaris was suggesting.

Hochverrat. High treason.

Wolff already stood accused of the lesser crime of war treason, which also technically carried the death penalty but which would more likely see him sent to the punishment battalions. There, sheer luck would decide his fate. But intriguing against Hitler and his bunch of fanatics was a different story.

That was a guaranteed one-way trip to the guillotine at Plötzensee prison, around half an hour's drive from where they sat. Not to mention *Sippenhaft.* The odious theory of collective family guilt for one relative's actions would see the Gestapo go through his background and ship anyone connected to him off to a concentration camp.

Which basically meant his fervently Nazi father. Their relationship was far from ideal, but he still could not countenance that. On the other hand, the chances of emerging unscathed from a year or two of cannon fodder duties were also low. Even if he did, by the time he returned to regular duties again, it would be too late.

Kuchler's 18th Army had recently 'freed' Riga from Stalin's clutches. He had to get there before the whole kleptocratic Reich administration was fully installed. He thought of the photo

Mammu had given him of their old home, carefully folded and tucked into his wallet.

She had asked him to promise something to her at that moment which was the one thing he still held sacred. He had brought the photo with him on every combat assignment he had undertaken since he was conscripted initially into the army before volunteering for the Brandenburgers.

A reminder that he had something else to strive for above simple survival. Wolff looked up from his introspection to find Canaris and Oster staring back at him expectantly.

"What do you wish me to do, sir?" he asked quietly.

Canaris looked across at Oster and smiled again, while for the first time, something approaching satisfaction appeared in the colonel's eyes.

3

"What the admiral is about to tell you is a matter of the highest secrecy known to very few people, Wolff. If you open your mouth about it to anyone else, you may well damage us, but you will also ensure your own death. Or if you don't, I will."

Wolff nodded at the bluntness of the warning from Oster, who had now resumed his default dead-eyed stare. Another threat from a superior officer to worry about. Canaris winced slightly, but made no attempt to rein in his subordinate. Instead, the admiral cleared his throat once more and began to speak.

"A few weeks ago, the Bulgarian ambassador to Moscow received a call from a high-level contact within the NKVD requesting a meeting. They met at a Georgian restaurant called Aragvi on..." Canaris glanced down again at the file on his desk.

"Tverskaya Street. Aragvi is Lavrenty Beria's favorite place to eat in Moscow, just a few minutes' drive from NKVD headquarters at Lubyanka. He keeps his own private dining room there. Best Georgian dumplings outside of Tbilisi, by all accounts."

Canaris looked over at Wolff again. "You do know who Lavrentiy Beria is, I take it?"

Wolff nodded. "Of course, sir."

For the past two months, he had been pretending regularly to be a Russian soldier. And every Ivan knew the name of the head of the all-powerful and hated NKVD. Stalin's henchman, who had orchestrated the Great Purge on the Soviet leader's behalf. Signing tens of thousands of death warrants and sending hundreds of thousands more to the gulags.

"Good," Canaris continued. "Anyway, the ambassador, Stamenov, was told he would be dining with Beria himself at the restaurant, but he never showed up. Instead, Stamenov met an NKVD officer named Pavel Sudoplatov, who claimed he had been sent in Beria's stead.

"Given that this meeting took place in Beria's private dining room, we must assume that was the case. Hard to judge why Beria did not go there in person, but we'll get into that later. Regardless, Sudoplatov had something very interesting to say to the ambassador.

"He had an offer of a peace deal for the Reich, which he portrayed as coming from Stalin himself. Stamenov was a touch vague on details when he relayed it to the Bulgarian Foreign Ministry, who in turn informed our people on the ground in Sofia."

Wolff kept his reaction to a mere nod. Internally, he was attempting to figure out why on earth Canaris was telling him this. Try as he might, he could not see the man's angle here.

"Thankfully, the Bulgarians went straight to the top Abwehr man at our legation in Sofia, Dr Wagner, who knew to come directly to me," Canaris went on. "The essence of the deal is broadly along the terms of the Treaty of Brest-Litovsk from

1918. We would get Ukraine, Belarus and the Baltics and all hostilities would cease. In theory, anyway.

"Is it genuine? A stalling tactic?" Canaris shrugged. "Who knows? You must remember, this offer came just as we encircled the Soviet 16th, 19th and 20th armies at Smolensk. They lost 300,000 men. Our information is also that, following the fall of Minsk at the end of June, Stalin had a nervous breakdown and locked himself away in his dacha.

"When Molotov and the others went there to coax him out, he thought he was going to be arrested and shot. After all, he had been warned by the British, by his spies here and even by ourselves that the invasion was coming, and he ignored us all.

"Not forgetting that the shambolic performance of his army is largely because he had Beria purge all the best officers in case they might pose a threat against him." Canaris shook his head in wonderment at such behavior, even though Hitler had done more or less the same thing to his former comrades in the SA militia during the Night of the Long Knives back in '34.

But Wolff was less concerned with that than with the fact that the head of Reich military intelligence had, for the second time in the space of half an hour, admitted high treason.

The Abwehr had tipped off the Soviets about the invasion!

He had heard Canaris had a reputation for scheming, but this was incredible. Was this a trap? As his mind raced, Wolff noticed Oster was carefully observing him, as if to gauge his reaction to what was being discussed.

He mentally ran over what he had already said in case the entire conversation was being recorded as some kind of bizarre test of his willingness to conspire against the state. "But even if the offer from the Soviets was genuine, sir, the Führer would never agree to it," he repeated.

Canaris smiled, as if amused by Wolff's understandable caution. "What matters more is what the deal represents rather than whether it is genuine or not. And do you know what that is, Wolff?"

Having just given himself a potential, if somewhat weak alibi should the Gestapo come storming through the doors, Wolff was loath to compromise it by offering a guess. In any case, he had no idea what answer Canaris was seeking.

This time, it was Oster who spoke, and his flat, slightly aggressive tone was enough to finally convince Wolff that all of this - unbelievably - was on the level. "It gives us a chance to at last eliminate the pig currently occupying the Chancellery over on Wilhelmstrasse," he said. There was silence in the room for a few seconds.

Each man was aware that what had just been said was enough to ensure all of them, even figures as highly placed as Canaris and Oster, would die the most horrible deaths. Canaris picked up the conversation quietly.

"What I told you about Colonel Oster and I being opposed to the Nazis earlier was not an exaggeration, Wolff. Nor are we alone in such views within the Reich. We are part of a small but important group which believes Hitler is leading Germany to its doom.

"The determination to drag us into war. The ridiculous obsession with Jews. The intolerance for other political views. We have tried to have him removed before. But always, somewhere along the line, something has gone wrong.

"When he issued the ultimatum to the Czechs to cede the Sudetenland or face war, we had men outside the Chancellery prepared to storm the building, have him dragged away and declared clinically insane. An hour before they were due to go in, the British prime minister Chamberlain announced he would fly to Berchtesgaden for talks and we had to call it off."

"He only had a dozen SS guards around him then," Oster murmured, almost to himself. "What an opportunity that was." Canaris shrugged in a 'these things happen' sort of way and for the first time, Wolff noticed a slight divergence between the two men.

"We gathered our forces once more a couple of weeks later when he appeared on the verge of taking over Czechoslovakia," the admiral continued. "This time Chamberlain went and begged Mussolini to help set up the failed Munich talks.

"Next, we contacted the British and told them we were prepared to act ahead of Poland and again before the invasion of France, but we could get no response from them. Each and every time Hitler took us to the brink, things went his way.

"His standing with the people soared and the cowards at Wehrmacht High Command, who are the only ones with access to him these days, dithered further. But this time, it really is different.

"When Hitler signed the Non-Aggression Pact with Stalin, we thought we'd underestimated him again. Sadly, the truth turned out to be even worse. Hitler thinks the war in the east has already been won, but the smart ones at Zossen know better. A fool could see that invading Russia will end in disaster.

"The generals - even chief of staff Halder - were uniformly against it, even if none of them said it aloud. But this offer from Stalin is a real chance. A chance to end it before it blows up in our faces and possibly even negotiate a lasting peace with the British.

"Something which should finally instill some backbone in our prevaricating High Command colleagues. Now we come to what all this has to do with you, a sergeant in the Brandenburgers, Wolff. The Soviets have proposed a meeting on neutral turf. Bulgaria, in this instance, and I want you to go as my representative."

The light sweat which had formed between Wolff's shoulder now felt like it was turning into a torrent running down his spine. He reached into his breast pocket and took out a handkerchief, pressing it to the beads on his brow. Rather than answer Canaris's last remark directly, he asked: "Would you mind if I opened a window, sir?"

Canaris nodded his assent and Wolff took his time doing so. He lingered at the sliding sash pane as if enjoying the breeze, even if there were none. He needed to get out of here, and not just because of the heat. He retook his seat. "With respect, sir, I don't know the first thing about negotiating international peace treaties! I only—"

"I'm not sending you as a negotiator, Wolff. I am sending you as a messenger. And one whose existence I will have to deny if it ever comes to it," he added. "But I don't believe that will be necessary. We have chosen you precisely because you are an unknown, Wolff.

"There are many members in our group, but not all are military men or intelligence-trained. Those who are, are too

36

well-known to risk sending on such a mission. They may be on the radar of our colleagues in Herr Heydrich's *Sicherheitsdienst*, who are always on the lookout for a scalp to triumphantly present to Hitler.

"But they shall know nothing about you." Mention of the *Sicherheitsdienst*, or the SD, as they were commonly known in military circles, did nothing to ease Wolff's discomfort. He was already a target for vengeance from within the SS. He could do without coming under the crosshairs of its intelligence wing.

Responsible for rooting out anti-Party sentiment within the Reich, it did not consider itself limited to spying on the ordinary citizenry. Army officers, civil servants and, of course, the SD's supposed colleagues in military intelligence were all fair game too.

Canaris was still going. "We must also consider the possibility that this is a solo run by senior NKVD figures who plan to remove Stalin from power. The Soviet equivalent of our little group, if you will. If that is the case, those loyal to Stalin may be aware of the meeting in Sofia and could represent another danger.

"Or it could be a straightforward disinformation trap, though I really don't see why they'd go to so much trouble. The Brandenburgers trained you to operate behind enemy lines, posing as someone else, in various weapons and unarmed combat," Canaris continued. "To be self-sufficient and make decisions for yourself on the spot.

"You speak fluent Russian. And most importantly of all, you have proven yourself through your actions to be as disgusted with this regime as we are ourselves."

"And if you are returned to the eastern front, the chances of you surviving multiple outings in a penal battalion are not very high," Oster chipped in again smoothly. This time, Canaris looked reproachfully at Oster, who kept his eyes on Wolff.

The admiral returned his gaze to their visitor. "I did not want to put it in such crude terms, but the colonel is correct," he said. Wolff stared down at the floor to give himself a chance to compose himself. There was a creak as Canaris sat back in his chair, his presentation over.

Neither he nor Oster said anything else, and Wolff suddenly realized they expected him to step forward for this job. Perhaps that was another reason why he was here. One of the many ways his regiment differed from every other in the Wehrmacht was its volunteer ethos.

No Brandenburger, no matter how lowly, could be ordered to undertake any mission behind enemy lines. It would be presented to them, and they could accept it or refuse to participate without any consequences beyond the potential disdain of their comrades. Similarly, he could not be commanded to take part in subterfuge against Hitler.

He would have to agree to it of his own free will. If not, he would simply go back to facing the consequences of his attack on Stumpfegger. Though Oster struck him as a man who might quickly ensure his penal unit was sent out on something from which it would never return.

One thing, though, was abundantly clear. This was far bigger than him. If he turned it down, Canaris and Oster would simply find someone else. And did he want to take part?

It was certainly true that he hated the Nazis. He had despised their obnoxious racial theories ever since his father had first explained them when ordering him to stop playing football with the black and mixed race kids along the wharves of Porto Alegre.

That contempt had only increased since his arrival in Germany and the discovery of the society they had constructed here. A society he had struggled endlessly, without success, to find his place in. Both as a foreign-born *Volksdeutsch* and as someone who had the apparently novel conviction that someone's color or religion did not define what sort of person they were.

What was it that Canaris was asking him to do, after all? Travel to a civilian destination, make sure he was not under surveillance and meet some Russians. Listen to what they have to say, return to Berlin and report back. And what then?

He cleared his throat. "And afterwards, sir?" he asked, his tone and phrase as casually non-committal as he could manage. But Canaris grinned like a salesman who knew he has already earned his commission.

"We shall find something for you then, Wolff. I will always have work for a man of your talents and attitude, not to mention linguistic capability. But one step at a time. First, Colonel Oster here needs to brief you on exactly what will be required of you in Bulgaria.

"Then, you will need some further training. We can have this done at our facility in Hamburg, which will also give you the chance to... see anyone you need to before you go to Bulgaria. Such as your father." For the last time, you mean? Wolff wanted to ask.

Nonetheless, Canaris's remark hinted at how risky the admiral obviously considered the mission to be. This would be a vastly different type of assignment from anything he had undertaken thus far. At the front, objectives were clear-cut and the enemy easily identifiable.

A bridge or town would be seized and held against counterattack. If something went wrong, you did the best you could and waited for the cavalry to arrive. In Sofia, judging by what he was being told, he would be all alone. Not only having to look out for threats from the other side, but from his own, too.

Bulgaria was nominally neutral, but as an Axis ally, it had allowed German troops through its territory to attack Greece. It was essentially a Nazi vassal state, which made it all the more puzzling to Wolff as to why the Russians had suggested a meeting there. But this was no time to worry about that, nor Canaris' curious faith in some sort of Wehrmacht uprising against Hitler.

Wolff had already seen how the army was turning a blind eye in the east while the SS were murdering women and children in cold blood, so he did not share such optimism. He looked up and across the desk. "I'll need some kind of orders, sir. To officially release me from military police custody."

Canaris smiled again. "Don't worry about that, Wolff. Just pay close attention to what Colonel Oster here tells you. Oh, and needless to say, now that you are working directly for the Abwehr, you do not tell anyone where you are going and what you are doing. And I mean anyone, Wolff, understood?"

Wolff nodded, and Canaris and Oster got to their feet, the talking clearly over. To avoid identifying commanding officers in hostile territory, Brandenburgers were allowed to shake hands with each other rather than salute.

But even so, Wolff was surprised when Canaris, an admiral, leaned across his desk to do the same, though he noted Oster made no such gesture. "Good luck, Sergeant," Canaris said, resuming his seat and taking another file from a drawer.

Oster gestured wordlessly with his chin towards the corridor and Wolff turned and followed him. He was about to step out through the double doors after Oster when Canaris's voice stopped him again.

"This pagan Baltic chieftain your mother named you after, Wolff, the one who led the rebellion against the Teutonic crusaders. Whatever happened to him in the end?" Wolff turned back for a moment.

"He was betrayed by those he thought were his fellow tribesmen and executed, sir. His head was given to his enemies as a peace offering."

Canaris nodded and smiled sadly. "Be careful, Wolff."

4

Wolff followed Oster down the hallway, still reeling from how he had entered Canaris' office a condemned man and left it paradoxically a free one with an even tighter noose around his neck. He had found himself constantly watching his words during the engagement with the admiral, but had the impression that he was a fundamentally decent man.

He had learned how to instinctively interpret body language. What a suspicious enemy sentry said was one thing, but their movements, gestures and expressions always told the real story. Everything about how Canaris had held himself in there indicated a sincere officer of the old school prepared to listen to opposing views.

Wolff got no such sense of the colonel striding purposefully ahead of him down the gloomy corridor. The sound of Oster's heels ringing against the parquet wood surface was the only thing audible in what otherwise appeared to be a completely deserted floor.

He could see now his initial reading of him as a typical stuffed shirt Prussian was entirely erroneous. The man was a zealot.

Oster opened the door of a much smaller office a few yards down the corridor. It consisted of a desk with a chair on either side, some shelving and the same view over the Landwehr canal, albeit without the French windows and balcony.

The strangest feature of the room, however, was the five separate telephones which sat in the center of the desk, leaving no space for anything else. Wolff wondered whether Oster spent his entire day making phone calls. There was certainly precious little room for writing reports.

Though his selection as Canaris' envoy had already been agreed, Wolff perceived that Oster was still against it. The colonel ignored him entirely as he took a box of Eckstein No 5 cigarettes from a drawer. Even the brand itself fit with Oster's political views: a formerly Jewish-owned company which had retained its Jewish-sounding surname.

Oster sat down, turned to one side and put his feet up on the tiny free area of his desk and carefully fitted one into a plastic holder before lighting it and inhaling. There was an elegant, arrogant precision to Oster's movements, as if he were determined to extract the maximum pleasure from his tobacco regardless of who else might be present.

Perhaps part of the attraction was that smoking itself was an intrinsically anti-Nazi act, given the party's attempts to discourage it in honor of their ascetic leader. Finally, the cigarette well aglow, Oster turned to Wolff and regarded him for a second, at last indicating that he could take the other seat in the room. "Well, Wolff?" he said at last.

Wolff was baffled. "Sir?"

"Do you feel up to this? This is a matter which could very well decide whether this country emerges from this mess in one piece or goes down the tubes completely. The admiral may have couched it in rather polite terms, so let me reinforce it for you, just in case.

"We are determined, utterly determined, to render this mad beast harmless. I myself passed the point of no return last year when I personally informed my Dutch opposite number that his country was about to be invaded.

"Unfortunately, like every other bunch of weak-kneed politicians across Europe, his government did not want to believe what they were being told. Now, Dutch people are being dragged out of their homes in the dead of night and sent to concentration camps."

Wolff sat there and allowed the latest casual admittance of high treason to wash over him. In the space of little over an hour, he had found himself up to his neck in a conspiracy he had no idea existed. That was not enough time for him to fully decide how he felt about it. For the moment, he had no choice but to play along to ensure his own survival.

Oster was still lecturing him. "Even here in Germany, after all that has gone on, there are people who don't get what they're up against. They want Hitler arrested and for a friendly psychiatrist to declare him insane, as if that will solve the whole thing.

"The point I am making to you is that, as far as I am concerned, there are no half measures here. You are either completely with us or completely against us. And if it is the latter, then I shall ensure some further trumped-up charges are brought against you and you shall end up in Flossenburg.

"I'm assured the chances of surviving forced labor in the quarries there are even lower than that with the penal battalions in the east. Concocting something shouldn't be too hard given your police record from Hamburg."

Wolff's stoic nods stopped instantly, and the polite smile on his face vanished. He said nothing, but Oster smirked, clearly aware the blow had landed as intended. "Yes, that's right, Wolff. This is a country where there is a file on everyone. The Nazis deliberately set it up that way so they could control it.

"Your *Baltendeutsche* heritage is currently enough to allow you Reich citizenship. Unless of course an objection were raised that you had previously engaged in behavior which indicated you were actually a 'race traitor'." Oster pursed his lips as he pronounced the last two words, making his disdain for them clear.

He put his legs down and turned to regard Wolff with a tinge of pity in his eyes. "Such as siding with a Jew in Hamburg following *Kristallnacht*. The fact you expected the police to do something about what happened indicates a charmingly naïve side to you, which evidently no longer exists. Nonetheless, the records remain."

Wolff said nothing, but his dismay increased. He should have realized. He should have known that they would have done their research before bringing him in here. Probed his weak spots, sought out his pressure points. So that if it came to his word against theirs, there was an established track record to point to as the icing on the cake.

The night he had been beaten up by thugs of the Nazi SA militia for attempting to stop them tormenting an old Jewish shopkeeper had stripped him of any delusions about the country to which he had moved. An incident in which, incredibly, he was the one who had broken the law.

Oster smiled at last as he stubbed out his cigarette. It was the smirk of a man who knew he was fully in control. "You know, I can see you're an alert fellow, and I hope you realize I'm doing you a favor by putting you completely in the picture here.

"The admiral is a good man, but he has a fondness for intrigue that occasionally exceeds its usefulness. He has known Reinhard Heydrich since the days when he was Heydrich's superior in the Navy.

"Now that Heydrich is head of the *Sicherheitdienst*, he's not interested in being anyone's subordinate. The Abwehr is supposed to be the primary intelligence agency for gathering information externally, while the SD hunts down enemies of the party inside the Reich.

"But Heydrich wants it all. He's endlessly scheming to find ways to encroach on Abwehr turf and make us look bad in Hitler's eyes. And he knows about the resistance movement. Remember the incident in Venlo in 1939?"

Wolff racked his memory. He vaguely recalled some triumphant nonsense in the Goebbels-controlled press about how the capture of British spies at the border with Holland proved the Dutch were conspiring with British intelligence to assassinate Hitler.

He had not paid much attention to it, aware that most of what was published in German newspapers these days bore only a passing resemblance to the truth.

Oster snorted. "What you probably read is that we captured two British agents who had supplied that Elser fellow with the bomb he used to try and kill Hitler down in Munich. What really happened is that we had been actively negotiating with the British behind the scenes about what they would accept for a peace deal. Chamberlain was aware of it all and was fully on board.

"Remember, this was not long after war had been declared between us. We had invaded Poland, but the rest was still to come. There was a real possibility a deal could have been worked out and Hitler deposed. However, the admiral and I were careless.

"We thought we had neutralized Heydrich's informants within the Abwehr, but apparently not. The SD got wind of what we were doing and sent their men posing as members of our group to meet the British in Holland. Heydrich used a major named Walter Schellenberg, who lured them to a meeting and abducted them across the border.

"Then Heydrich told Hitler he had caught the foreign agents who had given Helser the bomb. Heydrich got the glory, Schellenberg the Iron Cross and Hitler used it as the pretext to invade Holland after the Dutch ignored the warnings I gave them and...."

Oster trailed off and spread his arms in self-explanatory exasperation. Wolff recalled now seeing Georg Elser's defiant, sulky face staring out from the front pages of the newspapers, flanked by two men identified as British intelligence agents. The headlines crowing over a glorious German sting operation.

"So the British had nothing to do with Elser's bomb in the beer hall?"

Oster frowned. "No! Elser was a madman. He did it all by himself. A Bolshevik, but a brave one, I must admit. But Heydrich told Hitler what he wanted to hear."

He sighed wistfully. "I have to admire the bastard in one sense. He is utterly ruthless and will use anything to his advantage. In one fell swoop, he advanced further up the ladder and poisoned the chance of any further negotiations with the British. Since Churchill took over, he will not hear of anything further, apparently.

"This is the dirty game going on behind the scenes between the Abwehr and the SD, Wolff. The admiral and Heydrich are engaged in a battle of wits, and the stakes are enormous. I'm really not sure why Canaris is so courteous towards a man who he knows wants to destroy him.

"They go riding together every week in the Tiergarten. Heydrich bought a house right around the corner from his out in Schlachtensee. He comes over in the evenings to play the violin with the admiral's wife while Canaris puts on his chef's hat and cooks them all a saddle of wild boar.

"If it were me, I'd put strychnine in Heydrich's food. Unfortunately, the admiral is prone to a type of squeamishness that serves only as a hindrance in what, these days, has become our primary business."

Wolff recalled some gossip he had heard about Canaris following the Abwehr chief's visit to Brandenburger regimental HQ last year.

The admiral had been given a display of proficiency in silent killing and the demonstration of the garotte on a wooden dummy had left him distinctly green around the gills, according to some of those present.

It was the sort of macho talk common in a unit whose members considered themselves an elite and Wolff had not thought much of it. But it tallied with Oster's remarks. Wolff realized there were differing levels within the anti-Hitler movement into which he had just been invited. The man in front of him clearly represented the hardline faction.

"Questions?" Oster was regarding him sideways from his perch with his feet on the desk.

Wolff ignored the impatient tone and stared down at the bank of phones in front of him. It was clear he would be going to Sofia whether he liked it or not. Provided he took the required precautions for his own safety, it should be achievable. Once done, he would be free to resurrect his own personal quest to get to Riga.

Perhaps much freer, now that he had been removed from frontline duties. But first he needed as much information about the situation in Sofia as possible, and now was the time to ask. This appeared to be the briefing, and there would probably not be another.

"Will I be able to rely on this Dr Wagner you have in place at the legation for support?" he said, eventually. Oster's reply was instant and absolute. "No. Your cover will be that of an invalid soldier turned commercial representative selling tractors to the Bulgarians.

"The government in Sofia is heavily dependent on us for trade these days, we buy almost all their agricultural produce, and they rely on us almost totally for machinery. So, German businessmen are quite common there.

"Wagner is a good man, but his face is too well-known, so it is better not to involve him in this. We don't need to, anyway. Your main worries will be ensuring none of Heydrich's or Ribbentrop's stooges at the embassy are snooping around you."

The threat posed by the SD had already been outlined, but Wolff was confused at the mention of the Foreign Minister's name. Oster noticed his frown and sighed.

"What's going on at our embassies makes the jockeying for position here in Germany look like a picnic," he said. "Ribbentrop was sick of the SS trying to influence diplomacy abroad, so he made sure he put in place his own intelligence network reporting directly to him.

"So Ribbentrop has his ambassador and diplomats snooping about, and the SS has a Gestapo brigadier as the police attaché. Both of them, along with our man Wagner, are actively gathering intelligence and sending it back to Berlin.

"Even though Wagner's the only one supposed to be doing it. It's the same at all of our embassies and has led to some ludicrous face-offs. There was an attempted coup by the Iron Guard fascist movement in Romania last January.

"The SS were backing them, while our army was siding with the dictator Antonescu." He smiled. "Thankfully, Antonescu came out on top, though it doesn't always work out like that."

Oster sighed. "It's really quite tedious, but this is how Hitler set the whole system up. All the Reich agencies competing against each other so they would forget about working against him." Wolff blinked, taking it all in. One thing, at least, was clear. Nobody at the embassy could be trusted.

"What about the locals?" he asked. Oster, in the process of fitting another cigarette into a holder, took his time lighting and drawing upon it a couple of times before answering. He placed his feet back on the desk and crossed his ankles.

"You may find yourself coming in for some surveillance from them," Oster admitted. "The Bulgarians only ever used to worry about communist agitation and have long had a section within their Police Directorate monitoring Soviet activity on their territory.

"But the coup attempt next door in Romania put the wind up Tsar Boris something terrible. He's terrified of the same thing happening on his turf, which is why he set up a new unit, Department D, specifically to keep an eye on our people too.

"Don't be fooled by the fact Bulgaria has signed a treaty with the Axis powers. They are walking a tightrope right now, and they know it. As one of the few countries in the east to maintain diplomatic relations with the Soviets, they have acted as our default representatives in Moscow up until this point, which is why the NKVD approached them in the first place.

"The government and the tsar might be pro-Germany, but the people are generally quite pro-Russian. Slavic brotherhood, that kind of thing. It was the Russians who pushed out the Turks in the last century, so many of them feel they owe their independence to Moscow.

"I believe when the Spartak Moscow football team came to Sofia to play a local side in a friendly last year, they were given a hero's welcome.

"In any case, the Bulgarians' primary objective is to avoid being drawn into this war, so they would be delighted if this peace deal went ahead. They also seem aware of the *realpolitik* of the Reich, which is why they went straight to our man Wagner rather than the others."

"So they'll watch me, but they won't interfere then?" Wolff asked, attempting to simplify the complicated situation being charted for him. Oster blew out a stream of smoke and shook his head while he chuckled for a few seconds as if amused by the stupidity of the question.

Wolff's temper rose inwardly, but he kept his face impassive. Oster removed his legs from the desk and leaned fully towards him. "No, Wolff, that's not what I'm saying at all. Look, the intelligence business is about need-to-know, and only a select few within the Bulgarian government are even aware that this is happening.

"The tsar and those loyal to him are in the picture and very much want this deal to go through. But there may also be those within the upper echelons who don't, either because they're convinced fascists or because they see this as an opportunity to advance their own careers.

"There is a certain possibility that some of them may be in touch with Heydrich's people in order to further those aims. Then there are those further down the chain in this new Department D of their Police Directorate, who are completely in the dark about what's going on.

"They may spot you as an intelligence officer and may actively try to impede you, because that, basically, is their job. Understood?" Wolff nodded. He was beginning to realize the tightrope he might have to walk himself.

"So I have to watch out for the Bulgarians and the SD. What about the NKVD? The admiral said there might be factions within it opposed to this going ahead too." Oster had resumed his relaxed sideways pose and exhaled another long, perfectly formed stream of smoke. It made him appear an exasperated dragon.

"That is one of the great unknowns, Wolff. We have more questions in that area than answers. Why, for example, did Beria not meet the Bulgarian ambassador himself? Deniability? That wouldn't do him much good if it came to it. Is he acting on his own initiative here, or was he sent by Stalin?

"Who knows what scheming is going on behind closed doors in Moscow. It could well be that this offer is from Stalin. It could well be that Beria is planning to overthrow Stalin, and this offer is from him. It may also be the case that there is another faction in the NKVD hoping to seize control themselves.

"In the end, it doesn't really matter. The priority for us is to put some backbone into those gutless shits in Zossen to take action before we all end up in the soup. So that, in case you haven't grasped it, Wolff, is the objective of your mission.

"Return with proof of a generous peace offering from the Russians - whomever amongst them it is - that we can use as a springboard to at last get rid of this bastard Hitler. We'll worry about the details afterwards. In the meantime, expect the un-expected. As Old Whitehead said, you are used to operating in enemy territory. Consider this an extension of that."

Oster put down his cigarette carefully in the ashtray and rose to fetch a meter-long, rolled-up tube of paper from the top of a set of metal shelves to the right of his desk. He lobbed it casually across to Wolff, who had to scramble to prevent it falling to the floor.

Oster was grinning across at him again when he eventually made it safe in his grasp. "That's a map of Sofia city center there. As you can see, it's all rather grid-like. The names of the streets are in Cyrillic script, but that shouldn't be a problem for you.

"Take it home, memorize it and burn it. Completely, Wolff. Take no chances." He pulled out a drawer and took another folded piece of paper, which Wolff recognized as standard Wehrmacht issue. "Those are your orders enabling you to get to Hamburg first. They even include a promotion. Congratulations, you are now a lieutenant. Didn't expect that when you tried to wring that SS man's neck, did you?"

He sat down again and returned to the concentrated pleasure of his smoking. "You can report to army headquarters in the city, but you will be based out of a discreet building on Klopstockstrasse. I presume you know where that is?"

Wolff did. He had walked the street almost every day since he and his father had left Brazil behind to resettle in Hamburg. The grand tram-lined boulevard was traditionally home to some of the northern port city's richest merchants, and he was slightly surprised to learn the Abwehr had something as secret as a spy training school there.

Though then again, remaining inconspicuous was supposed to be the intelligence agency's speciality. "Captain Voigt is the head of *Abwehrstelle* Hamburg. He's one of us, but that doesn't mean you should volunteer any details on your mission, and he certainly won't ask you," Oster continued.

"They're taught all sorts there that you might not have covered in your Brandenburger training. Secret inks, dead letter drops, Morse code, Afu radio set operation, that kind of thing. Though I believe you were instructed in both of the latter?"

Wolff nodded. "Good," Oster said, as if he had just been relieved of a tedious yet necessary obligation. "But the most important part is the anti-surveillance end of it. I'm aware you were shown how to track Russians through the woods, Wolff. But not how to know if they were tracking you."

Oster snorted and got to his feet. "Otherwise, what the admiral said is correct. Go and see your father by all means and say you're home from the front on a few days' leave, everything's going great out there, *et cetera, et cetera.*"

He paused and gave Wolff a supercilious smirk. "Though if I picked up on matters correctly, that may not be your priority." Wolff just stared back at him. He was starting to intensely dislike this man, who he realized might be his main point of contact from now on. He swallowed his anger as he stood himself and forced a polite smile.

"Sir."

5

Wolff sat at the window and watched the flat green countryside of northern Germany roll by. There was a large group of naval cadets on the train from Berlin bound for Wilhelmshaven and their youthful good cheer contrasted sharply with his own tense mood.

He ought to be overjoyed. Canaris' intervention had saved him from being used as a distraction for Soviet machine gunners in return for carrying out what appeared to be a comparatively far safer endeavor. More importantly, after his discussion with the sneering Oster, he had asked to see Canaris again, where he had outlined his price for going to Sofia.

If they already knew everything about him, he might as well lay it on the table. To his relief, the admiral had readily agreed, and he had left the Bendlerblock elated. Both that his pledge to *Mammu* was once more viable and that such high-level opposition to this revolting regime not only existed, but was actively taking steps to overthrow it.

However, his excitement had given way to nervousness upon reflection. He was being drawn into a shadowy world of which he knew nothing, and where his fate could be decided by developments he might never understand. Canaris had been blunt about denying all knowledge of the Sofia trip if required, and both he and Oster might both be high enough up to protect themselves if it came to it. But Wolff would not.

He closed his eyes and winced as an image floated into his head of a confused Ludwig Wolff futilely waving his party branch founder badge at the Gestapo as he was roughly dragged out of his rathole apartment.

He had four days in Hamburg and had put off seeing his father until the end, telling himself he needed to concentrate on the intensive training which awaited him. He had a number of acquaintances in the city, of course, but none close enough to really deserve a visit.

They would all have been called up by now anyway, apart from Lothar, who was probably at work. Apart from that, it was just old Ludwig, who had been so desperate to volunteer for any kind of acceptance upon his arrival in the city three years ago that he had ended up in the SA militia.

The *Sturmabteilung* had greatly faded in importance since its powerful leadership was quite literally gutted during the Night of the Long Knives. Technically now in charge of military training for potential conscripts, it was really a home for Nazi thugs too old, fat or well-connected to be at the front.

With little else to do, some of them had begun to spend their time checking for blackout violations and other infractions, which would allow them to throw their diminished weight around.

Arriving amid the chaos at Hamburg train station, Wolff ducked his head and pulled the visor of his uniform cap down as far as he could just in case anyone he knew was on the platform. He was in no mood for exchanging war stories.

The naval cadets were spilling out of the carriages as he made his way outside and cadged a lift on the back of an army truck to headquarters in the city. Inside, his meeting with Voigt was mercifully perfunctory.

Wolff was clearly not the first person to turn up at the captain's office with mysterious orders about which he did not wish to know any more. Voigt told him to go to his accommodation and change into civilian clothes. His training was to begin immediately.

The city's sparse tram network did not serve as far as the Harvestehude district where army HQ lay, so Wolff decided to walk half an hour along the Outer Alster into the city center. He had not been to this part of the city since receiving his conscription papers two years beforehand.

Wolff remembered the massive lake from the summer of '38 as being alive with rowers on its waters, with young couples walking hand-in-hand along the shores. Now, there was only the occasional middle-aged man or woman hurrying along or some field gray or navy blue uniform visible in the distance.

He reached the building used by the Abwehr on the corner of Klopstockstrasse and Alsterglacis and looked up in surprise. He had frequently passed the non-descript brownstone, which jutted out like a ship's prow towards the Inner Alster lake, and had never thought anything of it. But then it was a secret training base for an intelligence agency, after all.

The front door was answered by an old man with a kindly face, and Wolff gave the codeword before being shown into a realistic-looking lobby area with a hotel-style desk. There, a woman who was presumably his wife was talking discreetly on the telephone.

The man fetched a key from behind the desk and led him up the stairs to a small, furnished room with a sturdy-looking bed and a wardrobe in the corner. Through the window, there was a beautiful view of the tree-lined Lombard Bridge, which separated the city's two great lakes. But he had no time to admire it.

He had barely unpacked his small valise and changed out of his uniform and into civvies when there was another knock at the door. They were outside waiting for him, the man from downstairs said quietly.

He went down the stairs and got into a car driven by a middle-aged man, who offered no greeting beyond a simple nod. Prepared for a long journey, he found himself driven just a few hundred yards to a building on Glockengiesserwall, next to the police presidium.

There, he was brought to a large windowless room, which was empty apart from Voigt. The captain bade him sit and immediately launched into a lengthy lecture on counter-surveillance techniques. Most of these seemed natural enough to Wolff, who had already had some training in how to monitor the ground in enemy areas for signs of troop movements.

The simplest way to detect a tail, Voigt said, was to bring them on a roundabout tour of whatever location you found yourself in and check suddenly and unexpectedly for any suspicious activity behind you.

The Abwehr captain walked up and down the length of the room as he explained how to suddenly increase and decrease the speed of his stride, turn corners and wait to see if anyone hurried after him and stop suddenly in the street to tie his shoelace.

More blatant strategies involved whirling suddenly and doubling back in the same direction, making eye contact with as many of those walking towards him as possible. "The eyes always give them away," Voigt said.

"Look for those who instantly avert their gaze or immediately find a nearby shop window inordinately interesting. Or, conversely, if they maintain eye contact. If a stranger stares at you in the street, your natural inclination is to look away casually.

"Anyone who doesn't do this is a potential tail. Pay attention to faces to see if the same ones pop up at different times. Particularly when leaving wherever you're staying, as this is most likely where they will try and pick you up.

"I'm told that your mission will be abroad and may involve surveillance from a third-party hostile agency. That's a positive, as it means they will probably have a limited amount of manpower and will have to use the same personnel, which will give you a greater chance of spotting them.

"However, there are certain things you need to be conscious of so that you do not make life easier for them. Change your clothing every day. If they are watching your hotel and you come out with the same coat on each morning, it will make you much easier to spot.

"The same applies to having your photograph taken surreptitiously. We tell all our operatives abroad to keep their heads down and use their hats to cover their faces when possible if they believe they are being observed.

"Apparently it has gained us the nickname of the *Schlapphüte* - the floppy hats - amongst our colleagues in the SD," Voigt added, the contempt in his voice audible. "Which is ironic, as we seem to spend as much time avoiding their surveillance as those of foreign agencies.

"We believe we've managed to keep most of our secrets from them. They have broken some of our low-level ciphers, but not the more important ones, as far as we know. The same applies to the secret inks we use.

"Heydrich's lot seem to believe we're still writing between the lines of postcards with milk, which has been around since the time of Moses. We tell our agents abroad to send back the occasional innocuous-looking one to their families.

"God knows how much time the SD spends holding their postcards over a flame waiting for messages that aren't there to appear. Thankfully, we have developed rather more sophisticated formulas than that for important messages."

Voigt then ran through some other basics, such as stopping outside a mirrored shop window to try to discern whether someone was observing from a distance or getting up abruptly from a cafe table and putting on a coat as if preparing to leave, only to simply switch to a nearby table.

The doubling back trick could be invoked naturally by passing a bar and turning around to enter it as if suddenly deciding to have a drink. "Many of those who will be following you will never have been properly trained to do so and will thus be easier to spot," Voigt said.

"Of course, another issue is what will happen if you do flush them out. Because at that point, only one option is left to them: taking you by force." Wolff smiled as he reassured Voigt that this was one area where he would certainly not be found wanting.

The next couple of days involved a series of lengthy, frequently tedious training exercises in which Wolff had to make his way around Hamburg and attempt to discern whether he was being followed or not. At times he would be, Voigt told him, at others not. On other occasions, it was Wolff who did the following.

Voigt randomly selected a number of individuals for him, ranging from policemen to women carrying shopping, and he successfully tracked them around the city center for an hour without being noticed. None of them would have had any real reason to expect they were being shadowed, but cover was thin enough in the deserted city, so it had not been without complications.

However, the training dragged up some unpleasant memories too. The second afternoon, one of his marks had turned onto Rathausstrasse, and he had trailed the man past the scene of the incident which Oster had brought up the day beforehand.

He recalled the humiliation he felt at being unable to defend himself against the group of SA thugs three years earlier. It had been a major part of his motive for joining the Brandenburgers once he had heard about the regiment's emphasis on unarmed combat.

That and his father's incandescent reaction. Wolff had thought the old man was going to hit him. He might have too, if Wolff were not by then bigger than him. He had little time to dwell on such matters though, as the pace set by Voigt was relentless.

Extra tasks involved the transfer of small items like a box of cigarettes or an envelope via a brush pass, which Voigt made Wolff spend an entire afternoon practicing until the Abwehr man was happy he could carry it off seamlessly.

Wolff was sent to look for good locations for dead letter drops and taught to devise his own simple code of chalk marks. He was given a Minox miniature camera, an ingenious device no bigger than a spectacles case, and sent into a tobacconist's to surreptitiously snap the front pages of the newspapers.

The Minox had been developed by a Baltic German from Riga named Walter Zapp, who had gone to work for the Nazis after being resettled in the Reich along with hundreds of thousands of others following Hitler and Stalin's ill-fated Non-Aggression Pact back in '39.

Would Wolff have been obliged to work for the regime similarly if his parents had never moved to Brazil? It was hard to say. Brandenburgers were all trained in radio operation and Morse code, though Wolff had been informed by Voigt he would have a reliable radio man in place at the legation in Sofia.

Even so, Voigt put him through his paces on the transmitter so notes could be taken on his "fist", the rhythm of each operator considered as individual as a fingerprint.

It was standard Abwehr policy to have a 'distress signal' - an extra letter, capitalization or deliberate grammatical error - inserted in all agent's transmissions. Its absence, or the presence of another, would indicate the message was being sent under duress. He would be given this key just in case.

Most evenings, he was so thoroughly exhausted from the constant subterfuge that he simply arrived back at the pension and went to bed. Still, by the culmination of it he had successfully spotted the tail on almost every occasion it was in place and could pull off a brush pass without breaking stride.

He also had a newfound respect for the Abwehr, whom he and his comrades at the front used to contemptuously dismiss as *Etappenschweine*. Rear pigs, hiding from the real fighting.

At the end of his last day, Wolff entered his room and took off his shoes to lie on the bed. His feet ached from doing various circuits of Hamburg city center, vigilant at once for Voigt's men and the possibility of running into his few old acquaintances.

He simply did not want to have to explain what he was doing back from the front. The last thing he felt like doing was going out again now, but it was unavoidable. He had put it off until the last moment, and now that moment had arrived.

6

Wolff had mulled long and hard about how to approach his father and had ultimately decided that bluntly outlining his plans to get to Riga was the only option. He was not expecting a positive response, but he had to try. Was there a chance that Ludwig Wolff could see through Goebbels' guff and realize what was coming down the tracks?

Not many of his fellow citizens could at that point. Not many of those at the front could yet either. He felt sorry for the old man at times. The house his parents had left behind in Riga at father's insistence had been grand. He could see that from the photo *Mammu* had given him.

Their home in Porto Alegre had also been comfortable if not luxurious. His father had expected to be welcomed in Germany like a brave National Socialist hero fleeing yet more oppression, but the housing committee had been uninterested in his tales of promulgating the party message in Brazil.

Instead, he had been shoved into a cramped little flat in Ottensen, one of the worst areas of Hamburg. No wonder the old man was so bitter. He had put his uniform back on, hoping it would soften his father up for what was coming.

He was still getting used to his lieutenant's rank and the salutes it drew from the occasional enlisted man he passed in the street. Ludwig would not be so deferential, but it would grant him more status than the private's rank he held when they last met. Arriving at the flat, he rapped discreetly upon the door.

Loud knocks these days signified only one thing. In any case, he didn't want to alert Frau Graf, the nosy old crone next door. In her own way, the shriveled pensioner had been the perfect introduction to life in the Reich three years beforehand.

His attempts to introduce himself and offers of help with her shopping had been met with suspicion and questions about his origins and accent. He had no wish to see her again now.

His father's initial reaction was almost exactly as Wolff had anticipated, only almost comically played out via visual expressions in a matter of microseconds.

First, he blinked in surprise that his son was standing there in front of him unannounced. That quickly gave way to a sour smile and was in turn replaced by intrigue as Ludwig took in the officer's braid and collar tabs. It was the last factor which was clearly the deciding one as Wolff Senior grunted a welcome and turned back towards the kitchen, leaving the door open.

The man had not seen his only son in months, and this was how he greeted him. But Wolff felt no disappointment. This was how things were between them now.

"Place looks well," Wolff said, as he walked inside. Ludwig glanced back at him, scanning for signs of mockery. In the two years since he had been away, his father had done nothing with the flat, probably in keeping with his assertion that the accommodation was "temporary".

The mold was still visible on the kitchen ceiling, and the same rickety chairs and uneven table stood in the kitchen. In the tiny salon, he could see the framed certificate declaring Ludwig Wolff the founding member of the *Nationalsozialistische Deutsche Arbeiterpartei-Ortsgruppe Porto Alegre*.

Prominently displayed to impress any visitors, though of course there were none. Wolff had once enraged old Ludwig by telling a plumber who had come to fix a leak that there had only ever been 15 members in the Porto Alegre branch anyway.

That was towards the end, when he knew he was being sent off to the front somewhere and no longer cared what his father thought of him. A more conciliatory approach was needed here, though.

"Aren't you going to offer me a coffee?" he asked with a smile. Complaining about the tasteless ersatz *Kornkaffee* available in wartime Germany had been one of the few areas where they had found common ground.

Both of them remembered the rich aroma of fresh beans which had filled Ludwig's warehouse back in Porto Alegre as they waited for export to Europe. Wolff had occasionally caught the same odor wafting from officers' tents as they moved from town to town in Latvia.

Saudade, they called it in Brazil. Melancholy for something which he would possibly never experience again.

"I can't stay long," his father gruffly interrupted his musings. "I have to go out and check for any blackout violations." Wolff looked at him and snorted. The transparency of the lie was intention: it would not be dark for at least another two hours. In truth, he should be thankful to the old man for saving him from wasting his time.

"No need to bother with the coffee, Father," he said briskly. "This won't take long. I've come to tell you that I have received permission to travel to Riga and—"

"Riga?" Ludwig Wolff looked at him, puzzled. "What on earth do you want back there for? There's nothing left for..." Understanding dawned on his face, almost instantly replaced by the familiar, infuriating contempt and a derisive shake of his head.

"Your mother," he scoffed. "You know, she asked me the same thing, at the end. I told her she was being ridiculous." Wolff was stunned. Not just because he had thought it a secret pact between him and *Mammu*, but also at the callous way his father was referring to his late mother.

But Ludwig was unstoppable now, off on one of his customary scornful rants. The motive for his visit was falling apart, just seconds into it.

"How could I ever have expected you to be a good German when she was filling your head with such nonsense?" His father pointed an accusing finger at him. "You now live in the most powerful country in the world, boy. You should be grateful for the opportunities it offers you."

Wolff's eyes went reflexively to the worn linoleum and the cracked plaster on the walls before returning his gaze to his father.

Nothing good would come of this, he knew. He should end the conversation and depart, leaving things on a reasonably civil level. But the glances, and the inherent challenge within them, had not escaped Ludwig's attention.

"I'm aware it's not palatial, but there's a war on. We all have to sacrifice a little. Once it's over, I can get something better. There'll be plenty of spare accommodation once settlers start moving to the east."

His father was eyeballing him, daring him to go further. Every conversation they had now ended up like this. Ludwig never tired of telling people how much better off they were in Hamburg than in Brazil, even if the opposite was actually the case. He would regularly raise the topic with Wolff, probing for agreement.

"Yes, father. I'm sure they'll have you in an apartment in the Altstadt in no time. The concierge can press your uniform every evening before you go out trying to peek in people's windows." The words were out of his mouth before Wolff could stop them.

His father's face tightened. This was achingly familiar ground for both of them. "Oh, you know better than me, do you?" he sneered.

"Well, one of us is actually at the front and the other is getting their information from the *Völkischer Beobachter*. So, yes. I do."

Unable to counter that argument, Ludwig changed tack. "How on earth did you get promoted with that shitty, defeatist attitude anyway? You know, I made some inquiries about that regiment you joined and the reports weren't very complimentary.

"A bunch of sneak thieves running around posing as Bolsheviks rather than standing and fighting like proper soldiers is what I was told. Why didn't you join a real unit? Streithorst's son is in the SS, and he has already been awarded the Knight's Cross.

"Of course, you probably aren't able for that kind of soldiering. You always preferred skulking around with blacks and other *Untermenschen*."

It was the negative comparison with the SS that did it. Wolff knew he was being baited by an ignorant old man who didn't know what he was talking about. It was not the first time his father had accused him of cowardice either, but the added provocation of lauding a bunch of childkillers was just too much to bear.

"Soldiering? What the hell would you know about it, you old fool? All you've ever known is how to run away. When things got too tough for you in Riga, you fled to Brazil. Then, when Vargas saw your beloved Nazis for the obnoxious thugs they really are and banned them, you scuttled off to Germany and dragged me with you.

"I suppose it was a convenient excuse, given that you'd run your business into the ground and had convinced yourself there was some sort of commercial paradise over here, waiting to be exploited.

"Instead, they treat you like a skivvy here and you lap it up, because you're afraid you'll be seen as a failure if you go back. And as for your heroes in the SS, let me tell you a little about them. The majority of what they do at the front has nothing to do with taking on the Ivans.

"They arrive after the fighting is done, round up all the Jews and take them off into the forest to shoot them in cold blood. I saw one of them put a bullet in a young girl's head in front of me.

"Perhaps that's what Streithorst's boy got his medal for, bravely taking on some unarmed women and children? And let me tell you something else. Those who actually understand military strategy know what a colossal mistake that little *Gröfaz* twerp has made."

Already taken aback by the ferocity of Wolff's response, his father's eyes widened in alarm at the derogatory nickname for Hitler. *Gröfaz* was a sarcastic acronym used extremely carefully at the front among like-minded colleagues. It stood for *Grösster Feldherr aller Zeiten* - the Greatest General of All Time.

Wolff's fury had been such that he had blurted it out without knowing if Ludwig would understand, but it was clear from his reaction that the term had already made its way back to Hamburg.

His father walked quickly over to the open back window and slammed it shut, as if he could somehow stop the insult floating outside to be picked up by listening ears. Wolff had gone too far. This was the sort of thing which could result in a Gestapo visit if overheard by the wrong person.

Like Frau Graf.

"Get out!" his father hissed furiously. "Get out! You're a traitor and a coward and I want nothing more to do with you. Get out and don't come back or by Christ, I'll report you myself. You're a disgrace to your people. I never want to lay eyes on you again."

Wolff saw no point in continuing the argument, though he very much wanted to. He had come to try to save the old man from himself, but had instead lost his temper and potentially placed both of them at greater risk.

Fuming at his own stupidity, he turned and stalked out.

7

Wolff was on his way from the building and heading to catch the streetcar back into the city center when he saw Lothar limping towards him. He forced himself to swallow his fury.

The lad from the flat underneath was probably one of the few positives from his time in Hamburg and someone with whom he had bonded well. They were both outsiders in their own way, Wolff as a 'booty German' and Lothar, who was nineteen, in an even less fortunate fashion.

A bout of polio as an infant had left his neighbor with a withered leg which dragged after him. A considerable impediment in life, but far more so in a society which talked openly of euthanasia for the "unfit". Both knew what it was like to strive for acceptance in the Reich.

Wolff had jokingly asked Lothar to teach him to speak with the Low German accent of Hamburg rather than the *Baltendeutsch* dialect he had acquired from his parents. Lothar had replied that he would gladly oblige, once Wolff would show him how to march like a proper *Landser*.

Both had also initially embraced the war as an opportunity to prove their worth to their peers. After being conscripted, Wolff had volunteered for the Brandenburgers so that he could serve in a regiment where his background would be an advantage rather than a hindrance.

For Lothar, the manpower shortages had seen him gain employment in a factory making tank parts, a job he would never have had otherwise. It was the war which had seen Lothar designated *k.v.H - kriegsverwendungsfähig Heimat*, or fit for service at home, a designation usually given to those with serious war wounds.

Though Lothar himself would frequently refer to the sardonic slang version of the acronym. *Kann vorzüglich humpeln*. Can convincingly hobble.

The teenager greeted him with genuine affection, and Wolff was reminded of his admiration for someone who he never saw without a smile on his face, despite having more reason to complain than most.

Thus, when Lothar suggested hopefully that they meet for a drink once he had changed out of his work clothes, Wolff readily concurred. The alternative - lying in a lumpy bed in an Abwehr safe house replaying yet another disastrous interaction with his father - offered little competition.

They agreed to meet at a tavern on Groninger Strasse that Wolff was not familiar with, but whose owner Lothar insisted was a friend of his. Wolff took that as meaning a place where Lothar would not be bothered by drunken Nazi louts, something which could not necessarily be taken for granted.

Wolff made it to the tavern first and ordered a stein and a shot of schnapps, starting as he intended to continue. He had taken a tram back to the guesthouse to change out of his uniform.

He meant to get good and drunk tonight and wanted to do it anonymously.

He was still seething over the run-in with his father, but the majority of his ire was self-directed. The conversation had degenerated so quickly, Wolff had not even broached the real reason for his visit.

In truth, the old fanatic would probably have rejected the offer out of hand anyway, though by allowing himself to be drawn into a shouting match, Wolff had ensured it. The exchange of insults had followed a well-worn path, but as always, it was the taunts of coward which burned deepest.

Before moving to Germany, he had never even been involved in a fight, despite Ludwig's frequent warnings about the dangers of attending parties in the *favelas* of Porto Alegre. Everyone knew the pale-skinned *alemão* there, the only one from his community who deigned to mix with them.

That had not gone unnoticed among the expatriate German community. When Wolff refused to take part in a lynch mob going into the Bom Jesus slum following the alleged rape of a white girl, it had distanced him further from what his father termed his "ethnic equals".

Reluctantly accompanying Ludwig to Germany after the Brazilian dictator Vargas outlawed Nazism had been a vain attempt to win back his father's respect. Instead, Wolff's palpable abhorrence for the cruelties of Reich society and then the incident with the SA had rendered him an even greater disappointment.

He finished his beer and ordered another round. The tavern was simple enough, though it bore some slight touches which indicated the owner was not entirely enamored with the Nazis. While there was the obligatory picture of Hitler glaring out from behind the bar, it was counterbalanced by a portrait of General Hindenburg, the last president of the Weimar Republic, which hung on a wall off to one side.

It was perfectly legitimate to mourn the passing of the hero who had secured Russia's defeat in the first war, but those with a knowledge of the Weimar Republic's demise also knew Hindenburg had been the last brake on Hitler's avaricious ambition. It was only after his death in 1934 that the Nazis had been able to seize power completely.

The black rim around Hindenburg's picture dragged his thoughts back to his father. During the endless marches forward in the east, Wolff had often pondered how his father might react to the arrival of the 'birds of death', as the junior party officials tasked with delivering the official letters were known.

For most families, it was the worst possible news, but Wolff could imagine his father welcoming it. He had visualized Ludwig solemnly inviting the visitor inside and gleaning as many of the details as were ever disseminated by the army on such occasions.

Later, he would mention the matter offhandedly while out tramping around with his SA colleagues and then stoically accept their condolences while tacitly encouraging them to ask as many questions about what happened as possible. Perhaps even bridging the gaps in his knowledge with some speculation of his own dressed up as fact.

He smirked sourly as he thought of Ludwig desperately trying to source an appropriate picture in uniform of the hero who died for the Fatherland to place beside his party certificate. They had barely spoken since he was called up, let alone exchanged photographs.

Lothar arrived then, receiving a nod from the bartender. Wolff had intended to take a table so they could sit down, but the lad insisted they stay at the counter despite the discomfort it would cause him.

Wolff did not demur. Lothar was already made to feel like a lesser man by official state policy, and he did not wish to add to that. Besides, remaining in place ensured no impediment between Wolff and the steady flow of alcohol.

Lothar quickly steered the conversation around to the topic of life in the east. He seemed endlessly fascinated about the places Wolff had been, the combat he had seen and asked how many men he had killed.

Wolff shrugged uncomfortably. He didn't know, he said. You never stopped to count such things. Lothar continued to ask all sorts of questions. "You're lucky, you know," he told Wolff after a while. "You have a chance out there to show you're a man. The best I can do is say I make tank parts."

Wolff grimaced. It was far too early in the evening for such a maudlin air to enter the conversation. "Oh, come on, Lothar," he replied, attempting to lighten the tone. "You work in a factory surrounded by women. Most of the fellows I serve with would swap places with you in a heartbeat."

But for once, Lothar's usual repartee was absent. "Not if they knew the truth of it," he answered bitterly. "Most of the girls on the assembly line are waiting for their sweethearts to come back and sweep them off their feet.

"They chat away amongst themselves about where their boyfriends are, which unit they're in. Where they're planning to live, how many babies they want to have. Things that women normally talk about only amongst each other. But they discuss it in front of me."

Wolff looked away, unsure how to answer. He had expected a night swapping acerbic observations *sotto voce* about the Reich, the usual conspiratorial form their conversation took. He had not been anticipating this. While he thought of how best to respond, his gaze drifted to the corner where two soldiers in uniform had come in and sat down.

One of the men seemed vaguely familiar and Wolff stared at him, trying to recall if he had served alongside him. The Brandenburgers did not generally mix with rank-and-file infantry to avoid tensions spilling over into physical confrontation.

As a result, their only direct contact with the army was at officer planning briefings, where the timing and terms of offensives were outlined, along with the priority of whatever enemy landmark they had seized. This man was definitely not an officer, though.

After a few moments, he looked up, seemingly sensing Wolff's eyes upon him. Wolff turned away and took another large mouthful of his beer. There was movement to his right and he raised his eyes once more to see the soldier had moved up to stand at the bar.

The man was about 10 years older than him, but shorter and built like a barrel around the middle. Now they were closer, Wolff could see the braid and pips of a corporal on his uniform, but there were no distinguishing insignia to indicate his unit.

Nonetheless, it was clear that the man recognized him too. His eyes traveled disdainfully over the jacket of Wolff's well-worn best suit. Before the war, Wolff would have looked away, avoiding a potential problem. But those days were long gone.

So Wolff stared brazenly back at him and the man gave an insolent nod before turning back to face the bartender, a slight smirk on his face as he paid for his drink. He nodded once more to Wolff and walked over to his companion in the corner.

Wolff watched as he sat down and, after a few seconds of whispered conversation, the second soldier's eyes flicked momentarily to him. It was evident that whatever history there was between him and the corporal, the man was relaying it to his friend.

"Who's that?" Lothar asked. Wolff shook his head. "I don't know. I can't place him. Perhaps someone I came across in the field." But Lothar had lost interest in the soldier. "What's it like out there anyway, once the fighting has moved on?"

Wolff looked at him. "Why are you asking all this, Lothar?"

The boy took a deep breath. "Well, they must need people, don't they? To run the place after the army has left. Clerical staff and people to administer the new territory."

Wolff shook his head. "Lothar—"

"No. Hear me out." There was a determined tone to Lothar's voice that he recognized. "They will need people to run things, won't they? Especially when they start shifting the settlers out there, allocating the land. I mean, I serve a purpose here, but I could do more there, couldn't I? Make a career for myself."

Wolff thought of what he had heard about the *Einsatzgruppen*, the SS-organized Special Task Forces, who moved in after the line pushed farther east to rid the area of "undesirables".

"I'm not sure that's really somewhere you want to go, Lothar." But his neighbor was not prepared to see his patently long-cherished idea dismissed so easily. Clearly, Lothar had ulterior motives for their meeting beyond a few drinks himself.

"Why not?" he persisted. "I'm wasted here making tank parts. Being treated as invisible by the girls on the assembly line. Out there I could be somebody. Maybe even get myself a sweetheart."

Wolff looked at him. Would it really be so bad? In the east, even with his disability, Lothar would still be part of the *Herrenrasse*, the master race. Worthy of some sort of respect, however diminished. Who was he to piss on the lad's dreams?

The conversation was interrupted with the bang of the front door behind them and Wolff saw the bartender stiffen. He turned his head to see the back of a broad-shouldered man wearing an SA uniform walking towards where the two soldiers were sitting.

Judging by the way both jumped to their feet, both clearly deferred to the newcomer. His back still to Wolff, the man sat down at the table and Wolff looked on with idle curiosity as the corporal gestured towards the bar.

The older man nodded authoritatively, prompting the corporal to lean in and lower his voice before murmuring something slyly across the table. Even if his eyes had not flicked momentarily over towards him, Wolff would have known whom they were talking about. When the burly newcomer turned to look back at him, he understood why.

He had last stared into that face three years beforehand.

8

The SA man had been part of a group Wolff had come across on a frigid evening in November 1938 as he made his way home from his job as a stevedore.

Kristallnacht, the Goebbels-inspired national night of terror that left broken glass and Jewish blood strewn across Germany's streets, had occurred the previous week, but some of its victims were still trying to continue life as normal.

Perhaps to pay the *Judenvermögensabgabe*, the ludicrous collective Jewish Capital Levy imposed by the Nazis upon them for the privilege of being beaten and murdered in their own cities.

Perhaps because they were trying to gather the money to flee abroad. Or perhaps because they simply didn't know what else to do or where else to go. Shocked by the economic cost of what they had instigated, the Nazi leadership had forbidden any further pogroms.

They had no wish for the Jewish property they planned to expropriate to be damaged further. But that did not mean its owners were off limits. One such individual was attempting to close up his drapery - or what was left of it - on Rathausstrasse that evening while three young yobs, no older than 18, waited for him on the street like hyenas.

Wolff had later tried to rationalize why he had stopped to watch what was happening rather than continuing on his way. He had spent the day working alongside Lothar's father, a left-wing former union official who had somehow managed to hang on to his job at the port.

On their lunch break, they had quietly discussed the events of the previous week. Like most people, Wolff had been stunned at the orgy of violence against defenseless people who a few years earlier had been respected fellow citizens, but his disgust was nothing compared to that espoused by Lothar Senior.

A Hamburg native, the man had insisted angrily that the anti-semitism of the Nazis had never fully put down roots in his traditionally left-leaning hometown and that the violence had been carried out by thugs brought in from elsewhere in Germany.

Wolff was not sure he believed him, but initially wondered afterwards whether some of the man's outrage had rubbed off on him that afternoon.

Though when he considered it fully, he realized he had been brought to a halt by the calm, unyielding dignity of the shop owner, a man in his sixties, as the trio took turns to push him around and attempted to provoke him into physically defending himself.

Before he knew what he was doing, he had bellowed at the three teenage thugs to leave the man alone. Unused to being challenged and unsure of what to do about it, they had. He moved a little closer towards the group, hoping the distraction would allow the old man to slip away unhurt.

And that was when the big man had emerged from the alley-way across the street, from where he had been watching it all. A billy club down by his side and a deeply unpleasant grin on his face.

The old man had fled, and the hyenas had let him go. Wolff couldn't blame him. He knew what was coming, even if this stranger intervening on his behalf did not. When they had finished with him, they called the *Ordnungspolizei* and Wolff had been arrested for assault. He remembered now where he had seen the corporal before.

The squat little man had arrived on the scene while they were waiting for police to arrive and had guffawed sycophantically as the older individual boasted of how they had done the badly-dazed Wolff a favor by informing him of "the true realities of the Reich".

The old copper who had taken him in was sympathetic enough and informed Wolff he would try his best to make it all quietly disappear, but there was only so much he could do. The *Orpo*, like everything else in Hitler's Germany, was under the control of the Party and would do what it was told.

In the event, Wolff's call-up papers came through some weeks afterward and he never heard anything more of it, though clearly it remained on file. Dormant, but ready for resurrection when required. He was left with a badly bruised face and body and the lasting disgust and shame of his father, who refused to listen to his explanations of what had happened.

All three sets of eyes were now firmly fixed on Wolff, and the large man placed his hand on the corporal's arm as if standing him down. He rose slowly from his own seat and straightened his tunic over his portly frame.

Beside Wolff, Lothar had gone mute, all talk of the front quietened. His neighbor had enough experience of men like this not to draw attention to himself.

The man sauntered over to the bar where the bartender was already reaching for and filling a stein from the tap. "*Hauptsturmführer* Fuchs," he murmured deferentially. The SA officer ignored him and grinned unpleasantly over at Wolff.

"Enjoying some leave?" Fuchs asked, accepting the stein proffered by the barman without taking his eyes from Wolff. Wolff simply nodded in response. It was evident from the other man's tone that he did not consider Wolff to be an officer.

Perhaps it was his relative youth, or the faded fabric of his suit. Up until a few days beforehand, he would have been correct. Still staring at Wolff, Fuchs offered some coins to the barman, who nervously protested there was no need.

Fuchs grinned again, as if he had expected this, and thrust the money back into his pocket. He gripped the stein in his other giant hand and lifted it to his mouth to take a long swig, with an exaggerated performance of savoring it afterwards.

"Good, good," Fuchs said. "Our fighting men should make the most of their time at home visiting friends and family. Isn't that so, Ziegler?" The barman smiled and nodded obsequiously, but quickly returned his focus to Wolff. There was a warning to his gaze now.

Fuchs' eyes slid to Lothar, whose own gaze was now firmly on the counter in front of him. "What about you, boy?" Lothar looked up and took a step back involuntarily, the movement betraying his disability.

"I-I work in the armaments factory in Altona-Nord," he mumbled quietly. Fuchs smirked. There was only one reason any man of Lothar's age would have such a job, even if the lad had not inadvertently made it clear.

"Good, good," Fuchs said again. "We must all do what we can to contribute to the war effort. Even those who might otherwise be considered...human ballast."

Lothar flinched at the term used to justify the Party's euthanasia campaign against "life unworthy of life". The Catholic Church, along with the rest of German society, had turned a blind eye to most of Hitler's atrocities.

But the gassing and lethal injection of physically and mentally disabled adults and children had been too much even for them. Aktion T4, as it was officially known, had been halted by Hitler just weeks beforehand following nationwide protests led by the Bishop of Münster.

"However," Fuchs added, making an even more ostentatious show of checking his watch, "there is a curfew at 10pm, so I'm afraid you'll both have to finish your drinks and go on your way." Wolff looked up at the clock behind the bar, which said ten minutes past nine.

His eyes met those of the barman, who gave an almost imperceptible nod in return. Evidently it was not the first time he had seen Fuchs act out this particular scene. "Yes, let's go, Ako," Lothar said beside him in a low voice, drinking the rest of his beer quickly and pushing the empty stein glass across the counter.

Wolff looked over at his friend and patted him on the arm, just as Fuchs had done to the corporal moments earlier. Then he lifted his own drink and took a long, leisurely swallow before setting it down. Fuchs' eyes narrowed, before a slow smile spread across his face, the challenge recognized.

"I am a lieutenant of the Wehrmacht," Wolff said, his gaze still on Fuchs. "As such, I am exempt from such regulations. My colleague and I are out enjoying a drink, as we are entitled to." In the corner, the two soldiers stood up.

Fuchs' head pushed back on his thick neck in feigned appreciation. "A lieutenant!" He swung his gaze round to the other two, who grinned back at him, clearly enjoying the theatrics. The only other people in the bar, a middle-aged couple, were looking fixedly into their drinks.

Fuchs picked up his beer and moved down the bar towards where Wolff was standing. His voice dropped a little, but remained loud enough so that everyone in the now silent room could still hear it.

"You might well be a lieutenant," he said. "But even if you are, I outrank you. So if I tell you to go home, you go. Take your little crippled pal here and scram. Otherwise, we might have to teach you a lesson. Again."

Wolff picked up his beer and made as if to finish it. In truth, he was unsure if what Fuchs was saying was true. The SA had lost much of its power since its glory days.

Even so, it was clear Fuchs felt the events of three years before gave him a hold over Wolff he could exploit. No army officer would want to become involved in defending him against a messy accusation of race treason.

Hence the arrogant self-assurance of Fuchs and his two companions. This would never become an official matter. Regardless of how it turned out, it would end right here. That knowledge, combined with a terrible day and the recognition that his evening's drinking had come to an end anyway made Wolff's decision for him.

As he lowered his glass after draining the last of the liquid from it, he turned the stein horizontally, pivoted and smashed it with all of his strength onto the bridge of Fuchs' nose.

Stunned, his opponent took a couple of steps backward and put his hand up to where blood was pouring from his nostrils. Then, with a roar of fury, he launched himself at Wolff again, meaty hands outstretched towards the throat.

Surprising himself with his dexterity despite the amount he had drunk, Wolff ducked and sidestepped, allowing Fuchs' weight and momentum to carry him forward, before driving his right fist into the bigger man's exposed kidney.

Fuchs screamed in pain, but still made a valiant effort to turn again towards Wolff, who stopped him in his tracks by driving his knee into the man's groin. He had no time to appreciate his handiwork as the corporal rushed at him with beer stein aloft, clearly intending to do the same to Wolff as Wolff had done to his friend.

Wolff grabbed the arm with the glass and the man's other flailing limb, but was pushed against the bar, falling backward over Fuchs' prone form and losing his balance as he grappled with his second opponent.

The corporal was as strong as a bull and Wolff realized he was in real trouble here if he fell to the ground. This time, the police would not be called. He could have survived some of the worst combat could throw at him only to be beaten to death in a dingy Hamburg bar.

The third man was on his feet now too, ready to assist once the corporal gave him an opening. Wolff was still being pushed back against the bar, but his opponent had over-extended himself and that gave Wolff an opportunity.

Twisting his body at a right angle, he shortened his grip down to the crook of the corporal's outstretched arm with the stein. He moved his other hand up to the man's opposite armpit and hooked his left leg behind the back of his opponent's knee.

Using the man's weight against him, he completed a classic judo throw to the floor, walloping the corporal's head off the edge of the bar as he did so. The corporal went down like a sack of potatoes.

The third soldier stood there frozen in panic for a moment, still unsure quite how his two companions had ended up on the floor in the blink of an eye. Finally, he charged clumsily in fear at Wolff, who easily sidestepped him and struck him in the throat with his fingers and thumb forming a rigid vee, leaving the man choking and clawing at his collar on the floor.

There was silence in the bar for a few seconds, the horrified couple gazing at him from their table where they were hunched over in terror. Lothar was staring at him with equal parts alarm and wonder. He looked back at the barman, who instinctively raised his hands defensively as if Wolff was about to turn on him.

He heard the couple get to their feet and scuttle out the front door while his attention was elsewhere. It was time to go now, before they found a passing *Orpo* patrol and told them what had happened. Or even worse, some of Fuchs' SA colleagues.

But in his drunken state, some of Oster's recklessness seemed to rub off on him. He was sick of running from these people.

The barman had his hands up defensively as Wolff approached the bar. "Look, I don't want any more trouble. Just take what you want and go. Please."

Wolff saw the genuine dread in the other man's eyes. He might be facing a visit from the Gestapo over this in an attempt to establish Wolff's identity, even though it was the first time he had ever been in this bar. He had also, he realized, ruined possibly the only place in Hamburg where Lothar was allowed to drink in peace.

"Oh, there'll be no trouble, Herr Ziegler," Wolff slurred. He felt himself swaying slightly.

Get out of here.

No, the hell with it.

"However, you must have some better schnapps here than what I've been drinking all evening?" The barman nodded frantically, ready to offer him anything as long as Wolff would leave.

"Well, we'll have two glasses of that for the road, then." As Ziegler reached under the counter to where the good stuff was kept for favored customers, Wolff looked down to his right, where the corporal was still out cold on the floor.

The third man he had dealt with was still curled in a ball, wheezing against his badly bruised larynx. Meanwhile, Fuchs had raised himself on one elbow, eyes above his bloodied face filled with hate but showing no desire to get up.

Ziegler placed two glasses filled to the brim on the bar and immediately moved backwards, as if not trusting Wolff to stick to his word after such a display of ferocity. "They're on the house, but afterwards, please, leave."

"No, no. I really couldn't accept that," Wolff smiled, holding up his palms as if offended by the suggestion. He bent down towards Fuchs, who shrank back against the bar as Wolff leaned over him, patting his pockets until he found the SA man's wallet.

"Here," he said, standing up unsteadily and handing the largest note he could find inside over to Ziegler.

"The *Hauptsturmführer* is paying. Keep the change."

9

Wolff tried to focus on the brochure in front of him, though its tedious contents, his still considerable hangover and the roar of the airplane engines made that difficult.

He would need at least some rudimentary knowledge of his wares in case he was challenged, but unlike some of the Ukrainian farm boys back in his unit, he had zero interest in the relative merits of the Mannheim company's Z-960. 'The Reich's premier tractor', as the document boasted with typical bombast.

Still, anything to take his mind off what had happened back in Hamburg. He and Lothar had left the pub after downing the schnapps, though Ziegler the barman had spoiled some of Wolff's fun by refusing to take Fuchs' money. Lothar had practically sprinted out the door afterwards despite his disability.

Wolff had cursed himself for his stupidity the following morning and had gotten out of the city as quickly as he could by train, half-expecting the arresting sound of footsteps behind him even as he waited on the station platform. If he had blown his chance at redemption through a second detention for assaulting members of the SA, Canaris and Oster would probably have washed their hands of him entirely.

But far beyond that, Wolff was shocked at the pleasure he had taken in the fight.

He had insisted on accompanying Lothar to his tram stop, almost hopeful that some obnoxious citizen would make further remarks about the lad. But there had been none, and while Wolff was high on the adrenalin of exacted revenge, Lothar was entirely silent.

There was no more talk of the east and the farewell was hurried and perfunctory. It was as if his old pal was now afraid of him.

The following afternoon in Berlin, he underwent a short further briefing from Canaris and Oster at the Bendlerblock before taking the flight to Bulgaria. Wolff had taken advantage of it to collect the documentation he would need for Riga.

He had also been given a signed letter from Canaris ordering all members of the armed forces to cooperate with its bearer's instructions. He read over the material in his lap again, attempting to commit its details to memory. Just in case someone from Bulgaria's Police Directorate decided to pull him in and test him on his cover story.

Of course, the whole thing was so transparently false, they probably wouldn't bother unless they were determined to lay down a marker of some sort. No tractor firm would charter a 17-seat Junkers Ju-52 just to fly a single salesman to Sofia so they could flog a few units.

Wolff had pointed this out in his bid to be allowed travel by train, but Oster had shut him down. There was no time to lose and this took priority over all other concerns.

As it was his first time flying, he had been unsure what to expect. He had skipped breakfast this morning in his haste to get out of Hamburg and he was damn glad of that. The way this thing was bucking in the sky - an entirely normal occurrence, judging by the pilot's demeanor - it would have come up by now.

As the 'Aunt Ju' touched down in Sofia and taxied to the terminal, Wolff could see he had a welcoming party. A German car, a Daimler, at least, whether that meant anything or not.

The individual in his forties leaning on it was clearly local, however. Wolff was unfamiliar with Bulgarian uniforms, but the man's age and the small row of decorations along his left-hand breast pocket indicated he was relatively senior.

Wolff disembarked gratefully and walked towards the car, which was parked directly in front of the entrance to the small terminal building. He could see his host sizing him up as he approached, apparently surprised by his youth.

Between them, Oster and Wolff had decided he would claim to be epileptic if challenged. It was the best way of explaining what an apparently able-bodied man of military service age was doing out of uniform.

This also banked on a degree of ignorance among the Bulgarians towards Hitler's loathsome eugenics legislation. Under the Law for the Prevention of Progeny with Hereditary Diseases, all epileptics were required to submit to forced sterilization.

Unfortunately, Oster had informed him with a smirk, there would be no time to inflict a fake vasectomy scar. It was just as well, Wolff thought, as he would not put it past the man to insist upon it. The Bulgarian lifted himself from the car as he neared, flicking away the cigarette he had been smoking.

"Herr Hermann Schreiber?" he said in heavily accented German, his eyes still probing Wolff's physique for any visible disability. Wolff smiled. "Yes? Would you like to see my passport?" He reached into his coat and handed over the freshly made document Oster had given him back in Berlin.

The officer took it from him, flicked it open and glanced at it before handing it back. Everyone knew how easily such material was faked in wartime. The Abwehr even had its own passport creation office for that very purpose. The Bulgarian did not introduce himself, but simply opened the passenger door of the car.

"Please".

They drove out of the airport unchallenged, the military sentry at the gate raising the barrier as the car loomed. "You are younger than I expected," the man said to him. He had still not introduced himself and was attempting to dispense with Wolff's cover from the beginning.

Wolff ignored the overt ploy. "I'm sorry, are you with customs? I was expecting to be met by someone from my hotel." The man looked over at him and smiled. "Yes, don't worry. We took care of that, Herr Schreiber."

"Where are we going?" Wolff asked. "Don't worry," the man answered. "You'll get to your hotel. There are just some...formalities to be taken care of first."

"What formalities?"

The man looked at him and sighed. "My name is Major Tashev. I am from Department D of State Security here. I simply need you to come to my office for a few moments before I allow you to continue on your...business trip."

Wolff ignored the bait contained in the inflection at the end of the sentence, and they drove on in silence towards the center of Sofia. Tashev had been quite brazen, considering Wolff was a citizen of an Axis ally nation.

Oster had mused aloud over whether the head of Department D would be senior enough to be in on what was happening, before deciding it was impossible to predict how closely the Bulgarians would guard details of the offer from Moscow. People gossiped, it was as simple as that.

Wolff sensed he would find out shortly. The river was on his left now, so by his reckoning this was Slivnitsa Boulevard they were traveling along. He had taken the time to memorize the main thoroughfares of the center, though Oster had conceded the city map in his suitcase fitted his cover and he was allowed to take it with him.

A few seconds later, his guess was confirmed by a Cyrillic street sign. They crossed over Lion's Bridge, its two bronze big cats mounting mute guard on either side. Tashev parked up outside a four-floor yellow building, which at once managed to be elegant and forbidding.

Wolff followed as the Bulgarian led him past a soldier on guard duty and up a dark stairwell. As they ascended, a double door on the first floor opened and a uniformed officer came out past them. Wolff had a brief glimpse inside of a large and busy office filled with others in uniform. Department B, which watched the Russians, he guessed.

On the next level, Tashev opened the door to a room and ushered him inside. Wolff found himself in a suite of equal size, but notably less bustle. In fact, apart from a female secretary sitting behind a desk, there was nobody there at all.

Department D was evidently still the poor relation. Tashev turned left and Wolff followed him through a doorway to a spacious office, where Tashev gestured towards a seat in front of a large desk. The single telephone which stood starkly in its center accentuated its size. There was a filing cabinet in the corner, but no other furniture.

Tashev took the seat opposite him, all business now. "May I?" he asked, reaching for Wolff's suitcase. Wolff handed it over, and the Bulgarian snapped the clasps. He lifted the lid and poked around inside, lifting out the map of Sofia and opening it with a snort.

Aside from Wolff's clothing, toiletries and some more brochures, there was nothing else. "Your passport again, please?" Wolff handed it over and Tashev left the office, presumably to photograph it.

Wolff sat there without the slightest idea how a spy was supposed to behave in such a situation. Affronted? Resistant? He wondered also how a genuine salesman would react to such unusual scrutiny. Polite and compliant to a point, perhaps, though not prepared to be pushed around endlessly.

Tashev returned with his documents and sat down behind the desk, staring at Wolff for a few seconds as if deciding what to do next. "So, Herr Schreiber," he said eventually. "You are here to sell cars?"

"Tractors," Wolff corrected him. It was a lame attempt and the Bulgarian's sour expression acknowledged it.

"How can I help you, Herr..."

"Tashev."

"My apologies." The silence lay heavy between them. Unwilling to put his cards on the table just yet, Tashev tried again.

"You are much younger than I expected. I thought a man of your age would be in the army."

"Yes, unfortunately I suffer from a medical condition which prevents me from serving my country."

"Ah, so you are...what's the phrase, kv....?"

"KvH," Wolff finished for him smoothly. Tashev was doing his level best to provoke him and Wolff found himself taking umbrage on behalf of his adopted legend.

"It was decided that I should help the war effort elsewhere by boosting the home economy. Germany needs foreign investment, and who better to seek it from than one of our closest allies." Tashev smiled politely at the unsubtle dig.

He picked up the brochure from Wolff's suitcase, which lay on the desk before him, and began leafing through it before stopping at a random page. "Would you be so good as to explain to me the function of the crankshaft within the Z-960, Herr...?"

Tashev looked up at Wolff expectantly. "Schreiber," Wolff prompted him quietly. He said nothing else, as stumped by the question as Tashev had anticipated.

Tashev smiled again, this time in triumph. "I don't know why you are here, but whatever it is, it was evidently organized quite hurriedly. In truth, it is the manner of your arrival which I find perturbing.

"There is no shortage of German military officers, or indeed intelligence people, stationed in Sofia, yet you have come in the guise of a civilian. It is as intriguing as it is disrespectful. It is almost as if you are hiding from your own people as much as ours." Tashev's lips pursed disapprovingly.

Wolff remained silent, though inwardly his stomach plunged. He had been in the country a little over an hour and his cover had already been comprehensively blown.

"My department was set up to monitor German espionage within Bulgaria's borders," Tashev continued. "As you can see, I am somewhat...understaffed at the moment compared to Department B downstairs, but that is simply because the communists have always posed a bigger threat.

"They have tried to overthrow the government twice in the past 20 years. On the second occasion in 1925, they almost succeeded in assassinating the Tsar. Your country, on the other hand, has proved a useful ally of late.

"Thanks to the German invasion of Yugoslavia, we have been able to recover the lands unjustly taken from us after the last war. We also took back Western Thrace from the Greeks and Dobruja from the Romanians. The return of these has been a huge boost to the nation.

"That does not mean we are prepared to allow your government to act as it wishes upon our territory. I am aware of the identity of your operatives here in Sofia, and they have always behaved in a courteous way in the past.

"It does not imply, however, that we will simply put up with anything, Herr....Schreiber." Tashev infused the last word with heavy irony. "There is a delicate balance in this country as a result of the war," he continued, "and it is my job to maintain that balance.

"As such, I can assure you of one thing. If I even suspect you are engaged in any activity which will damage this country's relations with the Soviet Union, I will have you arrested and thrown out, with a formal protest to the German embassy.

"Our Tsar, Boris III, has stated publicly that while he is in power, no Bulgarian mother will wear a black headscarf for a son or a husband killed in this war. Believe me, this is a pledge I intend to uphold.

"Furthermore, and I would imagine this goes without saying, if I discover there are any attempts to rile up our own fascist rabble, the Ratniks, in the same way certain figures from your nation tried to destabilize Romania, well…" Tashev trailed off.

"Who knows, Herr Schreiber? You may well find yourself meeting some of those communists I was speaking of. They don't like fascists very much. I've heard a favored trick of theirs is to cut off the balls off Ratniks and make them eat them. Imagine what they'd do to a Nazi."

Wolff said nothing, but wondered how his genitalia had become an apparently legitimate subject of public discussion. Tashev eyed him for a few more seconds before picking up the tractor brochure and tossing it into the suitcase and closing it. He snorted and pushed it across the desk to Wolff.

"I wish you the best of luck in boosting your economy.".

10

Outside, Wolff took a moment to get his bearings and recover his composure.

Tashev had seen through him instantly, but how much did that matter? After all, he was not here to start a coup or provoke trouble with the Russians. Quite the opposite, as it happened.

If anything, he decided, the meeting had shown matters were in his favor. Tashev's unsubtle attempt at intimidation indicated the man had little else up his sleeve. Perhaps Department D was even a one-man band, without the resources to accomplish much more.

There had been no body search either, for which Wolff was grateful. He did not want awkward questions about the documentation he was carrying. Or the souvenir Red Army scout knife at the small of his back.

Still, he would have to play it cautiously. Oster had made the limitations of his role clear the previous day. He had not yet been co-opted into the Abwehr proper. He was a *Vertrauensmann*, a trusted collaborator, hired for a specific task.

But to maintain that trust, a V-man had to perform satisfactorily.

He was trying to figure out in which direction his hotel lay when he heard a car start down the street to his left and slowly rumble towards where he was standing. It stopped in front of him and the driver, a German in civilian clothes in his late thirties, leaned over and opened the passenger side door.

"There you are," he leaned over, looking at Wolff. He assumed this was Captain Wagner, who was supposed to meet him at the airport. He got in and Wagner introduced himself and pulled away. He grinned across at Wolff.

"So, Tashev took you for a little chat, did he? He's getting quite cheeky. I was delayed getting out to the airport, and when I saw there was no sign of you, I figured out what must have happened." Wolff outlined the details of his brush with the Bulgarian.

Wagner nodded. "I see, you didn't tell him why you were here?" Wolff stared at him. "Of course not." He sensed Wagner's question had more to do with his own curiosity than anything else.

Oster had explained that the local Abwehr *Ast* was being kept out of the loop, not least because it was believed some of them were also providing information to the SD. They had been given a cover story about attempts to recruit sources of information on the recent partisan uprising in Yugoslavia, which it was believed the Soviets were aiding via Sofia.

It was clear Wagner did not believe a word of it, but he knew better than to ask openly. When Wolff did not volunteer anything else, Wagner pressed on. "My instructions are to take you to the places where business is done in this town and let you get on with your work. Do you need to report in first?"

Wolff shook his head. There seemed little point in explaining Tashev's welcoming committee to Berlin. He would leave that for Wagner, if he felt like passing it on. Judging by what he had seen of the Abwehr man so far, he doubted it.

Instead, he asked Wagner to take him to his hotel. After a five minute drive, the captain pulled up outside the Slavyanska Beseda, a modern seven floor structure overlooking a cobbled street. Wolff got out, and they agreed to meet in a few hours' time in a bar called Riunione.

It was where most foreign businessmen in town drank, as well as every spy pretending to be one. Canaris had explained that much of what passed for secret intelligence work actually took place openly.

Germans, Russians, British and Americans all hung out in the same places, alternately cooperating with and attempting to stymie each other, and sometimes both at once. All sorts of information was bartered and exchanged; the trick was filtering out the genuine.

Riunione was the spot where Wolff could show himself and wait for the NKVD to make their move. As the instigators of the offer, the onus was on them. After freshening up at the hotel, whose level of luxury surprised him, Wolff made his way to the bar, which lay five blocks down on Dondukov Boulevard.

Though it was early evening, there was already quite a crowd inside, and some looked to have been there all afternoon. The atmosphere was almost desperately festive, those present maximizing their time in one of Europe's few neutral corners while the rest of the continent burned.

Wolff felt several pairs of curious eyes on him as he walked inside and glanced around. The place was large, but simple enough, with a bar running down one side and seating booths along the opposite wall. There were also some tables in the middle, with a dancefloor sandwiched between these and a tiny stage occupied by a jazz band up against the back wall.

He was relieved to see Wagner standing at the bar, waving him over. "Well, at least I know how it feels to be Kristina Söderbaum," he murmured, referring to the beautiful blonde film star who was Joseph Goebbels' favorite muse. Söderbaum had ended up drowning tragically in so many of the Propaganda Minister's film productions, she was nicknamed the *Reichswasserleiche*, the State Water Corpse.

"Flattered by the attention?" Wagner grinned as he ordered whiskeys without asking Wolff if he wanted one. "That's the whole point," he said, once the barman had moved away. "I don't know what you're doing here and, for the record, I don't buy the line about recruiting locals either.

"But whoever you are in Sofia to meet, though, will likely be in here amongst the crowd somewhere. Here, or Etoile, or Maxim's or the Imperial. You see these girls walking around chatting to people?" Wolff looked around properly for the first time.

Riunione's clientele was almost exclusively male and primarily middle-aged. What females were present were virtually all young, pretty and well-turned out. Some sat in the booths occupied by groups of men, while others stood at the bar or against the wall trying to catch the eye of bored customers.

As Wolff's gaze moved across the bar, a couple of them looked directly at him and beamed. He turned back to Wagner, who was still smirking. "The locals call them 'taxi girls'. I think it's because they're the ones who hail a ride home for customers who are unable to do it themselves by the end of the night.

"Don't get the wrong idea. They're not whores, though I've seen some of them jump in the same taxi if the guy looks particularly well-off. Generally, they're here to charm the customers, make sure they have a good time, take them up to dance. That kind of thing.

"But what they also do is pass messages between people who don't want to openly approach each other. And they get well-tipped, so they're quite discreet about it. That's how business gets done here. There's a delicate balance, and the smart ones maintain it."

He grimaced and jutted his chin towards a table behind Wolff's back. "Unfortunately, not all of our compatriots fall into that category." Wolff turned to a booth, where five German airmen were loudly attempting to bellow something above the music of the jazz band.

Wolff recognized it as *Sieg Heil Viktoria*, a favorite dirge of the Waffen SS. The song seemed to be directed at a nearby table where three men with the well-fed air of Americans were doing their best to ignore it.

"That's the military attaché from the US embassy," Wagner nodded at the largest of the trio. "Those flyboys probably lost a lot of comrades during the Battle of Crete, shot down by aircraft supplied to the RAF under the Lend-Lease Act. There have been a few near-dust ups with the Yanks in here, but it usually peters out."

Wolff nodded. The Americans were nominally neutral in the war, but President Franklin D. Roosevelt had made their position clear towards the Axis by sending destroyers, tanks and planes to Britain since signing the Lend-Lease Act the previous March.

He was about to ask Wagner whether he should also be concerned about potential American surveillance in Sofia when one of the taxi girls appeared between them. She was petite, with brown hair cut fashionably short in a bob and wearing a floral dress which complimented her slim figure.

"And how are you gentlemen doing this evening?" Wagner looked at Wolff and grinned again before excusing himself, saying he had to talk to someone. The girl introduced herself as Anna and Wolff as Hermann. She accepted his offer of a glass of champagne.

Her accent was Viennese, and they chatted briefly before Anna pronounced herself "a bit bored", while complimenting the band on the catchy music they were belting out. Wolff took the hint and invited her out onto the floor.

He had been on edge since arriving in the city, but here at last was an arena where he would be in complete control. Wolff considered himself a man of many parts. He ascribed his level-headed, calm approach to life to his German blood and his ease with solitude to his Latvian side.

But his approach to having fun was entirely a product of growing up in Brazil. And no Brazilian male worth his salt was unable to acquit himself on the dance floor.

As he whirled Anna around, he caught occasional envious glances from other booths. Even the obnoxiously drunk pilots had stopped their screeching to watch them in action. His natural instinct was to stop, that drawing attention to himself was not how a spy should behave.

But then, Wagner had told him that this was where the approach would likely be made. Instead of stopping, he threw his dance partner around even more, using the movements to scan the crowd for stereotypical wide Slavic faces above the substandard cut of a Soviet suit.

Perhaps an NKVD man endlessly nursing the same drink, rather than having to explain a large bill to his superiors. But there were no such individuals, and it was hard to know how many of the eyes on them were actually attracted by Anna's lithe, gyrating backside.

When the band finished up, he took advantage of the break to move back to the bar and survey whether any gazes were still lingering. Anna too was almost out of breath and was beaming at him in surprise.

"Where on earth did you learn to dance like that?" she asked, before leaning in flirtatiously. "I thought the Reich had banned jazz as 'morally corrupt'?" Wolff grinned back and lowered his own voice to a stage whisper. "They did, but they created their own permitted version instead. They call it the Goebbels Two Step."

Anna threw back her head and laughed, and Wolff felt the natural ego boost of flirting with a pretty girl. Details of the *Reichsminister für Propaganda*'s deformity were widely known in Germany, if rarely commented upon in public. It was another one of Nazism's endless inconsistencies - a leading member of the supposed master race with a club foot.

Wolff was about to say something else when he noticed two men still watching them from one of the booths at the far end of the room. There was nothing distinctive about either of the pair's dress or mannerisms. At best, Wolff could say they were Europeans rather than *Amis*, but that was as far as he could go.

The men held his gaze for a few seconds before resuming the chat between them. Wolff kept looking at them, but aside from a few glances, the pair did not make further eye contact. Anna caught his stare and turned to look back before facing him once more. "Friends of yours?" she inquired teasingly.

Wolff looked at her, unable to keep the reciprocal smile from his face. He was starting to quite like this Viennese taxi girl. He was trying to compose a witty reply when all hell broke loose on the far side of the room. The Luftwaffe pilots had resumed their singing and were putting extra effort into the verse referring to the Allied leaders and their perceived American confederate.

"*Farewell, farewell, farewell,*" they sang, waving sardonically with one hand and thumping the table with the other. "*To Stalin, Churchill, Roosevelt. Farewell, Farewell, Farewell.*"

The most inebriated-looking of the airmen had been conducting his colleagues with an upturned empty champagne bottle, and when one of the Americans finally responded to the taunts with a middle finger, the Luftwaffe man hurled it at their table.

Displaying remarkable agility for such a big man, the US military attaché caught the bottle in mid-flight, reversed grip and then returned serve. The bottle soared back towards the German table and landed in the middle of the group's glasses, shattering them and sending champagne everywhere.

The five pilots were up in an instant and charging as one towards the American table, whose occupants seemed far steadier on their feet. In the seconds before the two sides clashed, Wolff noticed all three adopt the classic pugilistic stance.

But as punches started to fly and some of the participants crashed to the floor, suited men rose from their seats elsewhere in the bar and ran to join in. Within seconds, there was a full-scale brawl involving almost 15 males underway in the center of the dance floor.

Other non-combatants and taxi girls scrambled to get away from the ever-growing melee, which was also starting to draw in even more customers who objected to Germans and Americans crashing into their booths as they grappled with each other.

"We'd better get out of here." Wagner was at Wolff's elbow and dragging him towards the exit. As they walked swiftly outside, Wolff saw a group of about eight burly men, all carrying iron bars, stride determinedly towards Riunione, open the front door and go inside.

"Who the hell are they?" Wolff asked Wagner when they were safely clear of the bar. "They're what we needed to get away from," Wagner replied. "The taxi girls provide entertainment in this town, the taxi men take care of security.

"They'll go in there and lay out anyone and anything involved in the fight, and perhaps even quite a few who aren't." He looked at Wolff and smiled wistfully. "This isn't the first time something like this has happened. Reminds me of Berlin back during the Weimar Republic days.

"Come on, I'll take you to Etoile. If your contact was in there and got out in time, that's likely where he'll head. If he didn't, you probably won't see him again tonight anyway." They turned to go when a voice came from behind.

"Hermann! Hermann! Herr Schreiber!"

Wolff stopped and faced the bar once more. Anna was standing there looking at him expectantly with a nervous smile. She had disappeared in the mayhem which followed the outbreak of the fight, and Wolff had assumed she had either fled outside or to a safe backroom along with the other girls.

He walked over to say goodbye. He had no need of further complications tonight, even if he sensed the spark between them was genuine. As he took her by the hands and leaned in to give her a peck on each cheek, he was surprised to feel her press something into his palm.

"Goodbye, Hermann. I hope perhaps we can see each other again while you're in town. You never did explain where that unusual accent of yours is from." She smiled at him radiantly, and Wolff felt an overwhelming desire to dismiss Wagner and head off with her to another bar, or better still, directly to his hotel.

It was tempered only by a single thought. Obviously, he had been under surveillance inside and whoever it was had taken advantage of the confusion to pass Anna a message for him. But the origins of the *Baltendeutsche* accent he had picked up from his parents was not the only thing he had not revealed to her.

He had not given the surname of his cover identity either.

11

Wolff awoke early with a medium to strong hangover for a second day in a row, but pushed it from his mind and got down to do his daily exercise.

After leaving Riunione, he and Wagner had gone on to the second bar and he had quickly excused himself to visit the toilet. Once safely in the cubicle, he had opened the scrap of folded paper to see an address scrawled on it in Cyrillic script and the time of 12pm.

So the NKVD, or at least one of their local stooges, had been in the bar all along. He wondered where they had been sitting. It stood to reason they had been taking proper precautions. According to Oster, the Soviets involved in this would have just as much to lose if things went awry, even if they were operating with Stalin's full approval.

Wagner had asked him the night before what the Russians would do if they caught a Brandenburger party wearing enemy uniforms. The Abwehr man had so far spent the war in safety in Sofia and was morbidly curious about conditions at the front.

The same thing they would do to any *Landser* in Wehrmacht uniform, Wolff had informed him. Shoot them on the spot. Wouldn't they be taken prisoner instead, Wagner had queried further, in an attempt to interrogate them? Wolff almost laughed in his face and was only prevented from doing so by the man's superior rank.

There are few secrets on the Eastern Front, he told Wagner. Each side knows where the other is and what they have to do. Kill them. The only occasions on which prisoners were taken was when their numbers made shooting all of them too time-consuming.

Wagner had gone quiet then, perhaps reflecting on how lucky he was not to be out there. The conversation had moved on, and the subject had not come up again. Wolff finished his lot of push ups, sit ups and squats and took a breather.

The regular troops always looked upon his Brandenburger unit's morning workout with bemusement. It was another thing which separated the men Wolff led from their rank-and-file colleagues. The determination to maintain standards in a war which had lost them a long time ago.

He breakfasted at the hotel and sat for a while in the lobby to read the newspapers. A two-day-old copy of the *New York Times* told him Guderian's panzers were now 400 miles from the Soviet capital, having covered almost twice that distance in little over a month.

Though Russian resistance was stiffening, the paper said, the Wehrmacht was expected to take Moscow by November at the latest. Even allowing for the inevitable Goebbels-orchestrated exaggeration, the reports were likely to be broadly correct. No wonder the Ivans were so desperate to arrange some kind of ceasefire.

He had run through some of his newly learned counter surveillance exercises en route to Riunione the night before, but there were so few people on the streets, he quickly realized it would be impossible to set a tail on him. This morning was busier, and ensuring he was not followed to the meet would be more complex.

After quickly studying his map of Sofia once more, he was ready to go. Most of the old center was laid out in a classic grid pattern, and those parts that were not all led towards St Nedelya's cathedral in the heart of the city. He folded the newspaper under his arm and walked outside.

A quick scan of people sitting at the tables outside showed an old couple having coffee, two apparently foreign businessmen eating at separate tables and Wolff's choice, a fat man in a rumpled suit reading a paper of his own.

He turned right before strolling off at a leisurely pace. His objective was to head for the Kyulutsite neighborhood, a warren of small streets northeast of Sofia's historic center, where he could double back, speed up and lose whoever might be on him.

A couple of blocks brought him past the Bulgarian Army Theatre to the intersection with Tsar Osvoboditel Boulevard. There, a glance in the plate-glass windows of a building opposite, showed his overweight shadow bustling down the street behind him to keep up.

Wolff turned left, heading towards the old cathedral. If this clumsy fool was all Tashev could spare to monitor him, he should be fine. He followed the boulevard where it snaked between Tsar Boris's palace and the park known as the City Garden and took another left before swinging suddenly into the park itself.

He walked down one of the side paths and stopped, ostensibly to admire a pretty bed of flowers. Just then, the fat man came jogging into view through the park entrance, frantically looking left and right. Spotting Wolff, he immediately developed an intense interest in the time and stared at his wristwatch for a couple of seconds before dropping to one knee to fiddle with a shoelace. Wolff shook his head.

Voigt would have made mincemeat of this fellow.

Wolff turned again and ambled towards the eastern exit, which would bring him out in front of the tsar's palace once more. Then he went left, right and right again, which brought him back to the same spot where he had been standing between the City Garden and Boris' regal home.

Instead of reentering the park, however, he continued straight on towards the cathedral in the city center before swinging right onto Dondukov Boulevard, the street named for the Russian general credited with expelling the Turks over 60 years earlier.

The street sign underlined again why the NKVD had chosen Sofia as the location for the parley. The country's government might be nominally a German ally, but Bulgaria would always be friendly territory for the Ivans. A couple of hundred yards along the boulevard, Wolff cut left and was in the neighborhood of Kyulutsite where he wanted to be.

Several twisted circuits and double backs on the streets there a few minutes later confirmed he was indeed 'clean'. He grinned as he thought of his portly shadow sprinting frantically along a pavement somewhere, head turning this way and that in search of him. But now was no time to get cocky.

Now that he was free, he would have to ensure he remained that way. He took off his suit jacket and tie and removed the flat cap from inside the newspaper, placing it on his head. If Fatso had rung back to HQ to issue a description of his missing mark, it would throw any reinforcements off further.

Maintaining his own brisk pace, Wolff took a meandering route via Tsar Simeon Boulevard west to the intersection with Hristo Botev and then turned south towards his destination. The Soviets wanted to meet in a dingy beer hall on Positano Street, which struck him as an odd choice.

After ordering a lager and sitting at a table beside the window, Wolff waited for half an hour, constantly scanning the street outside. He kept his hat on, mindful of the warnings he had received from Voigt against being photographed.

It still took all of his willpower to remain in such a prominent spot, with every instinct screaming at him to move back into the gloom. He assured himself he was being ridiculous. The Soviets had not arranged this complicated meeting just to have a mid-ranking German spy of little importance taken out by a sniper on neutral territory.

While he waited, he thought about where his unit was right now. Wolff did not miss the front or the fighting, but he did miss the certainty of the unbreakable bond between them due to the simple expedient of relying on each other completely to survive.

To a man, they understood too well the problem of being outsiders in modern Germany. The Brandenburgers offered them an acceptance they would never obtain elsewhere in the Reich. Perhaps he owed it to them to be able to return home alive to a country where they would no longer be judged on their accent, nose length or place of birth.

Maybe, just maybe, it would also result in Ludwig finally recognizing that the ideology to which he so fervently pledged allegiance was built on foundations of sand. After forty minutes and with no sign of any contact, Wolff was on the point of leaving. It was then he was approached by one of the barmen with a message.

The man spoke in Bulgarian, and with some difficulty, Wolff deciphered what he was saying. There had been a phone call. Wolff was to go to the Kolos cafe on Stefan Karadja Street, a short walk away. But no sooner had he walked in the door of Kolos than he was handed a napkin by a smiling young waitress.

There was a crude map drawn on the back. This took him a further two streets southwest to another cafe on the corner of a small side street called Uzundzhovska. He took his time on the way there, intentionally going off course and doubling back to see if he had a tail again, but could discern nothing.

He made it to the cafe, a smaller, grubbier affair than the previous two establishments. There were no white-shirted waiters here, just a stout old woman who ignored him completely as he took a seat in a corner booth facing the door.

It was now an hour and a quarter after the originally scheduled meet, and he was growing tired of these games. However, ten minutes later, two individuals arrived who seemed as if they could be his NKVD contacts.

Wolff had never met a Russian out of uniform who was not a peasant, so he looked them up and down as they approached.

The first, who he took to be the leader, was in his early forties and pale, with a large nose that dominated most of his face.

His companion had mean-looking, squinty eyes and a sour, downturned expression. Both wore the kind of suit and hat to be seen on the streets of Sofia, and Wolff recognized that he would have been hard-pressed to pick them out as NKVD in any of the bars he had been in the night before.

Neither gave off an air which could remotely be described as friendly. Big Nose slid into the booth opposite him while Misery Guts remained on his feet, looking around. Wolff found their nervousness oddly reassuring. It was clear they were just as worried about Wolff's motives as he was of theirs.

They would have been warned about Heydrich's kidnapping stunt with the British at Venlo.

The two parties stared at each other for a few seconds before Wolff asked quietly: "Why don't you ask your colleague to sit down and stop drawing attention to us?" Big Nose blinked, as if taken aback by Wolff's fluency, though he must have expected a Russian speaker.

"Ilyin", he responded abruptly. "Schreiber," Wolff replied in an equally curt tone. Ilyin did not bother to introduce Misery Guts as the other man slid in beside him. There were a further few seconds of silence then, as both sides waited for the other to show their cards.

"What is your government's proposal?" Wolff said finally with a note of impatience. Ilyin grinned, as if pleased he had forced his adversary to go first. He turned to Misery Guts. "Get us some coffees."

"I'm fine, thank you," Wolff said quickly. He was damned if he was ingesting something in this place. Ilyin shrugged. "Suit yourself." He took off his hat and placed it on the table and sat back a little, clearly more relaxed now. "You know, I was expecting someone a little older," he said casually. "Do you actually have the authority to represent your government?"

Ignore any mindgames, Oster had told Wolff. *Make them lay it on the table.*

"The proposal?" he repeated.

Ilyin shrugged and lit a cigarette. "The proposal is as outlined via the Bulgarians," he answered through a cloud of smoke. "Broadly the same terms as Brest-Litovsk in 1918, excluding independence for Georgia. Comrade Stalin is not prepared to lose his homeland. However, it would include the Baltic republics, Belorussia and part of Ukraine.

"Not all of it," he added quickly. "How much of it?" Wolff asked reflexively.

"That is a matter of negotiation," Ilyin retorted. "We are talking principle at the moment. Our offer comes from the very top. The question is, who are you here representing? As I say, it does not engender much confidence that they send someone so young."

"All of our other Russian speakers are tied up on map-reading duties at the moment," Wolff said. Ilyin's nostrils flared. He did not appreciate the joke. Misery Guts returned with two coffees and set one in front of his superior.

It was thick, black and almost creamy in its texture. Wolff had received the same at breakfast and had been unable to drink more than a few sips. The Russians might have chased the Ottomans out of the Balkans, but their influence lingered.

"What we require from your side is proof of Hitler's interest," Ilyin continued. "That means someone senior, like Ribbentrop or his assistant, Reinhard Spitzy, in Stockholm or Istanbul. Discreetly, of course. But we would need such assurances to proceed. Then we can choose where we want to meet further."

"You are worried about a trap," Wolff said.

They are aware there is a resistance movement inside Germany, Oster had said. *What they don't know is how strong it is or who's involved.*

"I don't believe this is a major concern for the Soviet Union," Ilyin replied somewhat smugly. He reached inside the breast pocket of his overcoat and pulled out a dog-eared newspaper, which he threw across the table. Wolff looked down at the paper without touching it.

It had been folded over to display an article in Russian headlined 'Warnings against German rumors and propaganda'. He continued reading.

Comrade Lavrentiy Beria, Commissar General of State Security and chief of the People's Commissariat for Internal Affairs, has instructed citizens to beware rumors of a proposed 'armistice' spread by spies, wreckers and saboteurs.

Comrade Beria told Izvestia: "The enemy is aware of its impending defeat and is seeking the aid of anti-Soviet elements and counter-revolutionaries to demoralize and halt the advances of brave Red Army troops."

The article went on and on in the same bombastic vein, essentially pre-empting any German attempt to use the tentative

Soviet offer as proof that the USSR was suing for peace to avoid total collapse. It was an understandable move from the NKVD given how adept Goebbel's Propaganda Ministry was at seizing anything it could to churn out disinformation in favor of the Nazis.

Indeed, the tone of the piece was not that different from anything which would appear in *Berliner Tageblatt* or any of the other tightly controlled papers back in Germany. What the Soviets did not realize was that Goebbels and the Nazi hierarchy knew nothing and would know nothing about these discussions. At least until it was too late.

"Clever," Wolff said, pushing the paper back across the table. "But what does it mean by 'radishes'?"

"Those loyal to the old Tsarist regime," Ilyin answered. "Red on the outside, white on the inside. "Anyway," he continued, "this is the basis of the...suggestion. What reassurances can your side offer us?"

Bluff it out, Oster had told him, *emphasize that you are only an envoy. It's what they would expect at this stage anyway.*

"My role here is to see what is on the table," Wolff answered. "All I can tell you is that this has been discussed preliminarily at the highest level. Naturally, we will need to be sure of your government's commitment to any potential deal."

Ilyin's mouth pressed into a tight line. "Commitment? I will remind you of which side broke the Non-Aggression Pact and attacked the other."

"And I will remind you which side just took Smolensk and bombed the Kremlin last week."

We are in the ascendancy at the moment, act like it.

"We both know the Soviet Union needs this deal more than the Reich. So if it is to be approved, there will be conditions. Such as a withdrawal of your troops a certain distance from the new borders to create a buffer zone."

Ilyin nodded. The Russians would have anticipated such a demand. "Has this been presented to Hitler yet?" This was interesting. They were actually working on the basis that the agreement was being discussed among senior Reich figures before being presented to Hitler. Which, in a sense, it was.

"I am an envoy sent to see what you have to offer," Wolff repeated. "But as I said, you can be assured that this is being reviewed at the very highest level."

Ilyin frowned, but said nothing. In a briefing before he left, Canaris and Oster had predicted what the Soviets would expect of him, and it had been agreed to fulfill these presumptions as much as possible. As forecast, it had been the most cautious of dances.

"And now?" Ilyin pressed.

"And now we both report back to our superiors and communications will continue. Where can I reach you for further communication?"

Ilyin wrote the name of a cafe and a street on a piece of paper. Wolff did not recognize either of them, but presumed he would easily track the place down. "You can leave a message for me there. If we want to get one to you, we will go to Riunione."

"Fine," Wolff answered. He had no problem going back to where Anna worked again. He paused, remembering Oster's advice. "I need hardly mention the need for the utmost secrecy surrounding these matters?" Wolff said.

Ilyin was visibly affronted by the arrogant tone adopted by such a younger man, but it was the closing act of the choreographed performance agreed back in Berlin.

You're supposed to consider yourself a member of the master race. Behave like it.

"There will be no leaks from our side," Ilyin replied stiffly. "Very good," Wolff said. "I think it might be best if we left separately then. You and your comrade can go first." He smiled over at the other man, who glared back.

"I might have that coffee now."

He watched the pair as they left without another word and checked his watch. It had just gone 1.30pm, but it had been a very wearisome morning. He raised his arm to the old woman, who gazed back at him with disinterest.

"Schnapps, please."

12

The constantly shifting meeting point with the Russians had coincidentally taken Wolff quite near where he needed to go next. The German legation was in a grand Mediterranean Renaissance-style mansion on Patriarch Evtimii Boulevard in the very south of the old city center.

The fact it was lunchtime, when it would probably be mostly empty, was a bonus. Full-on rationing had not yet hit Bulgaria, though Wagner had told him of increasing episodes of what local restaurants termed "meatless Fridays", where the only thing on the menu was a plate of beans.

As today was Thursday, the majority of the diplomatic staff, including the nosy Abwehr chief, would be out getting their fill ahead of potential hairshirt provisions the next day. Only one colleague would not be joining them: the legation code clerk Pfeiffer, whom Oster had assured him was "one of ours".

Oster had informed the man that he would be required to stay at the legation all day for the duration of Wolff's mission lest he be required for any urgent messages.

Pfeiffer let him into the empty building and walked him down to the small, locked office which comprised the Abwehr section. Wolff got down to composing and encoding his message. In common with most military communications, it was terse and to the point.

The one-time pad he had been given by Oster was considered virtually unbreakable, but even so, his message would not be sent to the Bendlerblock. The bank of phones on Oster's desk was part of a telecommunications network known as the "A-net" for communicating with far-flung Abwehr offices.

While it was considered encrypted and thus secure, it was still possible the SD had managed to access some or all of its lines. Should their experts ever manage to decode the transmission to the A-net's telegraph machines, it would prove a death sentence for them all.

Instead, the note was transmitted to the headquarters of the Reserve Army, whose commander-in-chief, Colonel General Friedrich Olbricht, was one of Canaris and Oster's confederates. It was Olbricht's troops who would be ordered to accompany selected Brandenburger units in attacking the Chancellery and capturing the madman inside when the moment was eventually right.

Their weight of numbers would be enough to overcome even the elite members of *Leibstandarte SS Adolf Hitler* Division, who stood bodyguard around their beloved Führer. Message sent, Wolff set off back for his hotel, leaving instructions for Pfeiffer to call him as soon as there was a response.

The NKVD's cloak and dagger subterfuge and the need for counter surveillance measures meant it had taken him nearly three hours to reach the legation. Now, however, he reckoned he was no more than 20 minutes' walk from the Slavyanska

Beseda and planned to enjoy the stroll on a day of bright Balkan sunshine.

But a few minutes after leaving the legation, the same Daimler which had met him at the airport pulled up alongside. "Herr Schreiber," Tashev called from the back seat.

Wolff affected surprise. "Major, what are you... you're not following me, are you?"

Tashev grinned at him, seeming to appreciate Wolff's devotion to the game. "Following you? Not at all, Herr Schreiber. Though I gather such a thing could be quite difficult if attempted. A colleague of mine happened to be on the same street as you yesterday and saw you carrying out what seemed to be anti-surveillance maneuvers.

"He thought it was a rather odd thing for a commercial representative to be doing. No, I was passing by and recognized you. I thought I could give you a lift back to your hotel. Unless of course I can bring you to a commercial appointment you have?"

Tashev stepped out of the car and stood on the pavement, the door open. His obstructive body language was completely at odds with his words. "Please." Wolff reluctantly sat into the vehicle and Tashev went around to the other side, his uniformed driver already there ahead of him with the door open.

"How is your trip going? Sold many combine harvesters?" Tashev asked airily as the car pulled off once more.

"It's fine, Major, thank you," Wolff parried. "Unfortunately, I'm unable to discuss the details of my mission for reasons of commercial sensitivity."

Tashev smiled. "Yes, it's a competitive business you're in, isn't it, Herr Schreiber? Sales, I mean. There seem to be all sorts of figures arriving into Sofia these days on specially chartered planes just to flog different bits and pieces. Another two yesterday on an otherwise empty flight."

Wolff turned his head to look at him now and found Tashev staring back, all levity vanished. He passed Wolff a photograph of two German passports in the names of Rudolf Möbert and Alfred Bonsen. Evidently, it was now practice to record the faces of new visitors from the Reich.

The man who called himself Möbert was the senior-looking of the pair and stared out at the camera aggressively in the photo. Bonsen, meanwhile, had something approaching an amused leer on his face. The passports were unquestionably false, and the images struck Wolff as having been taken especially for them, so evident was the grim determination in both men's eyes.

It all pointed towards them being in Sofia for a specific purpose. Wolff hoped it was not connected to his own.

"Interestingly enough though, these two individuals seemed to have friends already in town," Tashev continued. "I sent two of my men, but they missed them as their flight arrived early. However, they did see who collected and drove them away. Brigadier Friedrich Panzinger, the Gestapo attaché at the German legation."

Tashev's eyes were boring into him now, scrutinizing Wolff's face for a reaction. "It's all quite irregular, you see, Herr Schreiber. A German of military service age arrives alone on a chartered flight and claims to be an agricultural machinery salesman.

"The following day, two more of his compatriots, also of military service age and in plain clothes, fly in on another one and are met by the resident Gestapo officer. And now I have no idea where these men are or what they are doing in Sofia. Whatever am I to think, Herr *Schreiber*?"

They had arrived at the hotel and Wolff turned and looked out the window, while he considered his response. There was a strained edge to the Bulgarian's tone, and Wolff understood he would have to give the man something to avoid creating a determined enemy.

Tashev obviously suspected the new arrivals were in league with him, though they might actually be SD men sent to counter Wolff's mission. The Bulgarian's role was primarily to prevent any incidents on home soil which might drag his country fully into the war.

But Tashev had another, even more pressing preoccupation. One which he shared with Tsar Boris III. Preventing a potential German-sponsored coup d'etat. Wolff could use that - and thus Tashev - to simultaneously remove himself from the spotlight and put it firmly on Möbert and Bonsen, which might help frustrate any plans they might have in place.

He stepped out of the car and turned back to the Bulgarian. "I can reassure you, Major, that I am not in your country to cause trouble. I can also reassure you that I know nothing of what these two men are doing here, but as you say, the manner of their arrival is somewhat odd.

"You may wish to look into that further. After all, we've all seen what *agents provocateurs* have done elsewhere in this part of the world."

He pivoted and walked into the hotel, feeling Tashev's eyes on him with each step he took.

***

Wolff's first instinct upon arrival at the hotel had been to immediately return to the legation to send another coded message outlining what Tashev had just told him. But upon mulling it over during a drink at the hotel bar, he decided it could wait.

Firstly, because if the two new arrivals were SD interference, he could well run into them there. There was also the possibility that Tashev was bluffing in order to test his reactions, though Wolff believed him. Last, but not least, was Wolff's sense of professional pride.

For most of the past year, he had relied on his wits and confidence to keep him alive. Sofia was nowhere near as dangerous as the front. Completing his mission whilst evading SD surveillance should be well within his abilities. It had to be, if he was ever to reach Riga.

With nothing else to do, he went up to his room for a nap and was awoken by a phone call from Pfeiffer an hour later. He told the code clerk to wait for him and got dressed for the short stroll to the legation.

This time, there were two of them on the terrace outside and in far better shape than the rotund individual from this morning. Both wore calf-length topcoats despite the heat, most probably to hide whatever weaponry might be underneath.

They made no attempt to disguise what they were doing, and Wolff made no attempt to shake them off. It would have been impossible anyway, given that they stayed no more than ten paces behind him. Right now, he was happy to have them there. They would act as a shield against any potential SD approach towards him.

He would figure out later how to deal with them in the event of another meeting with the Russians. After the earlier confrontation with Tashev, Wolff was eager to see the response from Oster, but it was rather a letdown. *String them along. Say we will meet in Stockholm, but will only send our ambassador.*

It was a smart move by Oster. The ambassador was not the senior Nazi official demanded by the Ivans, but was an identifiable figure nonetheless. The NKVD would be aware through their spies how tightly Ribbentrop controlled his ministry, so would naturally assume the Reich's foreign minister was part of the plot.

Wolff had no idea of whether Oster actually had a strategy or was merely making it up as he went along. However, he hoped he was not going to be the conduit for a prolonged back-and-forth between the conspirators and the NKVD.

He could only evade the SD for so long. Pfeiffer did not mention anything about Panzinger being seen at the legation with two new arrivals from Berlin, and Wolff did not ask him. Instead, he encoded another short message describing what Tashev had told him and gave it to Pfeiffer to send.

He checked his watch. It was almost 7.30pm. Time for another trip to Riunione. The quicker he could arrange another meeting with the Russians, the quicker he could get out of Sofia. And, he had to admit, the prospect of spending more time in Anna's company was also quite enticing.

He and his two stalkers returned to the Slavyanska Beseda, where Wolff changed into a different suit. He found himself wondering whether he was doing it for himself or to impress the Viennese taxi girl.

Having grasped the layout of the city, Wolff walked the short distance from the hotel to Riunione on Dondukov Boulevard, once more trailed by the topcoats, who adopted positions at the end of the bar. He was not worried about them seeing him with Anna, which he could plausibly pass off as a lonely stranger in town seeking some female company.

Despite the early hour, the bar was as full as it had been the previous evening. Wolff ordered a drink and scanned the lounge. There was no sign of either of the NKVD pair, which did not surprise him. He doubted Comrade Stalin would approve of them hanging out in a decadent capitalist drinking den unnecessarily.

Initially, he could not see Anna either, but eventually spotted her in a booth with what looked like a group of Italian businessmen. He felt an instant stab of jealousy and told himself to smarten up. He would be gone from Sofia within days and would never see her again.

He turned back to his drink and saw the topcoats being served obsequiously by the barman, who clearly recognized them. Wolff wondered if anyone else did. After a few more minutes, he felt a presence at his elbow and turned to find Anna standing there.

"Hermann, what a nice surprise!" There was a slight sardonic undertone, as if she had been certain he would be back. He smiled back, nonchalantly hiding the thrill he felt at having her next to him again. This girl depended on tips from the bar's happy customers for her living, he reproached himself. Of course she would be pleased to see him.

Still, he felt awkward and suddenly tongue-tied, so much so that he cursed himself for the words which tumbled out of his mouth next. "Have you any further messages for me?" Anna stepped back and looked at him mockingly. "Really Hermann? Is that all I am to you? A messenger girl?"

She looked away and feigned a pout. "I thought we could have some fun first." Just then the band struck up a livelier tempo, and Wolff desperately seized the initiative in the only way he knew how. As he guided her skilfully around the floor, he could see the genuine pleasure she was taking in it.

Other couples shifted back a little too and gave them room to perform. For a few moments, they were once more the center of attention. Wolff again felt the ego boost of having dozens of pairs of envious male eyes upon him. All too soon, the tune ended and they found themselves back at the bar, Anna flushed with the effort, but still beaming.

The thin veneer of coquettish charm she usually offered had been replaced by the unmistakable joy of moving in seamless rhythm to the music. "Where on earth did you learn to dance like that, Hermann? You're one of the few men, perhaps the only man I've ever seen, who has come in here and who can actually dance."

So Wolff told her. The summer nights spent in places like Areal da Baronesa and Colonia Africana, where the *forró* band members were migrants from Brazil's parched and poor northeast who had traveled hundreds of miles to the supposedly richer south only to end up in a different slum.

The neat footwork needed to keep one's partner at close quarters and avoid cannoning into other couples in the heaving shacks which passed for dance halls, thus potentially setting off a drunken fistfight. And the pride he took in learning and improving as he realized the locals had accepted him as one of their own, despite the discrimination and disdain they received daily from his father and other members of the German immigrant community.

Drinking late into the night before walking home unmolested through the makeshift dwellings because everyone knew who his pals were and the consequences of touching him. He was an *alemão*, a German, yes. But he was also one of them.

When he stopped, her eyes were shining, and he could see she now viewed him in a completely new light. Still, there was hesitation. "But what would your country's government think of such behavior?" she asked eventually. "Mixing with...*inferior races*?"

A test, clearly. But though his instincts told him what she wanted to hear, years of not saying the wrong thing in Hamburg held him back. Eventually, he relented. "I don't believe in any of that rubbish," he answered softly. "And I don't think I ever will."

Her expression softened. "Perhaps you could buy me a drink, Hermann?" So he did. Followed by another and another. They adjourned to one of the booths, which Anna said would make Mamichka, who he took to be the owner, mad, as it could seat six customers rather than just two.

She opened up to him then, at first a little, then more, before it all poured out of her in a torrent. She was not in Sofia by choice, she told him. She had left Vienna following the *Anschluss*, disliking the new Nazi regime and fearful of what was coming next.

Her parents were dead, killed by the Spanish flu which followed the Great War, and she had been raised by her grandparents, who sent her to the *Wiener Staatsoper* ballet academy, which she had loved. "Ah, you are a ballerina!" Wolff clapped his hands.

The reason for her grace and enthusiasm upon the floor was now clear to him, and he was pleased at the rapport building further between them. But the smile she flashed in response was not that of one who had discovered a kindred spirit. Instead, it was tinged with sadness.

She *had* been a ballerina, she said, but was not anymore. And she doubted whether she would ever be one again. Along with quite a few others at the academy, she had been forced to flee when Austria was subsumed into the Reich.

Unable to get a visa for Switzerland, she had gone first to Budapest, but had moved again as Hungary adopted more and more quasi-Nazi policies in an attempt to curry favor with Hitler and prevent a potential invasion. Now she was here, where night after night she smiled and danced with drunken men old enough to be her father, whose hands she had to move up to her shoulders as they 'accidentally' slipped down her back.

Mamichka treated her okay, but she could see things in Bulgaria going the same way as in Hungary. The government, albeit reluctantly, had introduced similar laws earlier this year, though they had yet to be enforced. If they started to do that, she could be trapped.

The Germans had occupied Yugoslavia to the east and Greece to the south. To the north, Romania was just as fascist as the rest of them and beyond that, the front lines. That left Istanbul, where the government had strictly limited immigration to those of the "Turkish race". Wolff could see clearly where this was going.

"You're Jewish?" She looked at him with pleading in her eyes. She had bared her soul, potentially placing her life in his hands. He knew as he said it he was making another mistake, but he could not stop himself anyway. "I'll get you out of here."

She stared at him, evidently desperate to believe his words yet also entirely aware he was a man she had only met the previous night and some sort of undeclared member of the Reich's military at the very least, if not a spy for the Nazi regime.

She had met enough of them to know them by their bearing, even if the subject had been delicately avoided so far. "To where, Hermann? How?"

"I don't know, and you'll have to give me some time," Wolff responded. "But I swear to God I will, if it's the last thing I do. And my name isn't Hermann. It's Ako." Hope flared in her eyes and Wolff suddenly felt terribly afraid.

The enormity of what he was promising was beyond ambiguity, and it would be yet another complicated favor he would have to seek from Canaris, doubtless enraging Oster at the same time. There also remained the possibility that this was a honey trap, designed to catch him *in flagrante* with an illegal immigrant of extraordinary acting ability.

Thus serving Tashev with the perfect means to have him booted out of the country for immoral behavior. If so, it had succeeded perfectly, because, under the full gaze of the topcoats at the end of the bar, Wolff was now a slave to his emotions and desires.

So when she leaned in and bashfully suggested that they go to his hotel, all he could do was nod wordlessly and signal for the bill, his mouth too dry to even utter the words.

13

Though the hotel was mere minutes away on foot, Wolff was in no mood to wait to be alone with this girl. They flagged down a taxi and he gave the driver the hotel name. Upon arrival, he threw almost double the fare at the man rather than wait for him to count out the change.

Up in his room, their first coupling was frantic and nervous. Afterwards, they held each other for a while, before he was ready again. This time, they took their time almost as if by tacit arrangement, and when they finally shuddered together, he felt a bond with this woman he had never shared with any of the few other lovers who had entered his life.

They lay together in the darkness then and she began to ask him more detailed questions about himself. He understood that this was not mere nosiness or making conversation, but information she needed if she was to put her faith in him.

So Wolff answered honestly. He outlined his parents' flight from Latvia after the last war at his father's insistence, Ludwig Wolff insisting that anti-*Baltendeutsche* discrimination had made it impossible for them to stay.

When he had pressed *Mammu* upon the nature of this injustice years later, she had smiled sadly and he had come to understand that this was merely the first in a series of excuses used by his father to bail out because things were not going his way.

That knowledge had created a secret bond between him and *Mammu*, who had grown to lead a separate existence from her husband in Brazil. She had despised the snooty local German immigrants, who saw themselves as a cut above both the native Brazilians and some levels of their own community.

Meanwhile, father had spent his time engaged in frantic social climbing, unaware according to his wife that he would never be fully accepted by those he viewed as his peers. Wolff had been schooled through German, but learned Portuguese at his father's warehouse, where Ludwig had used him as a translator and social buffer between him and the men who lugged his heavy sacks of coffee onto ships bound for Europe and North America.

There too, he had picked up Spanish and English from interactions with the crews of the freighters while they hung around waiting for their vessels to be loaded. But his mother had never managed to gather more than a few words of her new land's native tongue.

Restricted to interactions with people she felt contempt for, she led a desperately lonely existence and pined for home. She had insisted on speaking to Wolff in both Latvian and Russian in case they ever returned to Latvia, but both were smart enough to keep it from Ludwig.

He had become an even more strident bigot since discovering Nazism. Hitler's racial theories jigsawed perfectly with Wolff Senior's existing prejudices, and his son was forced to hide his friendships and football games with the local boys in order to avoid a lengthy, pompous lecture, a physical thrashing or both.

Wolff could see Anna wince as he described his mother's travails. The callousness of the Nazi male was no surprise to her, but he supposed she was horrified to see that the intolerance which she was attempting to flee also existed on the other side of the world.

"But what did your mother do in the end?" she asked, eventually. "Did she move to Germany with your father?" Wolff was silent for a moment. It had always been his private theory, never shared with anyone else, that *Mammu*'s illness had been nature's way to relieve her of that burden.

The clampdown on Nazi activities by Vargas was only part of the reason Ludwig Wolff made such noise about relocating to what he referred to ridiculously as his homeland. The truth was that his father's business was in trouble and Wolff Senior could not bear the loss of face that would come with it.

His mother, who had followed events in Europe closely, was aghast at moving to a country whose leader was clearly spoiling for war. As she lay dying, she had begged her son to convince his father to stay. But Ludwig would not be turned and reacted with increasing ferocity to attempts to change his mind.

When that became abundantly clear, *Mammu* had instead spoken to him of Riga and had pleaded with her son to travel there and find the one thing there she still held dear, despite all the time that had passed. And he had promised, with tears in his eyes, that he would.

Wolff could not see Anna's face as they lay there together in the darkness, but felt her arms around him tighten for a moment.

He realized she would have been both overjoyed and relieved at hearing such stories from the man in whom her hopes now lay.

"It sounds like your father has been very unfair to you," she said at last. "Did you think at all of staying in Brazil yourself and letting him return alone?" It had never occurred to him, Wolff admitted. As bad as things were between them, Ludwig was all he had.

Soon, Anna gently steered the conversation round to how he would help her carry out an escape of her own. Here, Wolff was short on detail, beyond a potential flight to Switzerland or Portugal. Brazil was somewhere where she could make a new life for herself, he insisted.

The country had its problems too and lacked the infrastructure of the old continent. But it was still somewhere she could find her feet and perhaps even resurrect her lost dream of becoming a dancer of some sort. A boat to Palestine, where many Jewish refugees fleeing the horrors of Europe were heading, was another option.

But for either to happen, Wolff would first need to carry out the task which he had been sent to Sofia to achieve. He would probably have to return to Germany - and hopefully Riga - for a time before he would be able to return to Bulgaria to help her out.

He was asking her to trust him, to hold out just that little longer so that he could put the pieces in place which would enable her to flee. Could she do that? Place a faith in him which he promised with all his heart not to betray?

There was no initial response and Wolff at first feared that she would reject such pleas, possibly because she had heard similar

pledges before, only for their utterance to disappear subsequently into the night. It was only when he felt the wetness on his chest
that he understood she was unable to speak.

The emotion welled up in him too, until they were both
silently weeping together for a few minutes. In embarrassment,
and to move the conversation onwards, he took the opportunity to press her for details which might help his mission, conscious also that any intelligence he could attribute to her would
strengthen his case for an extraction.

He hoped she realized he was asking this of her reluctantly,
that nothing came without cost in this vicious, loathsome war.
However, he feared that in doing so, he had nonetheless somehow left her disappointed, both in him and in her own naivety.

The system which operated at Riunione was relatively simple.
All messages passed by the taxi girls to customers came through
the head barman, Kostadinov, who would receive the responses
along with drinks orders. Kostadinov's motives were unclear and
the business was never discussed amongst the girls, at least not
with those with whom Anna was friendly.

She had always suspected the barman was a communist. He
had a fervid, secretive air about him, as if his surreptitious role
was in the service of a loftier purpose. Couldn't he just as easily
be a fanatical fascist, Wolff had asked. Then why hide himself,
Anna insisted in response.

Tsar Boris III had officially banned extreme right organizations like the Ratniks and the Union of Bulgarian National
Legions at the beginning of the war. However, their members
still paraded openly in the red shirts they wore in an effort to
'retake' the color from their hated enemies.

Not so the communists, who were actively suppressed since the attempt to assassinate the Tsar in 1925. All of this was a useful background for Wolff, but would be old hat to the likes of Wagner. The Abwehr would not care about the political leanings of a cabaret bar waiter.

The more information she could give him on Soviet activity within Sofia, he told her, the easier it would be for him to get her out. She was quiet then for a second, perhaps because all pretenses regarding his presence in Sofia had been dropped. It was possible that she wondered whether she had been drawn into a honey trap of her own.

She would try, she said, but she would have to be careful. She had never read the notes she passed from Kostadinov to customers, many of them were in indecipherable Cyrillic script anyway. But she would do her best. Wolff could hear the quaver in her voice, and his heart broke at what he was asking of a woman to whom he had become inordinately attached in the space of 48 hours.

She had left a short time afterwards, dressing with her back to him even in the faint light from the street coming through the curtains. Such bashfulness was to him further confirmation of her bona fides. After she had whispered goodbye, kissed him and left, emphatic that she would make her own way home safely, Wolff had lain there, mulling it all over.

Sleep had not been a problem since Wolff had been sent to the front and he had learned to snatch rest on whatever surface was available, uncertain when the next nighttime mission would come. But here in his comfortable hotel bed, it eluded him.

Part of it was excited disbelief at his night of passion with such a beautiful young woman who eagerly reciprocated his desires. The physical signs of her arousal had been obvious and undeniable. But there was also the imposing reality of his pledge to rescue her, which now lay heavily upon him.

He would need some time to work out the details, but he had sworn on the life of his late mother that he would come through for her. The mechanics of getting her out were relatively straightforward - bogus travel documents courtesy of Canaris would get her passage to Switzerland or further afield if she wished.

Obtaining those documents would require a successful outcome here in Sofia, and that was far from guaranteed right now. In the end, it was the insomnia that meant he was awake when they came in the first stirrings of dawn. That and the bulk of the fat man who had inexplicably been brought along.

Their first mistake was the noisy approach. The harsh command to the hotel flunky to open the door and the subsequent rattle of the key in the lock meant he was out of bed before they entered. There were no weapons to hand, so he had desperately grabbed a pillow, feeling faintly ridiculous as the door was shoved roughly inward and the incompetent, rotund surveillant bounded inside.

He was followed by an unsmiling Tashev, while behind them the terrified night manager turned and fled back down the corridor. The fat man was smiling, enjoying his moment of revenge as he leveled the Luger P08 pistol in his hand at Wolff.

Whatever it was about, it was serious, though Wolff's first thought was that Department D had a lot to learn about catching their prey unawares by visiting in the early morning darkness. He had no time to consider that further, however, as Tashev skipped the preliminaries and snapped: "Get dressed."

Wolff drew himself up and played for time. "What is the meaning of this, Major? I am a citizen of the Reich, and I can assure you I will be making a vehement protest to my legation." Tashev did not bat an eyelid. He held out his hand to the fat man for the gun and barked an order, prompting his subordinate to fish a pair of handcuffs from his pocket and move towards Wolff, who raised the pillow protectively.

"What is this about, Major?" Wolff shouted again, with far less bravado. There was no answer from Tashev, but the fat man obliged him in poor, heavily accented German. "We saw you with her last night. No lie to us."

For a second, Wolff thought he was being lifted as some sort of absurd vice crackdown, but another look at Tashev's face confirmed something far graver was afoot here. The fat man was up close now and angry. "You are not in Germany now, you cannot do these things." It hit him then, like a slap in the face.

Anna.

"What happened? Where is she? Tell me!" Tashev was looking at him differently now, as if recalculating the situation. There was a hint of regret in his expression. "She is in the morgue, Herr Schreiber," he replied, the abrupt manner gone now. "And I am afraid you are coming with us."

14

For a moment, Wolff was stunned into silence. The beautiful girl whose perfume still filled the room was dead, and it was because of him. His stupor allowed the fat man to move closer, jerking Wolff back to reality.

"Don't be ridiculous, Major!" he cried, pushing his would-be captor backwards. "I've been here all night! She left by herself hours ago and insisted she would make her own way home. Ask the night manager." But Tashev remained stone-faced, and Wolff saw then how stupid he had been.

Rather than protecting him, his liaison with Anna in front of the watching Bulgarians had given someone a chance to neutralize him in the simplest of terms. Whether it was the SD or a different third party was irrelevant right now. The mission was disintegrating before his very eyes.

He could see Tashev did not believe him responsible, but someone would have to pay for her death. If pinning it on Wolff simultaneously removed the stone from Tashev's shoe and nullified a potentially damaging inquiry into Department D's failure to control its patch, then it would be so.

Against all of that, finding the real killer of a female Jewish refugee was of little concern. At best, Wolff would be sent home in disgrace, Canaris' protection by necessity removed, the chances of going onwards to Riga extinguished.

At worst, a long sentence in a Bulgarian prison whose conditions would make Flossenburg look like a Bavarian mountain spa. Tashev gave the slightest of nods to the fat man, who opened both sides of the handcuffs and moved closer towards him. It was all Wolff needed.

He grappled with his opponent, using the man's bulk as a shield from the pistol in Tashev's hand. Tashev was shouting now at his incompetent underling, doubtless now wishing he had brought a better caliber of colleague with him. However, the fat man was no better at physically subduing a mark than he was at following one.

Panicked by Tashev's anger, he attempted to bring his weight to bear upon Wolff, who moved slightly. When his adversary tried to straighten to avoid losing his balance and falling, Wolff hooked a leg behind the other man's ankle and pushed, sending him staggering back into Tashev and pulling Wolff with him.

All three of them landed awkwardly between the bed and the wall, with Tashev at the bottom of their untidy pile. As they did so, there was the sound of a shot, and the fat man grunted and released his grip on Wolff's wrist.

Tashev was swearing loudly now at Wolff in Bulgarian. One of the major's hands was free, and he was using it to ineffectually flail at Wolff's head. Wolff could see the other, presumably holding the pistol, was trapped between Tashev's torso and the dead weight of his now still subordinate.

Maintaining his knee on top of both men, Wolff used his left hand to reach between the two bodies underneath him and pull the gun from Tashev's grasp. He then used his right to pat down the major while he lay prone on the floor.

He could not recall seeing Tashev armed during any of their brief encounters, but wanted to double check he had not missed a hip holster in the earlier confusion. Satisfied, he stood and used his leg to shove the bed aside and allowed Tashev to roll the fat man's body off him and sit up.

Watching Wolff warily, Tashev began attempting to persuade him to put the gun down, but Wolff pointed the pistol at him threateningly. "Shut up, Major." He bent and picked up the handcuffs from where they had fallen on the floor during the brawl. "Put those on."

As Tashev complied, Wolff thought about his next move. His own time in Sofia was clearly over, but that did not mean the mission was necessarily dead in the water. Now that contact had been made, it could be continued by one of Canaris' more senior envoys.

Wolff would inevitably have been replaced in the negotiations anyway, so he was merely moving the timeline forward. However, he would have to do so on his own initiative - contacting Oster to seek further instructions was out of the question.

There was also the question of what else the SD - assuming it was them - might have done to sabotage things. He turned his attention back to Tashev, who was watching him intently. "Sit on the bed and open your mouth only to answer what I ask you or I can promise you that you'll join your friend here.

"What happened to the girl?"

"A local police patrol found her down an alleyway. Her throat had been cut."

Wolff winced momentarily, thinking of the fun, vulnerable young woman whose warm naked body had lain next to him just a few hours earlier. He had failed her. He shook off the guilt and focused on the task at hand.

"Had she been tortured?"

Tashev looked at him for a moment before answering. "Not that I was informed, no."

"How much do you know about the head waiter at Riunione, Kostadinov?"

Tashev shrugged. "We're aware of him, that he's a commie and passes information to the Russians. But so far, we've left him where he is. Better the devil you know and all that."

"Do you know where he lives?"

Again, Tashev paused, trying to work out where this was going. But Wolff had no time for the Bulgarian's attempts to play the situation for his own benefit. He grabbed Tashev's tie and screwed the muzzle of the gun painfully into his temple.

"Yes! Yes. He has a room above the club."

Wolff relaxed his grip, his point made. "Who else knows about your trip here with fatso?"

"Nobody. I wanted to deal with this in-house. Listen, we can still sort this out, Schreiber. Or whatever your name is."

Wolff laughed at the half-hearted offer. The situation had gone far beyond cover-up, and they both knew it. "You have a car outside." A statement this time, not a question.

"Zhelev has the keys."

Wolff bent and patted the dead fat man's pockets until he found them. "Okay, you and I are going for a little drive. I think Kostadinov's life could be in danger, and whether you believe it or not, I am trying to prevent that. Not because I care about him, but because there are already enough inconvenient bodies around the place.

"If you behave yourself, you will live, and then you can spin whatever tale you wish to extract yourself from this situation. If you attempt to call attention to yourself in any way, I will kill you. There are important matters at play here, Tashev, and you are irrelevant in the grander scheme of things.

"You will be kept alive as long as you are useful. If not..." He jutted his chin at Zhelev's body. Tashev did not reply, and Wolff believed the Bulgarian understood the frankness of the threat against him. He dressed quickly, recovered what he needed from his suitcase, and they took the stairs down to the lobby.

Wolff removed Tashev's handcuffs but kept the pistol at his back as the major warned the terrified night manager that nobody was to enter Wolff's room under any circumstances on pain of arrest. The streets were virtually empty as they drove the short distance to Riunione. Tashev was behind the wheel of the Daimler and had recovered some of his composure. He asked Wolff what his real name was and who he was working for in Sofia.

Wolff considered threatening the man, but realized there was an opportunity here to lay a false trail which might work in his favor. "Who I am is none of your concern. I work for the *Sicherheitsdienst* and I am here on a matter of Reich national security in cooperation with the highest levels of your government. That's all you need to know."

It was a facile lie, but might help muddying the waters in attributing responsibility if everything went wrong.

Tashev was silent for a few minutes as he tried to gauge the truth of what Wolff was telling him, and Wolff was glad of the respite as he figured out how to play it with Kostadinov. Having Tashev along would be useful. The waiter would likely be more cooperative at the sight of a Bulgarian uniform than when pressed by an armed foreigner.

Wolff had heard of a Red Army colonel who had hidden a stick grenade down his trousers upon his capture, knowing he would be taken to a senior Wehrmacht counterpart for interrogation. When it began, he had triggered the device, killing himself and everyone else in the tent rather than be sent into forced labor.

Ideological fanatics were unpredictable, and it was impossible to know how committed Kostadinov was to his cause. As they turned onto Dondukov Boulevard, however, he could see that such precautions would be unnecessary.

A thick pall of smoke hung in the air above the street, attracting a crowd of gawkers as the local fire brigade tried in vain to extinguish the roaring flames producing it. Sofia's spies would have to carry out their note swaps at a different cabaret bar in future. Riunione and the two floors above it were completely ablaze.

More dangerously for Wolff, there was a policeman standing in the middle of the boulevard directing the low levels of traffic around the fire tender. The cop beckoned the Daimler towards him, and Wolff jammed the pistol muzzle into Tashev's kidneys and told him to drive past the obstacle.

If the major knew anything about gunshot wounds, he would be aware that such a shot would almost certainly be fatal. The cop moved aside to let the car approach, straightening and offering a salute when he saw Tashev's uniform behind the wheel. He then leaned down to the open window, glancing curiously across at Wolff.

Senior army officers like Tashev did not often chauffeur civilians around, particularly those roughly half their age. After a few seconds of chat, Tashev drove on. The fire had been reported around an hour ago, he said.

To Wolff, this looked more and more like the work of the SD, and they were moving quickly. He had to assume they had obtained what they needed from Kostadinov before setting the flames. Tashev drove a hundred yards past Riunione before pulling in at the side of the street. Wolff breathed a sigh of relief. The Bulgarian was acting smartly for the moment, at least.

"Where to now?" Tashev asked.

Wolff had not wanted to reveal his ultimate destination unless absolutely necessary, but it was clear it was now.

"Where do NKVD operatives usually stay in this city?"

Tashev blinked at the question, which was clearly unexpected, but answered without hesitation. "The Red Star on Panayot Volov Street. It's a flea pit up in Kyulutsite."

Tashev gestured at the neighborhood which lay north of the boulevard. "Appropriately proletarian lodgings," he added acerbically.

"Let's go," Wolff said, giving the Bulgarian another poke in the side with the pistol just to remind him who was in charge. He had no real plan for when he reached the hotel other than to play it cautiously. He was confident that he would be able to spot any Germans hanging around, and he doubted any Reich official would stay in such a cheap establishment favored by Soviets.

Tashev turned onto a rundown looking street and pulled up, pointing to a decrepit looking building a short walk down. Wolff could see the Cyrillic letters for 'hotel' on a sign hanging from its corner. Tashev had said nothing since they had driven past Riunione and was clearly trying to work out what was going on.

Wolff decided that taking him into his confidence to a limited degree was the best way to secure the intelligence officer's cooperation. If Tashev could be sure Wolff was out to prevent further bloodshed rather than create it, he would be far easier to handle.

Moreover, the man's uniform could yet again be extremely useful in securing otherwise reluctant collaboration, not to mention translation. The tables had well and truly turned since the head of Department D had met him personally at the airport just two short days before and attempted to intimidate him into revealing his mission.

Wolff turned to him. "I cannot tell you what is happening here, but you should have worked out by now that someone is on a killing spree and is attempting to frame me for it. I suspect those responsible might be in that hotel, and I'm going in to stop them.

"If they're not, I'll need you to help me warn the clerk. That said, what I told you earlier remains the case. There is something far bigger than you happening here, Tashev, and if you attempt to sabotage it in any way, I will kill you on the spot, along with anyone else who is watching.

"Play ball, and you will live to find a way to clean up this mess. Agreed?" Tashev nodded at him coolly. Wolff could see the Bulgarian trusted him now, though he clearly did not like being ordered around one bit.

He took a deep breath. "Right, look smart. We're going inside."

15

The bell on the front door sounded as Wolff pushed it in, but he could see nobody behind the front desk. The lobby was little more than an average-sized sitting room with a couple of threadbare couches and a tiny counter, behind which stood a doorway to a back office.

Wolff had the gun out and held low as he moved slowly inside. He was still not entirely sure how to play this. He may have met the Russians publicly under truce the previous day, but that was then and today their nations were still at war.

His first dilemma would be to persuade them that he was not there to kill them. Far more delicate would be how to explain that other Germans possibly were. Who exactly Wolff was representing had never been fully clarified, though Canaris and Oster had discussed how the Soviets would believe him an emissary for anti-Hitler figures within the upper echelons of Nazism.

It would not bode well for these figures' credibility if it emerged their activities had been discovered and they had been followed to Sofia by Führer loyalists intent on stopping them at all costs. Still, the very public way the SD had murdered Anna and torched Riunione left Wolff with little option.

The NKVD were no fools and would figure it out themselves, with or without his help. He gestured Tashev towards the front desk and allowed the Bulgarian to take the lead. Tashev strode forward confidently and shouted "*Politsiya!*", smacking authoritatively on the desk's tarnished bell.

When there was no response, he angled his head to look into the back office, before jerking back instantly when he noticed something on the floor behind the desk. Warily, Wolff followed his lead and craned his neck over the countertop.

The body of a man in his sixties lay on his back, the dark bloom on the front of his ragged green cardigan denoting the wound to his upper chest below. Gun raised, Wolff moved behind the desk now and checked the small room there, which was empty.

He touched the body, which still retained some residual warmth. The man had been killed recently, but Wolff had no idea at what rate a dead human being cooled. He picked up the cheap ledger used as the guest register from under the counter.

The man who called himself Ilyin was booked in under the same name on the third floor, in a room alongside another man called Kuznetsov. His coffee-fetching companion, Wolff thought. He flipped through the ledger.

There were around a dozen other names in it, but those were the only Russian-sounding ones, which struck him as incredibly sloppy tradecraft. Perhaps the NKVD had become so used to staying there that they had become lazy. He now had a decision to make. It was difficult to know what lay upstairs.

Two ransacked rooms, at the very least, or perhaps more bodies. Maybe the SD were still up there, tossing paraffin around the place with plans to set it alight. He walked over to the front door and turned the lock on it, pulling down the grimy blind.

"In there." He gestured to the back office with the pistol and saw the alarm on Tashev's face. "Don't worry, I'm not going to kill you. Quite the contrary. I have no idea what's up there waiting for me, and I'm not going to put you at risk. Or let you take advantage of any confusion and disappear, for that matter."

He took the cuffs from his hip pocket again. There was nothing in the room to which he could anchor Tashev. "Face down on the floor with your hands behind your back," he ordered the Bulgarian, who complied grumpily. Wolff clicked the cuffs into place, then rolled the man over and roughly removed his uniform tie.

"What are you doing?" Tashev demanded angrily. Wolff could sense his humiliation at being treated in such a way by a man half his age, but there was no time to worry about the major's ego. Wolff pushed him back onto his stomach and used the tie to bind Tashev's ankles together.

"You're leaving me helpless here!" Tashev protested furiously. "If whoever did this comes back, I'm a sitting duck." Wolff turned from the doorway. "Then I guess you'd better stay silent so they don't find you."

He advanced towards the rickety-looking elevator before changing his mind and making for the stairs. Emerging on the third-floor corridor, he walked stealthily along the hallway before reaching number 305, Illyin's room. The door was closed, so he listened outside for a few seconds. No sound came from within.

Holding the Luger down by his side, he tried the handle, which turned easily and pushed in the door. The room inside was dark, with the curtains drawn and a sour metallic odor that Wolff immediately recognized. He felt for the light switch and was about to turn it on when he heard the unmistakable click of a pistol hammer being drawn back.

"Put the gun on the ground and kick it under the bed," a gruff voice whispered in Russian. Wolff's first reaction was one of some relief that the man was not speaking German, before he caught himself. The NKVD were just as likely, if not more so, to shoot him as the SD. Especially if the smell in the air was what he thought it was.

He put his other hand in the air and bent down to comply with the order. As he did so, he made out the shape of his interlocutor on the far side of the bed against the drawn curtains. It was obvious from his stance that the man was pointing his weapon right at Wolff.

"Turn on the light and close the door and lean against it with your arms high," the Russian ordered him. Again, Wolff obeyed. The light from the weak bulb in the middle of the ceiling revealed the voice to be that of Misery Guts from the cafe, aka Kuznetzov, according to the ledger downstairs.

It also provided enough illumination to show Ilyin's body lying prone on the floor at the foot of the bed, eyes open and unseeing. An upended suitcase lay on the floor beyond Ilyin, the door of the wardrobe ajar, indicating the room had been ransacked before whoever had killed the NKVD man had fled.

Kuznetzov quickly and roughly patted Wolff down for other weapons. Satisfied there were none, he took a step backward and the next thing Wolff felt was the explosive spasm of the man's foot connecting with his groin. He crumpled to the floor in agony, his breath taken from him.

It was drilled into them again and again in training. In close combat, if you could land a blow to your opponent's balls, it was all over. Perhaps the NKVD man had had the same type of instructor.

Wolff pushed himself to his hands and knees and gulped in air as he fought the nausea that rose in his throat. "What did you forget? Eh?" the voice demanded from above. "What did you come back to look for? Stupid bastard."

The anger seemed to rise in the Russian, and he pointed the pistol at Wolff as if to shoot. Aware that his life depended on talking the man down, Wolff battled to overcome the crippling waves of pain spreading out from his nether regions and feebly flapped one arm at his interrogator, as if this would persuade him to lower his weapon.

"Kuznetzov? Kuznetzov, right?" he panted, recalling the name in the register downstairs. Misery Guts said nothing, but made no effort to contradict him either. With enormous effort, Wolff pushed himself back against the wall, so he could at least face the Russian. Were they....were they Germans?"

Kuznetzov frowned in anger, and for a second Wolff thought he would cross the room and attack him again.

"Of course they were fucking Germans!" he spat, raising the gun almost reflexively at such an idiotic query. "You think the Bulgarians would do this?" He pointed with the barrel at his dead colleague.

"It wasn't us, Kuznetzov," Wolff panted, still barely able to catch his breath and hoping the use of the name from the register downstairs would buy him some time. "It wasn't us. It was the *Sicherheitsdienst*. The SD."

"I know what the SD are," the man barked angrily. "Which organization are you from?" "The Abwehr," Wolff panted. "The Abwehr. Different...organizations. Rivals. Like the NKVD and Red Army intelligence."

Wolff had no idea if the rivalry between Beria's all-powerful state security and their eternal underdog rivals was anything like as antagonistic as that between the organizations run by Canaris and Heydrich. But he hoped to God it was.

He was seconds away from being shot, he realized, now that the paralyzing pain from his groin was subsiding. He had only one card to play here - the possibility that he might be able to save this man from the same fate as Ilyin if Beria caught wind of what had happened here.

"Listen," he said, his heaving finally under control. "This might sound stupid, but we're actually on the same side here. We need to cooperate if we're to make it out of this in one piece."

The slight smile on the Russian's face told him he had no intention of allowing Wolff to achieve that aim. He pressed on. "There are elements within the SD who want the peace deal to fail. They're connected to the big armaments firms, Krupps, Mauser. There are people making a fortune out of the war, and they don't want it to end.

"My people are the pragmatists. They can see how a war on two fronts will end, and they know it's imperative to close one of them off." He switched tack, desperately trying to keep the man from pulling the trigger. "What were they doing here anyway? What were they looking for? What did they take?"

Wolff knew exactly what they had been doing here: searching for proof to bring back to Berlin. However, to admit that right now would be a death sentence. Moreover, if he was to get out of here alive, he would have to either locate the SD men and neutralize them or discover what evidence, if any, they had gathered here and inform Canaris so a counternarrative could be concocted.

The Russian was looking at him differently now, as if sizing up what information he could obtain before killing him. After a few moments, he replied: "I was in the toilet at the end of the hall when they came. Two of them, I think, from the sound of it. I heard a shout, and then there was a shot.

"I knew whoever it was would come looking for me too, so I hid in the laundry cupboard. They went into my room and searched the toilet too, but they didn't find me. That was about an hour ago. When I was sure they had gone, I came out and found Morozov here," the man said, using what was evidently Ilyin's real name. "I was about to leave when I heard you at the door."

Wolff pushed himself up so his back was against the door, the movement sending pain shooting up from his groin anew. The Russian pointed his pistol threateningly, and he raised his hands to calm the man down. "What did they take?" he gasped.

The NKVD man studied him for a moment before responding. "It looks like his notes are missing."

"What was in them?" Wolff asked, without missing a beat. *Keep him talking.*

"Comrade Morozov was a very careful man," Kuznetzov went on. "He knew that when we returned to Moscow, we would face a thorough debriefing. Everything you said and the way you said it would be pored over and analyzed in an attempt to gauge which way your side is leaning.

"Immediately after meeting you, he came back here and wrote down everything that had been discussed before going to the embassy. To be honest, when we saw how young you were, we already realized the whole thing was doomed. Nobody who was serious about such negotiations would send such a...boy to represent them."

On the contrary, Wolff thought. *My side is deathly serious about the whole thing.*

"So they took his notes," he prompted the Russian. "Is that all? Is there anything else missing?"

"I haven't checked, but I don't think they took his *makhorka*," came the sour reply. The harsh pipe tobacco was simultaneously despised and a point of pride for frontline Red Army troops. Many Wehrmacht soldiers had taken it off dead Soviets as souvenirs, but its foul taste meant they only ever smoked it if they had absolutely nothing else.

"These notes, what did they look like?" The Russian looked at him for a moment and laughed as if amused, but Wolff could see a glimmer of hope in his eyes. "You kill me now, and the chance of an armistice dies with me," Wolff continued.

"My side will believe the NKVD ambushed me in a petty act of vengeance, and they will redouble their efforts to get to Moscow, because there is no other option. You can tell your superiors what happened here, but someone will have to pay. Who do you think that will be?"

Kuznetzov's mouth drew into a tight line, but Wolff drove home the point with sledgehammer logic. "If this all comes to nothing, do you think Stalin will let the few people who know he tried to buy off the invaders run around free with that knowledge? You'll be lucky if you make it as far as Siberia.

"Or," Wolff said, warming to his theme. "You let me go back to the embassy and report back. This conspiracy is being run from inside the SS. There are only a few of their people in this part of the world. It won't be too difficult to track down which of them it was once the squeeze is put on.

"Once we have them, we can get the names of those further up the chain and eliminate them all in one go. And the talks can continue. What happened to your comrade is unfortunate, but you can dress it up as something else. A knifing by some drunk Wehrmacht man down in a bar or whatever. I'm sure you have plenty of imagination."

Kuznetzov was staring at him now, and Wolff could see the barrel of the pistol propped up on the man's thigh had moved ever so slightly to the right so that it was no longer pointing directly at him.

"So," Wolff said with an authority he did not really feel, "what did these notes look like?"

16

"Find them."

The response from Oster had been succinct, curt and not overly helpful. There had been no time to send a coded message via the embassy or ring Olbricht's office at Reserve Army head-quarters to relay a message.

Wolff had rung the colonel on his A-net directly from the hotel's phone and discovered to his relief that Oster was an early bird when it came to work. Wolff then outlined in improvised coded terms what had happened.

The musician's friends had taken their dance partner's notes and run off home. There would be no concert now - and a very real risk of the others staging a recital of their own.

Oster had been silent for a moment, and Wolff had pictured him standing there in front of his bank of phones, absorbing the news that yet another bid to save Germany had been sabotaged by Heydrich, this time possibly with concrete evidence to expose it.

"Find them," he had repeated, "and get those notes back by any means necessary. Otherwise, we might have to play *Für Elise* ourselves. Understood?" The reference to one of Beethoven's most famous piano compositions had not required much translation.

Tales of the Führer's predilection for slowly strangling traitors with the tempered steel wire of a baby grand were well known throughout the armed services. The question was, where to start? The SD were not going to hang around to face the consequences of their actions at Riunione and the Red Star Hotel, not to mention the murder of Anna.

With Zhelev's body ripening in the summer heat back at his room at the Slavyanska Beseda and an irate Tashev lying yards from the similarly maturing corpse at his feet, Wolff had reasons of his own to get out of town fast.

But if he was to have any chance of getting the incriminating diary back from the SD, he would have to track them. And he would have to do so unarmed. Kuznetzov had gathered his belongings and fled, but had taken Tashev's pistol with him. They were still enemies, after all.

Wolff needed all the help he could get, but did not trust Wagner, who he felt was likely to give him up under pressure. He would have no choice but to rely on the code clerk, Pfeiffer.

Wolff dialed the legation and kept his voice low so as not to be overheard by Tashev through the now closed door to the back room. Someone eventually answered the phone, and Wolff asked for Pfeiffer. Mercifully, the code clerk was there, and he was transferred through within a few seconds.

Invoking his all-powerful letter from Canaris, Wolff told him to call the airport immediately and check for any incoming flights from Berlin before phoning him back. A few minutes later, Pfeiffer was on the line to him once more.

There was nothing due for the rest of the day, he said. Bad weather over the Reich's capital meant all flights had been canceled until further notice. Furthermore, he added, the Bulgarians had ordered that no planes be allowed to take off from Sofia until further notice.

It had caused quite a degree of annoyance among some Luftwaffe figures. Wolff smiled and threw a mock salute at the closed door behind which Tashev lay.

"Okay, Pfeiffer," Wolff said, taking him further into his confidence. "What I am about to tell you is a matter of the highest military secrecy, and divulging it may result in court martial, understood?" The code clerk confirmed that he did.

"I am attempting to follow and apprehend two individuals who may be attempting to make their way back to the Reich. These people are believed to be behind at least three murders here in Sofia, and their capture and discreet deliverance back to Bulgarian authorities has been deemed high priority.

"Failure to do so may have catastrophic political consequences for our relations with a fellow Tripartite Pact ally."

"I understand...Herr Schreiber." Wolff could hear Pfeiffer's difficulty in taking such instruction from a fellow Wehrmacht officer posing as a civilian, albeit one with a letter like Wolff had in his possession.

"If these individuals cannot fly from Sofia, they may try to exit the city by other means. What about trains? Could they attempt to get to Athens?"

Pfeiffer took a moment to answer. "There are direct international connections from Sofia to Bucharest and Istanbul. But if one wanted to head for Reich-controlled territory or anywhere else by train from here, one would have to go through Yugoslavia."

Wolff straightened up. That was it, he knew instinctively. The SD would have contacted Berlin and would almost certainly have been informed of the restrictions placed on outgoing flights as a result of their actions.

A butcher like Heydrich would not have cared about a few deaths in Sofia once he had evidence with which he could discredit his old Navy superior and wrest control of all intelligence facilities within the Reich.

But he also would have recognized his men had to get out of Bulgaria and the value of that evidence ruled out the potential risk posed by a lengthy train journey to Istanbul and a flight back from neutral territory.

Instead, the two SD assassins calling themselves Möbert and Bonsen would have been ordered to get to German-held territory as quickly as possible and commandeer a Luftwaffe plane back to the Reich along with the precious diary.

"Pfeiffer, if these individuals were fleeing by train to either Greece or Yugoslavia, what would be the earliest service they could take from Sofia? Could you call the main train station and check, please?"

"There's no need, Herr Schreiber, I have the schedules here in front of me." Wolff said a silent prayer of thanks for the innate organization of the German state official. "There is only one service to both Belgrade and Salonika today.

"But both depart at the same time. It's the one train as far as Niš and then passengers have to change to continue on north or south. It leaves from Sofia Central in one hour."

***

Wolff stood impatiently at the end of the very last carriage while he waited for the train to cross the border into what used to be called Yugoslavia. Like many of its counterparts, the country had suffered the consequences of standing up to the Nazis.

When Hitler had been refused free passage of German troops en route to invade Greece across Yugoslav territory, he had bombed the hell out of Belgrade and taken what he wanted anyway.

The price the Yugoslavs had paid was to see their country - never more than a patchwork of ethnic groups anyway - dismembered, with slices given to the Bulgarians, Italians and Hungarians.

The two largest remaining sections were Croatia, run by Germany's fascist allies the Ustaše, and Serbia, which was now under direct occupation and officially called The Territory of the Military Commander.

The old Yugoslav border lay a mere 60km from Sofia, but the train had not merely been over half an hour late in leaving, it had taken an age to cross the short distance to the frontier. The delayed departure had taken its toll on Wolff's nerves, but he had used that time to discreetly reconnoiter the various carriages from the platform at Central Station.

He was relieved to spot Möbert and Bonsen sitting amongst the few civilians on board, hats pulled well down and failing entirely to appear inconspicuous. *Floppy hats*. How ironic.

On the next carriage up was what appeared to be an entire company of paratroopers, presumably on their way to shore up the weak Wehrmacht presence in what used to be called Serbia.

From snatches of overheard conversation between the troops as they smoked on the platform, he learned they were on their way there to deal with the partisan uprising which had broken out following the invasion of Russia.

This was threatening to overwhelm the existing force of poorly equipped conscripts commanded by old hares, as the veterans of the Great War trenches were known. The battle-hardened *Fallschirmjäger* onboard were being sent from Greece, where they were no longer required, to help stamp the rebellion out.

None of them were any older than Wolff, but there was a swagger to them which was all too familiar. The confidence of those who had seen combat and come through the other side. It was clear from their disparaging repartee that they were looking forward to showing their comrades in Serbia how such things were done.

As the train at last pulled into Kalotina, the final Bulgarian station before crossing the border, Wolff watched keenly out the window. It had been almost three hours since he had abandoned Tashev back at the hotel, and he had probably worked himself free by this stage.

Now was the moment he would learn whether the major was smart or stubborn. Of the four murders committed by the SD, three could be covered up by local police as either failed robberies or an accidental fire death.

The fourth, Ilyin's, would probably be smoothed over by the NKVD themselves. Tashev's airport and airfield checks had presumably been imposed when he believed he was hunting Wolff over Anna's murder.

It was likely he had imposed similar restrictions at Bulgaria's borders. Now that it was clear he was dealing with something of far greater proportions, he might have withdrawn them to ensure the troublemakers removed themselves from his patch. Assuming of course he had indeed managed to free himself by now.

He watched on edge as two Bulgarian border guards made their way down through the train to the last carriage in which he was standing. Both had their rifles slung over their shoulders and were carrying sidearms in holsters.

Neither seemed particularly alert, but Wolff had the Red Army knife up the sleeve of his shirt, ready to drop into his hand. The Russians called it the *finka*, as it had been adapted from the traditional Finnish blade for gutting fish into something to be used on far larger objects.

He had brought it from Germany simply because he had nowhere else to leave it for safekeeping. Along with his documents, it was the only thing he had taken from his suitcase before leaving his room at the Slavyanksa Beseda hours beforehand. Kuznetzov had missed it while patting him down earlier and he was damn glad of it now.

If the two guards tried anything, he would kill them on the spot, jump off the train and make his way across the frontier on foot. It would make following the SD men to Belgrade a lot harder, but it was still infinitely better than being sent back to Sofia.

The two guards reached him and the first held out his hand for Wolff's passport, while the second stood back, looking him up and down. He passed over the documents in the name of Hermann Schreiber, and the first man pulled out the permission slip identifying him as a sales representative.

He turned and muttered something to his companion, who studied Wolff more intently now. Wolff pointed his arm down toward the floor, ready to let the knife slide out and into his palm as he played out how he would tackle them in his mind.

He would let the blade drop with one hand and use his other to push up the first man's chin while slicing across his windpipe in one smooth motion. The second guard would most probably attempt to unsling his rifle from his back, allowing Wolff to go for his unprotected neck or side.

The priority was to silence them quickly, before a shot could be gotten off. The two men had finished with his passport, but had not yet given it back. They exchanged glances, and Wolff discreetly adjusted his feet as he let the sharp point of the knife fall gently onto his curled fingers.

Suddenly, the second guard grinned and gave him the thumbs up. "Mannheim Z-960. *Gut!*" Wolff's shoulders sagged with relief as he smiled and held out his free hand to get his papers back.

He had almost murdered a couple of Balkan tractor aficionados.

The train crossed into Serbia, and the whole process was repeated at the next station of Caribrod, only this time with a couple of typically garrulous teenagers from the Rhineland in field gray.

They asked him a couple of questions, puzzled in particular as to why he was sitting in third class when he had a second-class ticket. Wolff deflected the query with a smile, explaining that he was just stretching his legs along the length of the train and had decided to sit down.

He asked how long the journey to Belgrade would take and was told it would be six hours. "Whenever the new driver shows up," the older one rolled his eyes. Now that the train had crossed into Serbia, the journey had to continue with an engineer from what used to be known as Yugoslav Railways.

Most were less than punctual. Word of this had clearly spread, and many of the passengers had disembarked to wait on the platform. Wolff would have liked to join them to escape the stifling air of the carriage, but he stayed where he was. There was too much risk of being spotted by his quarry.

So he remained in place at the very back of the carriage, watching what was taking place outside. Around half an hour later, the train moved off, and Wolff refocused on how he would overcome the SD men. The two conscripts had confirmed that the six-hour slog to Belgrade would be punctuated with a stop off in Niš, where those heading south to Greece would change services.

That seemed to him to be the ideal place to strike. There was no food or drink service on the train, and everyone on board would undoubtedly get out in Niš in order to procure something to eat.

It was now mid-afternoon, and Wolff had not had any food since being rudely roused from his bed by Tashev at dawn. His stomach was rumbling fiercely. Möbert and Bonsen were almost certainly suffering the same pangs.

He leaned against the window, pulled his hat over his face and settled down to nap for a couple of hours. The last carriage of the train was for third-class passengers, where seating was little more than uncomfortable wooden benches and there was a pervasive smell of chicken shit from the caged poultry a couple of peasants had boarded with.

He slept fitfully, awakened periodically by the jolting of the carriage and always with a microsecond of confusion as to where he was before he caught his bearings. At last, the train pulled into Niš, and Wolff opened his eyes as he sensed the train slowing to a halt.

The peasants and their chickens were all getting off here, and Wolff used them as cover while he walked onto the platform himself and took up an observation post behind a convenient pole. Passengers were spilling off the train now, among them the older SD man, Möbert, who walked quickly towards the station toilets, clearly intent on beating the rush. Wolff didn't blame him.

The stench coming from some of the lavatories on board in the August heat would deter all but the most desperate of travelers. Wolff considered following the man inside, but decided against it. The chances of overcoming Möbert in the packed loos were minuscule, and there was a strong risk he would be recognized.

A few minutes later, the SD man reemerged and went back on board. Now Bonsen disembarked and had his turn using the conveniences. Wolff swore in frustration. These two were not going to let their guard down, even now.

A few minutes later, Bonsen came back out and headed to the cafe where many of the troops on board had already gone. Wolff edged up along the platform, careful to keep his back to the train carriages to avoid Möbert spotting him.

He peered in the window of the cafe, like a traveler attempting to decide whether the crowds were too much to bother with. The place was indeed packed, almost completely with Germans, and the man and woman behind the counter were frantically attempting to serve their new customers as quickly as possible.

There was a mirror on the wall behind the counter, and Wolff could see in its reflection that Bonsen was already at the head of the queue. This told Wolff that he must be at least above sergeant level, as there were several NCOs in the line.

It was potentially useful information should any situation arise in which rank mattered, though it didn't help one bit now. He watched in the mirror as Bonsen handed over some cash and picked up some sandwiches. Wolff ducked his head out of sight and sidled back down the platform, from where he watched Bonsen emerge onto the platform again.

The SD man looked up and down the platform as if deciding what to do next and Wolff hoped for a second that he might decide to make another trip to the toilet. However, after a few seconds Bonsen seemed to make a decision and boarded the train again.

Wolff swore under his breath. Patience. It would have been suicidal to make a move here. Other opportunities might present themselves later.

The train whistle sounded for departure, but was ignored by the majority of the paratroopers, some of whom were smoking on the platform. The others dribbled out of the cafe eventually and joined them.

The whistle sounded twice more impatiently and eventually some of the NCOs appeared and began herding the men onto the train like teachers rounding up their unruly pupils. Wolff got on himself ahead of an elderly local woman laden down with a couple of suitcases.

He helped the woman with her baggage, receiving a quick smile of thanks and a deferential duck of the head in response. Having deposited her suitcases inside, the woman leaned out the window of the carriage door, waving farewell to someone, only for the door to open outwards again suddenly under her weight, sending her tumbling out onto the platform.

She seemed unhurt, yet embarrassed, and the girl to whom she had presumably been waving goodbye ran forward to help her off the ground. An officious local conductor, who had stood silent while the troops took their time getting on board, now approached the two women and began berating them in Serbian, the younger of the two answering back in a pleading tone.

A few of the last paratroopers waiting to board looked on amused, while another local man smoking and leaning against a pole watched the scene in silence. None came forward to assist. Wolff got back out again to help the old woman back up.

He glared at the smirking paratroopers and the idle smoker before cutting the conductor's tirade off with a few choice words in German. He assisted the woman in climbing back up the steep steps and onto the train once more.

He received the same bob of the head in gratitude from both women, with the younger one pointing to the door and attempting to explain something he didn't understand. Obviously, the door locks were not to be relied upon.

The whistle sounded again, this time a long, impatient blast, and the conductor shooed the younger woman away. The train began to slowly chug forward and Wolff assisted the woman with her baggage down to the third-class carriage.

The conductor was standing on the platform, glowering in at him over his public humiliation, the smoker behind him still watching impassively. Wolff winced. It had been stupid of him to draw attention to himself in such a fashion. What if either Möbert or Bonsen had been attracted by the noise and had glanced out the window themselves to see what was causing the delay?

Wolff resolved to set any further acts of chivalry aside until after the mission was completed. It was clear he lacked the self-centered dedication required for the cold, hard calculations of the intelligence game. He resumed his seat at the very back of the train and thought about his next move.

As no opportunities had presented themselves in Niš, he would have to find another way. His quarry would probably want to use the toilets upon arrival at Belgrade again. He would have to find a way to subdue one or both of them there and take the diary.

If discovered, he could screech loudly in German about a partisan attack, pin it on some hapless local and disappear in the confusion. It wasn't much of a plan, but it was better than nothing. There seemed to be no chance of attacking them on the train without drawing the attention of the paratroopers in the next carriage.

Wolff fought down a rising sensation of panic which threatened to overwhelm him as he considered his position. He still had the crucial element of surprise, and it would be a matter of finding the opportunity and acting upon it. He began to formulate a rough plan in his head, again based on silently overpowering one of the pair in a toilet with his knife.

He could then stash the man in a cubicle with his feet visible underneath the door and wait til the second came to investigate, before delivering him the same fate. If Möbert, who presumably carried the diary, was the first one into the toilet, he might not need to kill Bonsen at all. He could simply take the evidence and disappear.

It all depended on quite a few factors, of course, such as entering unobserved after his quarry and being able to get the better of him or them without the alarm being raised. But it was not impossible. Furthermore, both SD officers were in civilian clothing, so the discovery of their bodies would not lead to the same immediate outcry as those of men in military uniform.

It was a different task to any he had faced so far, where there had always been the comfort of knowing that your comrade had your back and you had his. Here and now, Wolff had only himself to rely on.

Once more, he fell back on the words of Sergeant Major Salomon, his old training officer at Quenzgut, as the finishing school for Brandenburgers was known. They had served him well on numerous occasions and he sought their comfort once again, visualizing Salomon parading before the young men in front of him as he prepared to send them off to subterfuge and dicing with death behind enemy lines.

Don't concentrate on the advantages you lack, concentrate on those that you have.

Salomon knew what he was talking about. He had served in the Great War under General Paul von Lettow-Vorbeck, the legendary *Lion of Africa*. Between them, they had tied up a combined Allied force of 300,000 with just 14,000 men of their own, mainly native *askaris*.

As a member of Lettow-Vorbeck's colonial protectorate *Schutztruppe*, Salomon had lived off the land and his charges' knowledge of it to evade defeat for four years until forced to surrender by the 1918 armistice.

It was a far more difficult mission, with many more moving parts in an inhospitable environment with a constant threat of betrayal, yet he had done it. And for four long years. Compared to what Salomon had faced, overpowering these two thugs was relatively straightforward. Especially as he still had the element of surprise.

Wolff was beginning to feel vaguely confident about his chances of success when he felt a presence at the doorway to the carriage. He looked up.

There, carrying a pistol and with a triumphant smile on his face, stood the SD man who called himself Alfred Bonsen.

17

"How did you track us?"

Bonsen's demeanor was part angry, part fearful, and it took Wolff a second to grasp why. Just as Canaris was aware he had figures within the Abwehr reporting to Heydrich, Bonsen obviously believed the admiral had moles within the SD.

Playing on that fear might be the only thing preventing Bonsen from shooting him right here. Bonsen had patted him down and found the knife. He had made Wolff remove the tie he had put on in Sofia in an effort to look less bedraggled and had bound Wolff's wrists with it.

Bonsen peered across at his captive from his seat on the other side of the now empty carriage. There was no chance of Wolff overpowering the man. His body would be tossed out the back door onto the track, all identifying papers having been removed first.

No glorious funeral at which Ludwig could shake hands solemnly and accept condolences from the few who might attend. Instead, his son would officially be classified a deserter in yet another crushing disappointment for a middle-aged, failed businessman whose life had become an endless series of them.

"I'm afraid I can't tell you that," Wolff replied, receiving a gratifyingly infuriated look in response.

"Think you're clever, do you?" Bonsen sneered back. "We've been onto you from the very beginning, when you turned up at the Bendlerblock." The remark hit home as intended, and Wolff was unable to keep the shock from his face.

Now it was Bonsen's turn to adopt a victorious smirk. "Yes, that's right. We had you checked out, and something didn't add up. Why would Canaris drag a man facing a court martial in the east all the way to Berlin? Even if it was a member of one of his half-breed units who had attacked an SS officer.

"We're aware of the admiral's envy toward the *Schutzstaffel*, but that would be extraordinarily petty, even for him. But then it all became clear. You have nowhere else to go, do you? Even with that ludicrous volunteer creed, it was guaranteed you would accept whatever he was offering. We just had to figure out what it was.

"And by God, the admiral didn't disappoint, did he? Negotiating with the enemy behind the Führer's back?" Bonsen shook his head in something approaching admiration. "*Obergruppenführer* Heydrich has been waiting a long time to catch the old traitor red-handed. And you led us right to the evidence."

He smiled pityingly, but Wolff's eyes were drawn to the rectangular outline of something which bulged against Bonsen's chest in the inside breast pocket of his suit jacket.

Did Bonsen have the diary on him?

"You must have thought you were pretty smart, did you? Shrugging off the Bulgarians?" Bonsen continued to lecture him smugly. "We were following their man, so when you lost him, we lost you. But the girl...."

Bonsen shook his head again, this time in derision. "Couldn't even keep your *Schwanz* in your pants, could you? Did you know she was a Jew? A brave one, I'll give her that. She tried to protect you at first, but she opened up once she saw the knife. She didn't know much, but she knew your connect, the waiter at Riunione. Once we had him, we had everything."

Wolff stared at him with pure loathing. Bonsen ignored the look and cocked his head curiously. "How did you get away from the Bulgarians anyway? We saw Tashev going into the hotel with that fat buffoon." When Wolff didn't reply, he shrugged. "Leave it to the professionals, son. You're completely out of your depth.

"Even back at the station in Niš. Do you know how I spotted you? The reflection in the train window. When I came out of the cafe, I could see you peering out from behind your pole, then jerking your head back in when I looked in your direction."

He chuckled, and Wolff felt the intense burn of humiliation and shame. His blundering and underestimation of the ruthless lengths to which Heydrich and his underlings would go had gotten Anna killed and tightened the noose not only around his neck, but those of Canaris and Oster.

Someone would have to take the fall for all this, and it was not hard to imagine who it would be.

"So who is the mole?"

Wolff did not respond, but adopted a defiant jut to his jaw.

Concentrate on the advantages you have.

Bonsen eyed him curiously. "I don't think you actually know. Let's face it, it's quite a bit above you, and we all know how careful Canaris is to compartmentalize these things. Still, we'll find out soon enough when you're handed over to the Gestapo in Belgrade, won't we?"

Bonsen wrinkled his nose, as if viewing the torture required to extract such information as distasteful, before getting to his feet and looking around. "This carriage stinks. We're going back up to first class. *Hauptsturmführer* Udolph is delighted with how things have gone so far. Presenting you to him will be the icing on the cake.

"Neither of us can read that ridiculous Slav alphabet in the *Bolo* diary, but I'm sure there's mention of a Herr Schreiber in there somewhere."

Udolph. So that was Möbert's real name.

"It's a few hours to Belgrade, and you've got a decision to make. Think about your future, boy. These traitors are going down with or without you. If you cooperate, you might even get a short sentence and be back at the front again in a few years." He grinned unpleasantly. "Though not as a lieutenant, I'm afraid."

Wolff got to his feet slowly, using the time to weigh up his options. Even with his hands tied, he might be able to subdue the man if he could get a clean strike to the jaw with one of his elbows while in the corridor. If Bonsen had the diary, he could dispose of him, take the evidence and simply disappear at the next station.

Or wait and kill Udolph or Möbert or whatever the hell he was calling himself to be sure. The bastard deserved it anyway after what he had done to Anna. But Bonsen was no fool. He constantly maintained at least a meter of distance between them.

"I need to use the toilet," Wolff said in an attempt to buy time.

"You can shit your pants for all I care," Bonsen replied. "That's probably going to happen at some point when the Gestapo get their hands on you in Belgrade anyway. Keep moving."

They passed through another third-class carriage and then three more second-class ones, all the occupants averting their eyes at the sight of a man with his wrists tied being ushered along by another man pointing a pistol at him. Better not to know.

Wolff walked as slowly as he could, hoping that the constant jerking and rocking of the train would bring Bonsen within range. On a couple of occasions, Bonsen came tantalizingly close, but he knew instinctively that it was not close enough.

They were on the verge of entering the wagon next to the one filled with the paratroopers when the train lurched sufficiently violently and Bonsen stumbled, falling for a split second against his prisoner.

It was all Wolff needed.

Spinning around, he used the outstretched palms of his bound hands to push the pistol to one side, just as Bonsen let off a shot which reverberated loudly throughout the carriage. For a split second, Bonsen's chin was unguarded, and Wolff put his wrists between his legs, bent his knees and then used his upward momentum to drive his clasped fists into the man's throat.

Already off balance but clinging to his gun, Bonsen grabbed desperately with his free hand at Wolff's bindings to steady himself for another shot. Instead, Wolff ran at him so that the SD man tottered backwards.

Together, both men crashed into the carriage door behind them, which gave under their combined weight and opened outward, sending the pair of them crashing from the moderately speeding train to the earth outside.

They landed heavily on the side of the track, Bonsen's body acting as a cushion under Wolff, who nonetheless had the wind driven out of him. After a moment of shock, Wolff scrabbled to get his bound hands up to his opponent's neck to finish him off.

But there was no resistance, and when he looked into Bonsen's sightless eyes, he could see why. The man's head was at a slight angle where it had fallen against a small rock, half buried in the soil bordering the incline from the rail track.

Whether it was the blow to the back of the head or a snapped neck, Bonsen would not be torturing or murdering anyone ever again.

Wolff got to his feet and looked at the receding carriages in the distance. If anyone had noticed two passengers falling together through the door, they had certainly not raised the alarm.

Doubtless, like every other population currently under German occupation, they had learned that the less interaction they had with their new colonizers, the better. With difficulty, Wolff rolled Bonsen onto his front and pulled the *finka* from the back of his waistband.

He dropped to his knees and jammed the handle of the knife between his thighs with the blade upwards, before using its edge to saw through the tie around his wrists.

Wolff's next thought was for the bulge he had spotted in Bonsen's jacket, and he rolled the dead man over once more and pulled his suit coat open. He reached into the pocket, pulled out the notebook jammed inside and opened it.

He knew immediately it was not what he was looking for. The writing inside was in Roman letters, not Cyrillic, and in German. These were Bonsen's notes. He swore again loudly.

A quick flick through the entire notebook confirmed it. There were short annotations with dates and times, the last one from the day beforehand when Wolff had managed to shake his clumsy Bulgarian tail.

Subject has engaged in anti-surveillance maneuvers, is clearly an experienced intelligence agent. Suspect he has met with contact while unobserved.

"Thanks for the compliment," he muttered at Bonsen's corpse. There were no further entries. The two SD men had obviously decided not to record their murders of an innocent woman, a nightclub waiter, a hotel receptionist and an NKVD agent.

He patted Bonsen down further, finding a leather wallet identifying Bonsen as Lieutenant Andreas Axmann of *Ausland-SD*, the foreign intelligence arm of Heydrich's organization. In another pocket, he found an identity card for a Captain Kirill Igorevich Morozov of the People's Commissariat for Internal Affairs.

Morozov/Ilyin's shifty eyes stared out either side of his voluminous nose. It was hard to know whether Bonsen had kept the dead NKVD agent's card as evidence, or a souvenir, or both. It would certainly have formed part of the evidence gathered by Heydrich, but was still secondary in importance to the diary.

He tossed both the wallet and the card into the long grass bordering the track and forced himself to analyze the situation logically, something else which had been drilled into them by Horst Salomon.

To be able to exploit the advantages available to you, you must first know what they are - as well as what obstacles you face.

On the positive side, he was uninjured and had managed to neutralize one of his two opponents, seizing a key piece of proof of liaisons between the Abwehr and the NKVD in the process. Moreover, judging by what Bonsen/Axmann had told him, his senior partner, Udolph, was unaware of his presence on the train.

Bonsen had been intending to parade him up to his superior and present him like a trussed-up trophy. Thus, the junior SD man's disappearance would eventually be noticed and might serve to further hold up Udolph's flight towards Berlin, potentially allowing Wolff to catch up with him.

Wolff still had his knife and could now add the dead man's pistol to his weaponry. Against that, Wolff was stranded in the middle of the countryside with no idea where he was, with his remaining quarry getting further away with every passing minute. He swallowed his despair.

Given the ruthlessness with which the SD had acted so far, it was quite possible that Udolph would go on ahead to Berlin as quickly as he could, leaving the hunt for his missing subordinate to others. Also, even if Wolff did manage to catch up with him, Udolph would be even more on edge due to the unexplained disappearance of his comrade and was less likely to let his guard down.

The best Wolff could hope for here was to get to the nearest German garrison, flash Canaris's all-commanding letter once more and demand to be brought instantly to Belgrade, where Udolph was headed. He could deal with how to kill the SD man there.

Decision made, he bent down and grabbed Bonsen's jacket by the lapels, dragging his heavy corpse with some difficulty into the long grass. He picked up the dead man's gun from where it had fallen and tucked it into the small of his back, sliding the *finka* into the back belt loops of his trousers too.

Then he began trudging down the track in the same direction as the train from which he had just fallen. The going was slow, not just because of the need to step evenly on the sleepers to avoid twisting an ankle. But after a while, he fell into a kind of rhythm, whilst constantly scanning the horizon for any signs of habitation and listening for any traffic from a nearby road.

After around an hour, he came upon a tiny, deserted station, little more than an uncovered stretch of poorly maintained concrete at either side. There were no signs to tell him where he was - these had probably been removed by the Yugoslavs as soon as they could see their country was being invaded and had yet to be replaced.

A narrow, dusty road led from one side of the weed-strewn, rundown stop-off, though where it went was anybody's guess. He estimated that a station so minor was unlikely to serve an outpost big enough to warrant a German garrison and labored on.

The hot Balkan afternoon sun beat down on him as he walked along, and after another hour, he was grateful when he saw he was approaching an area of railway line bordered on each side by coniferous forest. As he came closer, he stopped and observed it from a few hundred yards away.

It was against all his hard-won military instincts to move into such terrain. He decided to leave the track and step into the trees and continue walking parallel alongside. It would not offer much defense, but would prevent him being caught out in the open like a sitting duck should there be any hostile parties alongside.

He took out Bonsen's Walther PPK and checked the cartridge. The *Polizeipistole Kriminalmodell,* used before the war by police, had also been issued to the SS and SD to set them apart from their lesser Wehrmacht colleagues. Even Hitler had been given his own gold-plated, monogrammed version for his 50th birthday in 1939.

But like the army-issue P38, it carried eight rounds, which left him with seven bullets given the shot fired by Bonsen during their struggle on the train. If he got into a firefight where he needed more than that, he was probably doomed anyway.

He stepped into the trees, which had thicker trunks and were closer together than they appeared from the track, meaning visibility was reduced to a few yards in the gloom. The density of the forest also made progress more difficult, and he was acutely aware of the noise he was making as he moved forward.

After 15 minutes of this, he stopped. At the front, they referred to it as *Kriegsspielen,* or war games. That instinctive, inexplicable sense gained through combat of knowing when one was in imminent danger. As silently as he could, he cocked the pistol and began to advance more cautiously.

Emerging into a natural gap between the pines, he looked down at the ground. Some animal tracks were visible in the mud, which remained soft here in the gloom away from the sun's rays. Movement caught his eye to his left, and he turned with gun raised to see a boy in his mid-teens step out from behind a tree.

The lad looked about 15 and was scrawny and in worn and dirty clothing. His stare was at once hostile and fearful, but his hands were empty. Wolff lowered the pistol slightly and was considering what to do when he heard a slight noise behind him and the unmistakable feel of a gun barrel being pushed into the base of his neck.

Wolff froze as the Walther was grabbed from behind and the knife yanked from the small of his back while he was roughly, yet thoroughly, patted down. A female voice hissed an order to him in what he presumed was Serbian, and he was grabbed by his collar and roughly pulled back, forcing him off balance.

The gun was jammed painfully into his side, and he was turned and forced to walk, hands raised.

Away from the track leading north to Belgrade and deeper into the woods.

18

Wolff snatched a glance at his captors as they led him further into the shaded twilight. The woman holding the pistol and giving the orders stood a consistent two yards behind him, ruling out any attempts to allow the gap to close and attempt something.

She was young, perhaps 19, but with a fierce look on her face accentuated by her short hair. The odds were even further against him, as the boy with her who had searched Wolff maintained the same distance to one side while clutching the Red Army knife.

He was in his mid-teens, and his attempts to portray the same aggressive air were somewhat undermined by the fear which seeped through beneath it. Both bore the unwashed air that Wolff recognized so well and he knew what he was dealing with.

Not for nothing did the *frontschweine* of Army Group North refer to the lice which inevitably plagued them after a few weeks as 'partisans'. It was a backhanded compliment: both were incredibly persistent and could survive even the harshest of attempts to exterminate them.

It was the girl that worried him the most, though. The female partisans in the east were known as *Flintenweiber* – shotgun hags – a term which indicated the depth of fear they inspired.

They were often far more violent than their male counterparts, perhaps to dissuade potential sexual predators that they might offer easy pickings.

This one was no hag and in peacetime would certainly have had her suitors. Wolff just hoped that he would not become a means for her to demonstrate she could be just as bloodthirsty as any man.

His captors walked him up the increasingly steep hill of the forest until they crested its summit and the trees began to thin out. They crossed several fields of untamed, calf-length grass and entered another, even thicker forest, which stretched as far as the horizon.

They walked for around three miles further, and Wolff noted they were heading west in a fairly straight line, betraying their lack of experience in handling prisoners. Both, though, were too smart to fall for any of his bids to draw them in.

After his third attempt at stalling led to a vicious jab in the shoulder from his own knife, he gave up and marched onwards without resistance. As he moved, he racked his brain for what he knew of the situation here.

The uprising had begun last month following the German victory the previous April. Two different groups were involved, the royalist Chetniks - soldiers from the defeated Royal Yugoslav Army who had taken to the hills - and the ever-present communists.

It was difficult to know which side had taken him, but he would find out soon enough, he supposed. Whoever it was, he could not expect any outside assistance. Nobody knew he was on the train, and there would be no search parties sent out for him.

After half an hour of further trekking through the woods, they reached the partisan camp, a rough circle of worn, dirty and sagging canvas tents held up by guy ropes stretching to nearby trees. Their arrival drew a crowd of other thin and shabbily clothed figures who had clearly been out here for some time.

There were up to 50 of them, but despite the spittle and slaps across the face Wolff received from some of those present, it was evident they were waiting for someone else.

A man eventually arrived at the camp with two or three others, all of them carrying the stiffened corpses of rabbits. As all eyes turned to him, Wolff could see that this was the outfit's leader. The man was as thin and as hollow-eyed as the rest of them, but carried the definite air of authority.

Ignoring Wolff, he went over and began angrily haranguing the girl, who responded just as sharply. Serbian was a considerably different language to either Russian or Latvian, but as far as Wolff could discern, he was berating her for failing to follow orders.

It was also clear that there was some sort of relationship between the two. Brother and sister or cousins, perhaps. The girl looked too young to be the man's lover, though who knew these days. The argument eventually subsided as the girl's verbal resistance petered out and the man, whose name he had gleaned from the shouting match as Darko, turned his attention to Wolff.

After looking his captive up and down curiously, he barked a query at the girl, who responded sullenly. Darko then patted down Wolff's suit pants before pushing open his jacket and retrieving his wallet from the inside left breast pocket.

He examined the sizeable wad of Bulgarian currency it contained with interest before replacing it and tossing the wallet to the girl. Darko then tried the pocket on the other side and came across what Wolff was hoping he would miss.

His *Soldbuch*.

The paybook issued to all German soldiers also served as their main form of ID. Wolff's had been altered to show a ficititious unit, as per Abwehr policy. But there could be no question of his identity now due to the photograph of him in field grey uniform.

"Alfredo," he said, reading out the middle name given to Wolff by his mother in anticipation of his parents' much-discussed move to Latin America. "*¿Hablas español?*"

Wolff's heart sank.

There was only one place a Serb would have learned Spanish and only one reason he would have traveled there. The issue of which type of partisan had taken him was no longer in doubt. If the man was the kind of dedicated communist who had gone to Spain to fight, Wolff was in even deeper trouble than he had thought. Darko was still looking at him expectantly. He nodded curtly.

"What does this say?" Darko had unfolded Canaris' letter ordering that all and any assistance required should be rendered to its bearer. Evidently, the Serb had little or no grasp of German.

The truth, Wolff decided, was the one thing which might actually work in his favor here. "It's a letter from the head of German military intelligence, Admiral Wilhelm Canaris. It orders all members of the German army to do as I request."

Darko frowned. He was clearly not expecting such a response. The others were watching them even more closely now, aware from their leader's body language that something intriguing was afoot.

"And why would you require such a thing?" Darko asked finally. "Because I was sent to Sofia to carry out secret peace negotiations with the Soviets."

This time Darko's head jerked back on his shoulders. He stared at Wolff, scanning his face for any sign of insolence. Wolff looked back at him with as transparent and calm an expression as he could muster. Darko barked another command over his shoulder, this time without looking.

A few seconds later, someone appeared with a rope, which was used to tie his hands behind his back. Darko pressed his hand firmly but not roughly down on Wolff's shoulder. "Sit down and make yourself comfortable," he said. "We have a lot to discuss."

The partisans busied themselves for a while preparing some food. A couple of the scrawny-looking rabbits were held over the fire on long sticks to roast. There was also some bread and a few canned goods.

Wolff had not eaten all day, but was not offered anything as the clearly ravenous group set about making their dinner. From time to time he caught others checking him out curiously.

It was evident to them that whatever he had told Darko had made an impact, but the partisan leader was not for sharing: an attempt by the girl who had captured him to re-engage him in conversation was tersely rebuffed.

That Wolff could understand. Darko was obviously running it over in his own head and perhaps preparing mental traps to catch out any lies in the interrogation which would follow.

At the very least, he mused, the man was not the kind of a fanatic who would instantly reject the idea of the noble Bolsheviks engaging with the evil fascist invader. And that gave him some hope that there would be a way out of this. Darko eventually came and sat beside Wolff and ate noisily while peppering him with questions.

Why was Hitler holding talks if he was clearly winning?

What was the aim of the negotiations? Why Sofia?

Why had he been on a train to Belgrade rather than a flight back to Berlin?

Wolff answered each as honestly as he could, using logical guesses to fill in any gaps in his knowledge. Darko asked where Wolff had been heading at the moment of his capture, and Wolff again responded candidly, prompting another chuckle of disbelief from the Serb.

The partisan turned to the girl and questioned her at length, evidently searching for any fabrications in Wolff's story.

Darko seemed satisfied with her explanation, and Wolff could tell he was still dumbfounded with what he was being told. He could empathize. Until a week beforehand, he would have reacted similarly.

The conversation then moved onto Wolff and his background. Where had the name Alfredo come from? Why wasn't he in uniform? What was he planning to do if he had managed to kill Udolph, the second SD man otherwise known as Möbert?

Wolff found himself outlining his life story to a complete stranger. He stayed away from any embellishments of his anti-Nazi credentials, especially as Darko's eyes narrowed as he went over details of what had happened at the village in Latvia.

"Why would you care what happens to a bunch of peasants?" he asked scornfully. "I fought for the Republicans at Brunete, and I saw what your Condor Legion did to civilians. They came in and bombed villages and strafed civilians."

Wolff looked him in the eye. "That is exactly why I agreed to travel to Sofia. We are on opposite sides, true. But some of us believe the war can be conducted, if not honorably, then at least without deliberate murder. Do you know what an *Einsatzgruppe* is?"

Darko shook his head.

"It translates as 'Special Task Force'."

"I don't know this phrase in Spanish. Get to the point."

"They are units of the SS who go around gathering people the Nazis consider 'undesirables' and then bring them off to be shot."

"And who are these...undesirables?"

Wolff shrugged. "In Poland, it was the priests and the aristocracy. After that, the Jews and the gypsies. I didn't see it myself because we had always gone ahead to where the fighting was. At the beginning, they came in after we left and carried out their crimes without anyone looking.

"It's different now. They come right in after the army secures a location and get to work immediately. In the Baltics, they have been mainly killing Jews and communists. Political commissars are shot on the spot. They do their work separately from the army, but everyone knows what's going on.

"Including the Soviets, by now. That is why this war must be stopped now, and Hitler overthrown. Because otherwise Germany can expect no mercy if the tide turns.

"The Americans are already openly favoring the British by giving them ships, tanks and aircraft through their Lend-Lease program. If something happens to bring them fully into the war on the Allied side, it would be disastrous for Germany."

Wolff was exceedingly grateful at this moment for the briefing Canaris had given him back in Berlin, which he hoped he was repeating correctly.

Darko was looking at him thoughtfully. "Even if what you say is true," he answered eventually, "it sounds like Germany is doomed anyway. When the Americans enter the war, then your country will be caught between them and the Red Army and they will lose.

"If a peace deal occurs and Hitler is overthrown, Germany will remain a fascist state with all of its Nazi infrastructure in place. That cannot be allowed to happen."

"*If* the Americans enter the war," Wolff corrected him. He had a sense his arguments were starting to work on the partisan leader. "They still have a strong isolationist lobby, and it is far from clear that they will, or if they do, when. The question is, will the Soviet Union still exist at that point? When I left the front, the Wehrmacht was advancing at a rate of forty miles per day, and right now, they are two weeks away from Moscow if things continue as they are."

Wolff was counting here on the fact that Darko had regular access to Yugoslav newspapers. Even if those papers were subject to Nazi censorship, they would still be faithfully reporting German victories in the east. "The Red Army was doing the best it could, but it was still being beaten back again and again.

"My co-conspirators have shown me Wehrmacht projections," he added, mixing a little lie in to bolster the truth. "They expect to have taken the Kremlin by Christmas. Where will Stalin go then? Siberia? He made these overtures because he knows peace is his only hope of survival."

Darko said nothing, staring ahead.

Wolff decided to hammer home his point. "In Spain, Hitler and Mussolini sent aid to the fascists. Who was the only one aiding the republicans? The USSR is the world's first communist nation and it has not yet survived 25 years. If it collapses, what kind of a future do you see for your cause?"

Darko turned towards him, and Wolff could see from the anger on the man's face that he had miscalculated. "You may have seen combat, but in terms of understanding how the world works, you are very much still a boy," he sneered. "Stalin's people spent as much time in Spain trying to gain control of the Republic as they did helping it.

"There were a lot of people mysteriously killed well away from the front line. Stalin does not represent Marxism, and if he is beaten, the revolution will simply continue in another form. It will not die. It has too many people across the world fighting for it for that to happen."

They lapsed into silence then, Darko clearly feeling he had put his prisoner in his place and Wolff simply without any further argument to make. It was dark by now, and shortly afterwards, the partisans began to make preparations to sleep. A rope was looped around Wolff's ankles and over the binds on his wrists.

A thin, filthy blanket was thrown at him, which he would have to pull over himself with the aid of his teeth. He lay uncomfortably on his side, nothing within range for him to use as a pillow.

Perhaps he would be shot in the morning.

19

A couple of hours after daybreak, Wolff sat back against a tree, and watched the partisans argue over how to best make use of him.

Five of them were involved in the discussions a few yards away from the main camp, while the rest sat and watched. He was stiff, sore and cold. They had left his hands tied all night and bound his feet too, just to be sure.

There had been a light rain and the blanket and his clothes had soaked through. When he had attempted to shift his position against the tree to something slightly more comfortable, one of the main group had approached him on his blindside, delivering a vicious punch to the face.

A petty revenge taken while the group leaders were distracted. Wolff could not blame the man. He had seen far worse dished out by his own side in Russia. He leaned back against the trunk, ignoring his aches, chills and the lump which he could feel rising on his cheekbone.

Was this to be it?

Death always came as a surprise. He had seen too many badly-wounded men slip away not to understand that by now. Each and every one of them with that same shocked expression on their faces.

That one of those bullets zipping around had actually hit *him* and that now it was his turn to bleed out as his comrades stood around him and whispered patent lies about how he would be fine.

Lies which were, without exception, desperately believed until the light faded from their eyes. For who wanted to consider that his life was about to be extinguished? It made crazy sense. A man could not function properly if he constantly thought about where the end was coming from.

And if this was his finale, what had he achieved? He had led as honorable an existence as he could in an increasingly revolting world where human life was valued less and less. He had no regrets, bar that of his unfulfilled vow to *Mammu*.

A promise whose accomplishment may have been impossible anyway, though he would never know that for sure. Much had changed since his mother had left Riga nearly two decades earlier.

That and Anna. Poor, sweet, trusting Anna. She had placed her faith in him, and he had failed her. He had killed Bonsen, but could not erase the man's taunts about how he and the other animal had murdered the girl.

He sucked in his breath involuntarily as he thought of the shock and terror in those beautiful brown eyes after one of the pair drew a knife suddenly across her throat. There was nobody holding her hand, nobody telling her she was going to be okay. She had died afraid and alone.

There was a whistle from a few hundred yards away in the forest, which Wolff assumed was one of the sentries. He looked up to see the youth who had helped capture him arrive into the camp.

The boy had a triumphant expression on his face and went straight to where Darko and the girl were sitting to hand something over to them. Wolff watched with interest as Darko glanced over at him before beginning to examine the items one by one.

There was a flash of bright red, and Wolff's spirits suddenly soared as he realized the partisan was holding a red NKVD identity book in his hands.

They had sent the boy off to look for Bonsen's body, and he had found it!

However, his initial early enthusiasm soon dissipated somewhat as a meeting was called. Darko, the girl and three others sat at the top, while the others gathered around them in a rough semi-circle. This was akin to a drumhead court martial, and the evidence the teenager had returned with would form only one part of it.

Like all such proceedings, the leanings of the self-appointed judges would matter far more. There appeared to be five of them, their status made clear from their seats apart from the rest of the group. Though he was too far away to overhear anything even if he understood Serbian, the respective body language shown by each made their positions clear.

Darko appeared to be on one side, while two others adopted various tones of frustration and pleading and the girl engaged in the most vociferous opposition to the partisan commander. The fifth individual, a man in his twenties, initially stayed silent but later seemed to intervene more and more on Darko's side.

The rest of the guerrillas just sat and watched the rapid-fire debate with keen interest, one or two raising their hands at one point to make deferential-sounding contributions which did not appear to gain much traction. Wolff counted thirty-six of them, in total.

Fewer than the fifty or so he had initially supposed, but still far too numerous for him to try anything should the opportunity arise. The numerous glances towards him throughout the debate removed any doubt that he was the main topic of discussion.

He prayed he had convinced Darko of the bona fides of his mission the night before and that the partisan was suggesting that he be released to continue it. If so, Darko's attempts were meeting a considerable degree of resistance, not least from the girl, who punctuated her increasingly irate assertions with finger-stabbing gestures towards where Wolff was sitting.

He wondered how many comrades they had lost so far and how big a part that would play in deciding his fate. He had heard one of the reasons the Republicans had lost the civil war in Spain was because some of the communist movements had no central command structure and insisted on taking a vote on everything before any decision was made.

If Darko was commanding that kind of operation here, he was doomed. After about an hour of this, the girl stood up and stormed off, effectively putting an end to the discussion. It was a positive indication, but nothing more. Perhaps he would not be executed today, but there was no guarantee of tomorrow.

To distract himself, his mind again sifted over what he had seen and how he might use it if an opportunity to escape presented itself. It stood to reason that there were other sizable towns along the train line heading north for Belgrade, so he would have to shadow it while keeping out of sight.

Who knew how many partisan groups were operating in this area? It would be too much of an irony to free himself from one only to end up in the hands of another. Getting back to German-controlled territory would only be the start of his problems, of course.

It was impossible to guess how far away Udolph was now or how he had reacted to his sidekick's disappearance. If he were in the SD man's shoes, he would be heading straight for Berlin.

It began to rain again, more heavily now than the night before, and most of the partisans retreated to their tents and lay down or sat in the openings staring out at the downpour. Wolff was left in place and pressed himself up against the tree trunk, though it did little to save him from being soaked. To compound his misery, the wind whipped up, driving much of the rain in on top of him.

Around an hour later, there was another arrival into the camp. The man was a short, stocky figure clad in a raincoat with the hood up to ward off the deluge. He glanced over to where Wolff was sitting and stared at him for a long moment.

Wolff watched as the man studied him intently, though he could see little from underneath the hood except the bottom of the man's face. Then the man went into the tent in which Darko and the girl were sitting. Darko stuck his head out through the flap and issued a command and the three others who had earlier discussed his fate emerged from their own tents and entered his too.

Perhaps this newcomer was a partisan commander from elsewhere brought in to make a decision, and the court martial had been reconvened.

It was quite cramped inside, and Wolff could see the outlines of the group's backs protruding through the canvas. Another agitated discussion with raised voices ensued, and he was quite sure his fate was the subject of discussion once more.

After about an hour of this, Darko emerged outside. The rain had lightened now, but the wind was still blowing in fits and gusts. The other partisans also came out of their tents and began dismantling them. They were breaking camp. It was never smart to stay in one place for too long. Guerilla groups had to stay light and mobile to avoid capture.

To have with them only what they could carry and be free of encumbrances such as spouses or children.

Or prisoners.

Darko walked over to where Wolff was sitting, his face tinged with an expression of resignation. He studied Wolff for a moment before he took the confiscated *finka* from the small of his back and removed it from its metal scabbard. Wolff instinctively pushed himself as far back against the tree trunk as he could.

The partisan looked at the blade, which Wolff had always kept honed to a keen edge. He seemed reluctant to carry out whatever he was going to do next.

"It's ironic," he said at last in his heavily accented Spanish. "You took this from a dead Soviet soldier as a souvenir, and now here it is, in the hands of another enemy thousands of miles away. You might call it fate."

He bent and leaned over Wolff, pushing his shoulder to one side. Wolff winced as he braced himself for the sharp pain of the knife point sliding into his torso. A deadly wound, albeit one which would kill more slowly and agonizingly than a simple slash across the windpipe.

Images flashed into his mind of the warning tales told around the campfires of Army Group North. What had happened to Wehrmacht infantry captured in partisan attacks. Their fly-covered bodies found hanging from trees, minus their ears and noses.

Stomachs slashed and genitalia cut off and stuffed into their mouths, the extent of the wounds indicating they had been left to bleed out.

But instead, Darko put his hand on Wolff's upper back, forcing him to double over before sawing through the bonds which held his arms behind him. Wolff slowly brought his hands around to his front, massaging his wrists to get some of the circulation back into his limbs.

He wondered what was in store for him now. Perhaps they were taking him with them. "My comrades think I'm a fool," Darko continued. "They want you disemboweled and hung from a tree in the nearest garrison town as a message. However, your story is so bizarre, I think there's a chance you're actually telling the truth.

"The boy found the body beside the tracks and the documentation on it. The crows led him there." He looked at Wolff, searching for a reaction. Wolff offered none. He could not have cared less if wolves had scattered Bonsen's remains across the entire Balkans.

"We have another witness from the train who says what he saw of you is in line with what you have claimed. So you're either a storytelling genius or genuinely engaged in an effort to free Germany of the most evil man in Europe. Time will tell.

"We Serbs have a saying: a dead man pays no debts. On that basis, I think the chances of you succeeding are worth leaving you alive. If you are lying, and send your comrades in here looking for us, I promise you, you will regret it. Though in doing this, I may have signed my own death warrant.

"Right now, my sister would be first in line to carry it out."

He held the knife upright by the blade in front of Wolff. "This will be given to you upon your release. Hopefully, it will remind you of your obligations and the fact that it could just as easily have been used to kill you. The gun, we will keep. Our need of it is greater than yours."

Another partisan came over and retied Wolff's hands, but this time looser and at the front. The man stood there, gripping Wolff's forearm forcefully while he waited for a comrade carrying a rifle to finish speaking to Darko.

Darko's tent was the last to be taken down, and as its guy lines were pulled up, Darko's sister and the mysterious visitor who had vouched for him came out from inside. The man still had his hood up, but it was caught and forced back momentarily by a gust of wind.

The visitor hastily turned sideways as he scrambled to conceal his features again, but it was too late. Wolff had recognized him. It was the conductor from the train station back in Niš.

His mind whirled. The man had been as obnoxious as possible to an elderly woman who had accidentally delayed the train's departure by a few minutes, even though it was already very late.

He had obsequiously withdrawn once Wolff established himself as a German. As a cover for a partisan informant, it was genius. Wolff turned his own head away quickly lest the man look up and see his identity had been compromised.

Wolff left the camp in the company of two other partisans, walking northeast for three hours. His guardians were clearly in Darko's sister's ideological camp, judging by the number of prods in the back he received from their pistols initially.

Eventually they had stopped beside a road bordered by the forest, and one of the men had untied Wolff's hands and said something terse in Serbian while pointing north. He had finished his instructions by spitting in Wolff's face and waving his pistol aggressively and, for a moment, Wolff thought he was about to disobey Darko's instructions.

Instead, the pair melted back into the trees, leaving Wolff to walk north along the road. Once they had disappeared, he began to run, fearful they might change their minds and return.

As he double-timed it, he thought about the conductor, one more surprise in a war whose battle lines were increasingly unclear. The man was presumably a communist and a sworn enemy of the Nazis, yet his input had helped ensure Wolff's freedom.

Allowing him to remain in situ would almost certainly result in the deaths of many German soldiers, but Wolff could not envisage himself condemning his unlikely savior to a horrific death at the hands of the Gestapo. He mentally pushed the matter aside until later.

He had bigger problems to focus on right now, though he doubted it would be the last time he would face such a dilemma before this war ended. After around 40 minutes, he came to a small, nameless town with a meager German barracks. Darko had taken his gun, but returned all of his documents.

One flash of Wolff's letter from Canaris and he was at the front of a Wehrmacht truck carrying 10 infantry regulars. After hearing of Wolff's capture at the hands of the partisans, the old hare sergeant in charge of the garrison was taking no chances.

He had been radioed from Belgrade about the disappearance of an SD officer from the train and orders had been passed on for all the stations between Niš and the Yugoslav capital to be checked. However, the man had not come through two wars so far without learning anything.

Wolff did not offer an explanation as to what he was doing on foot in the middle of the Serbian countryside and the man did not ask him for one either. He would be relieved to get this potential troublemaker off his hands as soon as possible.

***

"I want nothing to do with this."

Wolff stood in the Belgrade office of Major General Friedrich Weber of the 65th Special Corps, alternately attempting to threaten and cajole him into cooperating. Once more taking a calculated risk, Wolff had rung Oster on the A-net and explained where he was.

Oster had described Weber as a 'former friend', whom he had not spoken to since his posting to what used to be Yugoslavia. Wolff had grasped the improvised code: Weber had been a member of the resistance once, though this was no longer certain.

Oster had added that Weber might have forgotten him given all that had happened since and might require some 'reminding'. Wolff could see now that Oster had been somewhat understating the point. The mixture of fury and panic on Weber's face could not have been plainer. It was hardly surprising.

Weber was only one of a hotchpotch of German military officers behind the puppet regime which ruled the Territory of the Military Commander in Serbia. Among his colleagues, however, was SS Colonel Wilhelm Jürs, who had been appointed to oversee all SS and SD operations in the newly conquered addition to the Reich.

It was Jürs that Udolph would logically approach for assistance, thus the fear which had overtaken Weber, even though he technically outranked the SS man. What Wolff needed to know was whether any Luftwaffe planes had already taken off for Berlin with Udolph on board, or whether he still had a chance of catching up with the man.

As it happened, Jürs was on one of his periodic forays to Croatia to ensure that the Nazis' local fascist allies, the Ustaše, were properly rounding up local Jews. But Weber was still terrified that any inquiries he made about flights to Berlin would reach the SS man's ears.

The nominal head of the military government in Belgrade was a Luftwaffe general and nobody knew what way he leant. Wolff sensed it was time to up the ante in terms of intimidation.

"With respect sir, I'm not sure if you understand how pressing this situation is," he said to Weber, who had a look of barely concealed hatred on his face. "If this individual makes it back to Heydrich, we could all be in terrible danger."

Weber looked up sharply at Wolff's use of 'we', as Wolff had hoped. "The only way to prevent that is to catch him and, er, talk with him before he can leave Belgrade. You say there is no scheduled connection to Berlin until tomorrow evening.

"This man is going to want to get back there before then. I need to find him, but I have no idea where he is. So I have to know if there have been any special requests for planes so I can intercept him." Weber fidgeted, still refusing to look Wolff in the eye.

"And how do we know he won't have told some of Jürs's people?" he snapped back. "Then if he turns up dead - and I presume that's what you have planned for him - there'll be a huge investigation. What then?"

"I don't think he will have," Wolff insisted.

"Oh, you don't?" Weber sneered.

"No sir, I don't," Wolff answered, an assertive brazenness entering his tone. "Because he doesn't need to. You need to understand what's happening here, General. Udolph is in somewhat of a precarious position himself. His instructions were to observe, gather evidence and report back. They most certainly were not to murder a local hotel owner and a Soviet diplomat on the territory of a Reich ally."

Wolff was improvising now, just as he had seen his former Brandenburger superior do in the past with nervous Russian sentries before his death. "This is going to cause uproar in Sofia.

The Bulgarians told me the dead hotelier is a brother-in-law of a government minister. If Udolph gets back to Heydrich with his…information, then all that will be brushed aside.

"But until then, he's not going to risk blabbing about what he's been up to in Bulgaria and risk having it make its way back to the wrong ears in Berlin so it can be used against Moses Handel." Weber flinched at Wolff's use of Heydrich's naval nickname over his supposed Jewish heritage.

"He probably doesn't need to anyway," Wolff continued, now in full creative flow. "I imagine he has his own one of these." He waved his all-important letter from Canaris. "So if he wanders up to the airfield and starts demanding his own flight home, word is going to get around, isn't it?"

Weber nodded almost unconsciously, as if trying to convince himself of Wolff's logic. Wolff decided to go in for the kill. "Now is the time to act, General," he said gently. "If they start arresting people in Berlin, who knows what will be said under torture."

Weber's head whipped back into the moment, and he jumped to his feet. He unbuckled his holster and extended his pistol over the desk, so that it was no more than a few inches from Wolff's nose. "I don't take kindly to threats from junior officers," he snarled. "I could shoot you right here, and that would be the end of it. Nobody would ever hear of you again."

Wolff raised his hands placatingly. "It's too late for that, General. I've already telegraphed the Bendlerblock," he lied. "Besides, I'm not the threat against you. We're on the same side here, remember?" Weber lowered his pistol.

An hour later, Wolff found himself at Belgrad-Zemun, ignoring the stares of the Luftwaffe ground crew as they muttered amongst themselves. This must have been the most exciting thing they had seen in weeks. The airfield had only a skeleton crew as it was so far away from the front lines, and primarily functioned as a refueling stop for flights heading south to Greece or returning north once more.

Now, in the space of a few hours, first Udolph and now Wolff had turned up with important-looking pieces of paper and announced they were requisitioning aircraft to head back to the Reich. Wolff had been lucky.

The combination of the train delay necessitated by the search for Bonsen and more fortuitous summer storms overnight had meant his prey had been unable to leave Belgrade until this morning. Udolph had not been happy at the hold up and that too had worked in Wolff's favor.

The man's typical SD arrogance had so infuriated the Luftwaffe major in charge of the airfield that he had radioed the office of the Luftwaffe general in charge of Serbia - and had been quickly ordered to do whatever Udolph wanted.

Having been told to obey once, the major would not be checking again as to whether he should obey the latest command from Wolff. Wolff's more apologetic attitude had also allowed him to gain some vital details. Udolph had taken off in a Storch a little under an hour earlier and was bound for Budaors, another airfield used for refueling near Budapest in Hungary.

The Storch was a slow-moving single-engined plane primarily used for transporting functionaries. It would take up to two and a half hours to reach its next stop, and that gave Wolff another advantage. The Lutfwaffe major displayed definite curiosity as

Wolff asked him which aircraft would allow him to catch up with or overtake the SD man.

If Wolff was somehow going to cause trouble for Udolph, he was more than happy to assist. The major pointed to an Athens-bound Junkers Ju-88, which was refueling on the grass runway. The twin-engined *Schnellbomber* had a top speed of over 500km per hour - almost three times that of the Storch.

"I'm afraid I'm going to have to commandeer that one then," Wolff said. He received a shrug and a grin in response.

"If you must, you must."

Wolff nodded his thanks and handed the man a sealed message which was to be immediately hand-delivered to Weber for coded transmission to Reserve Army headquarters. He smiled as he imagined the cowardly artillery major general's fury at discovering his earlier lie about having already sent a message to Oster.

Wolff had been assured Reserve Army commander Olbricht was not under suspicion, but still left out the specifics of what had happened and boiled it down to as little as possible without risking Oster missing the meaning of it.

Interrupted, but resumed. Target in air, bound for Budaörs, then Billy Goat. Pursuing.

If the SD were listening in, then they would have to bring the message to Heydrich himself to fully understand it. Wolff smiled as he thought of Heydrich attempting to outline the import of the message and what action his subordinates should take in response.

Without explaining the nickname gained during his Kriegsmarine days due to his high-pitched caprine laugh.

20

The Ju-88 bounced again on an invisible bump outside and Wolff swallowed down the nausea.

He had spent most of the hour-long journey to Budapest emptying his stomach amid extreme turbulence.

The pilot, whose name was Sauer, had initially been highly amused at Wolff's blatantly obvious fear of flying. Then, he became concerned his cockpit might be potentially rendered uninhabitable by the stench of vomit and ordered his passenger further back into the fuselage.

Like the Luftwaffe major back in Belgrade, Sauer was intrigued by what was going on and tried to winkle as many details as possible out of Wolff, who stuck to the basics and told him he needed to have an urgent "meeting" with Udolph.

What form that meeting would take would depend on quite a few factors, but there was a high probability it would end badly for one or both of them. As they came in to land at Budapest-Budaors, the pilot pointed out the Storch a little off the runway with a fuel truck already heading towards it.

There was no sign of anyone in its vicinity, so Wolff surmised Udolph must have headed for the large terminal building in the southwest corner of the airfield to wait and perhaps radio ahead to Berlin.

Budaors had been the civilian airport serving the Hungarian capital before the war and offered more comforts than the average Luftwaffe refueling spot, so there might even be food or drink of which the SD man could avail.

Wolff instructed Sauer to go to the end of the runway, far enough away so that he would not be recognized as he got out. No sooner had the Junkers come to a stop than he was out and walking towards the hangars which flanked the runway, looking for a way to approach the terminal unseen.

Sauer had radioed ahead before leaving Belgrade, saying he was bound for Berlin from Athens and would need to stop at Budaors, though he had plenty of fuel. As he exited the plane, Wolff could hear the control tower squawking angrily on the radio, asking why Sauer had gone so far down the runway. He told the pilot to ignore it.

He could see a Horch 108 jeep heading their way at speed, a man imperiously upright, Rommel-style, on the passenger side. No doubt en route to find out why Sauer was being so awkward, but Wolff hoped a discreet showing of his Canaris order would be enough to ensure the man's cooperation.

The jeep braked sharply and the man on the passenger side jumped down and walked briskly towards where Wolff was standing. He had his hand half inside his breast pocket, pulling out the letter when the man, who wore a Luftwaffe ground crew's overalls, surprised him.

"Lieutenant Wolff?"

He nodded.

"My name is Schönebeck. I'm here to meet you on behalf of a mutual friend. He said to tell you Old Whitehead sent me."

Wolff relaxed somewhat. Such a message could only have come from the barbed tongue of Oster. "You're aware of the situation?" Wolff asked guardedly, his eyes on the driver a few yards away.

"Yes. You didn't give us a lot of time here." Schönebeck looked back at the driver and waved vaguely. "Don't worry, he's with me. Get in the back."

Wolff complied and the jeep took off again at speed towards the terminal. Wolff slouched down in the backseat as Schönebeck turned back towards him. "Our recently arrived friend is going to develop a little engine trouble with his Storch once it has refueled.

"Something with the ball bearings, I believe. He's almost certainly going to demand another aircraft, so I suggest you tell your pilot here to make himself scarce for a while."

Wolff nodded.

"There are no other flights expected here for another couple of hours," Schönebeck continued. "Or at least that's what he'll be told. There's a Heinkel on its way from Berlin right now with a couple of our people on board. They'll take him and keep an eye on him and see what they can do."

Wolff stared back at him angrily. "Keep an eye on him? What good will that do? You do know what he has in his possession?"

The Horch stopped with a jolt outside the hangar nearest to the terminal, and Schönebeck got out and strode towards it. Wolff followed him, pulling down the brim of his fedora over his face. He had found himself doing this more and more over the past few days as he tried to hide himself from omnipresent, hidden enemies.

In a sense, it embodied what he was becoming. A floppy hat.

"Why don't you just let the Storch go on with him on it and shoot it down with the Heinkel?" he demanded as he caught up with Schönebeck.

Schönebeck looked back at him with an expression of pity. "Have you ever been in a dogfight?" he asked.

"I fight on the ground, not in the skies," Wolff responded curtly.

"Indeed, and it shows," Schönebeck replied, still walking purposefully. "Firstly, we are in possibly the safest air corridor on the entire continent here. The nearest enemy aircraft are 1,500 miles away in Kharkov, and they have enough to do right now.

"Second, shooting down a plane is not an exact science, least of all with a Heinkel He 111. It's a bomber, so the only guns it has are defensive ones in its nose, behind the cockpit and in its belly. The Storch is a much slower aircraft, so they'd have to make several passes at it, which would allow its pilot plenty of time to radio that he was being attacked by his own side.

"Might cause a bit of a stir, don't you think? No, it's probably best if we avoid that approach, Wolff, if we're to come out of this with our heads on our shoulders."

Wolff looked at him, then stood slightly to one side and began appraising the terminal two hundred yards away.

"He's in there, is he?" he asked.

Schönebeck chuckled and shook his head. "I'm afraid you can forget about that too, unless you're planning on killing everyone here, plus the pilot that flies you out of here." He stepped back and looked Wolff up and down. "Were you planning to use a knife or a garotte?"

Wolff glared back at him. "I don't think you realize how serious this is."

"Oh, but I do, Lieutenant," Schönebeck murmured back. "I most certainly do. However, your role here is finished. You had the chance to catch him, and you blew it. You're going to have to leave it in our hands now."

***

Wolff was in a filthy back office, watching through a grimy window as Udolph remonstrated furiously with Schönebeck, who responded with a constant series of helpless shrugs. News of the Storch's sudden technical issues had not gone down well.

There were a few other Luftwaffe ground staff working on other disassembled planes, who stopped as the Storch was towed into the hangar to complete the charade. Presumably they would be reporting their findings directly to Schönebeck, who appeared to be a genuine Luftwaffe officer.

Udolph stomped around furiously for a while, before eventually settling down on a bench and lighting a cigarette. The man was carrying a briefcase under his arm, which he kept tightly to his side even as he sat down.

That's where the diary is.

Schönebeck had passed him a Walther P38, though that was as good as useless in such a public setting. Even if he had somehow convinced Schönebeck to discreetly clear out the hangar,

Udolph was almost certainly armed and he had zero chance of covering the few dozen yards between them without being spotted.

The sound of a shootout would bring everyone within half a mile swarming all over the place. A feeling of helplessness swamped Wolff as he watched Schönebeck return from the terminal and pour something from a thermal flask into a mug before offering it to Udolph, who grabbed it angrily from him.

He had tried to get a few more details out of Schönebeck about what exactly Canaris and Oster had planned to stop the SD man once he landed in Berlin, but he had been infuriatingly vague. The only thing Schönebeck would tell him was that Udolph would be required to report directly to Heydrich.

Of this, he was adamant. The head of the Sicherheitsdienst was a man who guarded information like a commodity more valuable than gold. Even his otherwise trusted deputy, the hero of Venlo, Walter Schellenberg, would not be informed until Heydrich decided he was ready to move.

The good news was that Heydrich was currently at Hitler's Wolf's Lair headquarters in east Prussia, from where the Führer was personally directing the assault on Russia. Access to the complex was highly restricted, so Udolph would have to wait for Heydrich's return to the capital, which would give the conspirators a couple of days.

To Wolff, it still seemed impossible. Udolph would almost certainly bring the evidence directly to lodge it at Heydrich's office at Prinz Albrecht Strasse for safekeeping, after which everything else was irrelevant. What would happen to Wolff then?

If Oster was anything to go by, the conspirators were fanatics in their own right, rather like mirror images of the Nazis they were so determined to depose. Despite what Oster had told him about deniability, he doubted whether he would be allowed to fall into the hands of the Gestapo if it came to it. It was too risky.

He might simply be made to disappear. It was not that hard to imagine Oster issuing the order, with or without Canaris's approval. After all, what records were there of his movements? Wolff had been collected from the cells in Brandenburg by an Abwehr man and brought straight to Canaris's office.

Nobody except the SD had seen him enter or leave and they would not be inquiring after his whereabouts. Oster would make his transfer orders and promotion disappear from the records. The Brandenburgers were directly under Abwehr control, after all.

Wolff would become one more casualty of the great game between Canaris and Heydrich. The admiral would be damaged, true, but he would live to fight another day. Wolff would not.

In such circumstances, Wolff's next course of action was obvious. If Canaris and Oster were determined they would take care of the diary problem from here on out, it was indeed completely out of his hands, as Schönebeck asserted. His part in this was over.

However, the second part of his deal with Canaris, the real reason he had agreed to go to Sofia, was still very much alive. He fingered the letter inside his breast pocket. He had complete authority over his own long-range fighter bomber.

He remembered reading once that it was around six hundred miles from Berlin to Riga, so presumably it was in or about the same from Budapest. That would still allow him to reach Latvia in under three hours, not counting refueling stops along the way.

He would be stopped eventually, but Canaris could hardly afford to put out an alert for him with Heydrich monitoring every Abwehr move. It would give him a chance to do what he needed, to fulfill the promise made all those years before.

There was the deafening drone of a large aircraft coming in to land and, moments later, a plane Wolff recognized as a Heinkel taxied past towards the large concrete circle in front of the terminal building to perform a turn. Udolph jumped to his feet and started off towards the runway, still tightly clutching the briefcase against his frame.

It really was up to Canaris and Oster now. Schönebeck was coming back towards the office, sauntering carelessly with the carefree cockiness Wolff had seen in so many Luftwaffe flyboys in the past. They all thought they were invincible.

Schönebeck ignored him and placed the flask on the filthy desk, which was strewn with smudged technical documents. "He's just taken off, so you're free to leave whenever you please."

"Yes, I saw you playing the genial host," Wolff snapped sourly. "Why didn't you make him a sandwich while you were at it?"

"Indeed, real coffee," Schönebeck replied, almost sadly. "A pity to waste it so, but the idea was to keep him happy rather than having him asking too many questions about what was going on."

Wolff's anger at the man's nonchalance exploded. One of the only positives from his trip to Sofia had been the chance to drink something other than ersatz rubbish in a cafe, even if he wasn't particularly fond of the thick, black Ottoman brew the locals favored.

Now here was Schönebeck confirming he had been pampering the man who had murdered Anna and who quite literally held Wolff's fate in his hands. Especially given that Wolff himself was fighting to keep his eyes open. He sat forward and grabbed the flask from Schönebeck. "Give me that."

The Luftwaffe man watched with the same infuriating half-smile as Wolff poured himself a measure into the lid and shrugged. "Suit yourself."

Wolff stood and watched as the Heinkel with Udolph on board began to gather speed down the runway as it prepared to take off. When he heard the change in engine pitch which indicated it was airborne, he slammed the plastic cup down without another word and strode out to find Sauer from wherever he had stashed himself.

21

Wolff awoke with a start as the plane jolted down roughly on the runway. He checked his watch and saw three hours had passed since they had taken off in Hungary and he had slept the entire way. The exhaustion from his uncomfortable night in the Serbian woods had caught up with him at last.

"Riga-Spilve," Sauer turned and shouted from the cockpit over the noise of the engines. Wolff gave him the thumbs up and stumbled towards the door. They had agreed before leaving Budapest that this was where they would part ways.

Wolff had no idea how long it would take him to do what was required in Latvia and Sauer was supposed to be thousands of miles south in Greece. Wolff would have to hope he could commandeer another aircraft when it came to it.

"You've caused a hell of a stink, you know," Sauer had told him just after taking off from Budapest. "The head of the Eleventh *Fliegerkorps* got on to Canaris's office from Athens and demanded to know what the hell was going on. I hope it was worth it."

"Time will tell," Wolff answered, in possibly the only straightforward, truthful remark he had made to the pilot since Belgrade. He got out and stood on the runway, surveying the damage around him.

Spilve had been the main Red Air Force base in Riga and had been heavily bombed by the Luftwaffe the previous month ahead of the capture of the city. The control tower had been vaporized when a fuel depot went up and Soviet prisoners had been put to work clearing the rubble away.

He waved his thanks to Sauer and strode over to the Wehrmacht NCO overseeing the work detail and presented his *Soldbuch*, seeking a lift into the city center. If the man was surprised by the unusual sight of an army lieutenant in civvies, he gave no sign of it. Perhaps the floppy hats were frequent arrivals out here.

Ten minutes later, Wolff was en route to the city center in the truck used to transport the prisoners to the airport from the camp which held them. The city center was 10km away, and as they drove, Wolff looked around. He had been a toddler when they left and was too young to remember the land of his birth.

From his mother's old photographs, he had expected grand homes with large gardens. Instead, the road into the city alongside the River Daugava was lined with rundown old farmhouses ringed by shabby, unpainted fences. Wolff had hoped to experience some sense of belonging upon his return to the land of his birth, but he felt nothing.

Latvia had undergone considerable change since his parents had emigrated, particularly in the last couple of years, during which two sets of invaders had attempted to put their stamp on the country.

A brand new sign welcoming visitors to the Province General of Latvia, part of the *Reichskommissariat Ostland*, had been erected on the roadside. On the ground, peppered with a few bullet holes, was an equally newish one in Cyrillic script hailing the entry of the Latvian Soviet Socialist Republic into the USSR.

The chatty young Hessian private delegated to drive Wolff into town told him with a certain boastfulness about the effusive welcome they had received from locals as they marched into Riga without firing a shot. Wolff thought again of the bombarded village 150 miles from Riga which had been preparing to do the same, but said nothing.

The driver interpreted his silence as disbelief and babbled on. The joy had been genuine, he insisted. "They hate the commies here," he chattered happily. "And the Jews. Though I'm not sure how many kikes are left anyway. Stalin sent a lot of them to Siberia after he took over."

After no response was forthcoming again, the private sensed Wolff's lack of enthusiasm for the conversation and switched to discussing the local watering holes.

A few minutes later, they crossed over the Daugava on a pontoon bridge - "the Ivans blew up all the others as they left" - and onto the eastern bank of the city. There, Wolff noted another freshly hand painted sign for Kaiserwald.

This was where his parents had originally settled after their marriage, until his father's disgruntlement at perceived discrimination after Latvia declared independence in 1920 had taken them thousands of miles across the Atlantic.

Not all the ethnic Germans in the Baltics felt this way, according to *Mammu*. She had always sighed quietly and rolled her eyes at Ludwig's rants about intolerance back in Riga. Her family had been resolutely half and half, as at home conversing in Latvian as they were in German.

Father's side, though, had known just enough of the local tongue to get by and resolutely shunned using it amongst themselves. For such *Baltendeutsche* in Riga, Kaiserwald had been a safe, leafy enclave on the northwestern fringes of the city, freeing them from having as neighbors those they openly considered inferior.

The suburb had been renamed Mezaparks under the pre-war nationalist government which Ludwig Wolff blamed for so many of his ills, but had now reverted to its German name under Latvia's latest period of subjugation. It was there that Wolff would begin.

Ideally, he would have liked to have had his own transportation to drive the streets of Kaiserwald, which had up to a thousand separate residences over a wide area. He had the photograph of the property *Mammu* had given him, but God knew how it might have changed in the interim.

However, attempting to use his letter to requisition an automobile for an unknown length of time would not be a smart move. Riga was a small city, and word would get around. Nor was a Wehrmacht vehicle the most inconspicuous means of avoiding unwanted attention.

According to his garrulous chauffeur, the arrival of the Germans had seen numerous local collaborators come forward eagerly to offer their services in the hope of sharing the spoils of war. It was one such group that Wolff encountered shortly after getting out of the truck and beginning his walk around Kaiserwald.

The well laid-out area seemed a lifetime away from the horrors of the front just a few hours' drive away. There were signs of life inside most of the *art nouveau* houses, though several of them were already falling into disrepair. The grandeur of the location was completely at odds with the dust-streaked green Ford-Vairogs V8 which pulled to a halt a few hundred yards away as he walked along Wilhelmstrasse.

Wolff could see through the windscreen, the only clean part of the vehicle, that its three occupants were attempting to size him up. He was not local, clearly, given the style and cut of his suit, but not in military uniform either, despite his relative youth.

But what, then? Gestapo? A civilian administrator?

Perhaps one of the rich *Baltendeutsche* former residents of the area, most of whom had been forced to leave for eastern Prussia following the signing of the Molotov-Ribbentrop Pact. Their properties had been ceded to the Reich's Main Welfare Office for Ethnic Germans, who had sold them off for a fraction of their former value to fund the reluctant emigrants' new lives.

Whoever he was, the three young men inside the car decided, he was someone worth acting deferentially towards. The trio got out of the car and the driver, quite obviously their leader and only a couple of years older than Wolff, strode ahead of the other two.

Like his companions, he was wearing a red and white armband, which Wolff took to be the insignia of some local pro-fascist militia. That suspicion was confirmed when the man got to within a few yards of Wolff, snapped to attention and delivered a Heil Hitler of which an SS man could be justifiably proud.

Wolff performed a languid, more understated response. He was determined to take control of this situation from the outset. "Konrads Kalejs, sir. We are members of the Latvian Auxiliary

Security Police, tasked by Brigadeführer Stahlecker with looking for bandits in this area. We've had reports that some Jews are still hiding out in this area."

Wolff nodded.

The private from their airport had told him about this group too, known less formally as the *Arajs Kommando*, after their leader, Viktor Arajs. He looked Kalejs up and down in the same imperiously arrogant way he had seen SS and Gestapo men do to others so many times in the past.

Kalejs stiffened under his gaze, unconsciously straightening his stance. "Lieutenant Wolff," he said curtly, walking over to the Vairogs and peering disdainfully inside. The other two occupants attempted Hitler salutes, which were comically restricted by the confines of the vehicle. There was a chest of drawers beside the man on the backseat.

"Are you aware that looting is punishable by death under Reichskommissariat regulation 221, clause b?" Wolff asked, making up a law and a penalty on the spot.

"We did not steal it, sir," Kalejs responded hastily. "It belongs to my companion's mother. He was taking it to be mended."

Wolff looked haughtily at the Latvian. "I am awaiting a driver to be sent to me, but he seems to have gotten lost. You can bring me around in the meantime."

"Of course, sir." Kalejs almost fell over himself in his haste to be helpful.

He walked quickly over to the car and barked an order at the man sitting in the front passenger seat, who got out, opened the back door and removed the chest of drawers before placing it on the curb.

Belongs to my companion's mother. These cretins. Wolff got into the vacated front passenger seat and looked around the interior. Despite the dirt on the outside, the Ford-Vairogs looked relatively new. Probably also looted.

Kalejs kept up a steady stream of commentary in passable German on he and his fellow yobs' thuggish achievements since the Wehrmacht had arrived in Riga. How many Jews he had rounded up, his close collaboration with Stahlecker, who Wolff assumed was the local Special Task Force commander charged with slaughtering as many human beings as possible.

They drove around for a while until they turned onto yet another conifer-lined road. A sign in Cyrillic proclaimed it Strupovich Avenue, presumably retitled the previous year after some Bolshevik flunkey. According to Kalejs, some members of the new communist elite had moved out here, but most had preferred to remain in the city center to keep an eye on each other as the jockeying for power rolled on.

But the original name was still visible on a stone plaque implanted into the ground which, judging by the chips missing from its edge, had survived a degree of force intended to remove it. *Hamburgas Iela.* Wolff's pulse quickened.

He recalled his mother mentioning the name before in a slightly mocking way relating to his father. That her husband had proudly talked about his family's Hamburg ancestry, but that the closest he had gotten to the place was the street on which they had lived back in Riga.

They continued along the road and, a few rows down, came upon the house he recognized from the photograph.

"Stop here," he told Kalejs, and the Latvian obediently pulled to the curb. Wolff got out and walked up the path to the front door. The house was built in the intrinsically German *fachwerk* style, its exposed wooden beam and whitewashed facade topped by a red-tiled sloping roof.

The windows on either side of the stout oak front door were firmly boarded up, and as Wolff walked around the side, he could see no signs of life. When he returned to the front, Kalejs and the other two were now standing outside the car watching him and talking in a low voice amongst themselves.

"I have been tasked with finding appropriate accommodation for Reich officials who will take over governance of the city," he said to Kalejs. "Are there many other homes of this type in the area?"

"Plenty, sir," Kalejs answered. "Many of them a lot bigger than this one. I would be happy to show you some more."

"No. I think I shall walk around to get a feel for the neighborhood and inspect them at leisure. My driver will be here soon enough anyway. You may go, Kalejs."

"Thank you, sir." All three men threw up a Hitler salute, though only Kalejs clicked his heels together, Nazi-style. They got into the car and drove away. Wolff could have used all three men's heft in finding a way into the property, but he had already made a mistake in showing such interest in it in front of them and had no wish to compound that.

He had come across such individuals again and again as they advanced east. Men eager to ingratiate themselves with the new conquerors and willing to sell out their compatriots for the slightest reward, whether that be monetary gain, the chance to settle old scores or a combination of both.

He had seen that same look in Kalejs' eyes, the swift calculation of how he could turn a situation to his advantage. It was better to get rid of them before he went any further. He returned to the rear of the house and examined all the apertures again.

The front and back doors were both solid-looking and had withstood considerable effort to break them down, judging by the numerous marks they bore. The windows also seemed tightly nailed shut, though brute force would more likely stand a chance of success here, provided he could find the right battering ram.

There was a shed at the bottom of the large garden, so he went and had a look inside. Anything of any value had long since been removed, but some firewood remained, mainly large, uncut logs which would have been too heavy for the scavengers to carry away on foot.

He picked up a stout pine trunk, which still had a number of branch stubs protruding from it that would act as handles, and lugged it back to the rear veranda. He tested the right upper corner of what he presumed was the window over the kitchen sink given its location.

There had been the slightest give in it compared to the others. Attacking it here would mean swinging his heavy makeshift breaching tool over his shoulder rather than the more convenient underhand, but there was no other way for it. He took off his jacket and set to work.

Mercifully, the back of the house was still in shade, but even so, he was soon perspiring heavily in the afternoon heat. After around fifteen minutes of cacophonous, arm-wrenching work, he had managed to knock the corner of the thick plywood sheet back through the nail which held it in place inside.

He put the log down for a few minutes to rest his aching shoulders, before climbing onto the railing which ran along the edge of the veranda. With one foot as an anchor, he began kicking with his heel where the board was nailed to the window frame.

A further twenty draining minutes of this and the board lay inside on the kitchen floor. He vaulted inside over the sink and countertop and stood listening to the sounds of the old house. The air was stale and fetid, but there was an underlying stench Wolff recognized and which immediately put him on edge.

Human waste. Someone, very recently, had been relieving themselves here.

Given that it was an old house with the privy out the back, that meant someone who was in hiding. If they were still here, they could not have failed to hear his entry.

Wolff took the Walther P38 given to him by Schönebeck from his shoulder holster and cocked it as silently as he could. He focused his eyes away from the shaft of sunlight coming in through the window and allowed them to adjust to the gloom.

The kitchen ran in a long rectangle along the back wall of the house and at the far end opened out into another room. Listening carefully for any sounds of occupancy, Wolff moved around the corner and found himself in a large salon with a sofa and a couple of armchairs taking up the center of the floor.

The smell of shit and piss was stronger here, but there was still no sign of anyone. Dust floated lazily in the limited beams of light streaming from the edges of the wooden coverings over the windows. He moved carefully over towards the door leading to the hallway and staircase outside, testing each floorboard in front of him before committing his weight to it fully.

The door was ajar and as he neared it, the stench worsened further. Whoever was fouling up the house was doing so in the hall. Pistol extended, he pulled back the door. A chamberpot could be seen beside the front door at the base of the stairs.

Wolff advanced slowly into the corridor and paused at the bottom step, ignoring the vileness at his feet. If there was anyone in the house right now, they were on the upper floor. He listened for a few seconds but could hear nothing. They would have heard him, of course.

Slowly, and again testing each step carefully while keeping his eyes trained upwards, Wolff began to mount the stairs. At the top, he paused and cocked his ear again. Nothing. There were four bedrooms, a small one on his right facing the staircase, two in the middle and the last on the left, overlooking the street outside.

None of the upper windows had been boarded up and the drawn curtains were doing a poorer job of keeping out the afternoon sunlight. Wolff was able to clear the first small room in front of him as its door was open, while the fourth appeared similarly empty.

That left the two middle bedrooms, the doors of which were both shut. He stepped forward as silently as he could and placed himself against the section of wall which divided the two doorways before trying the handle on his right. It was unlocked and he pushed it inside, the door creaking noisily as it went.

Wolff held his breath and listened. He knew, just knew that there was someone inside. *Kriegsspielen*. War games.

"I'm coming in and I'm armed," he shouted in Latvian. "If you haven't got your hands up, I'll put a bullet in you." He repeated the warning in Russian. There was no response.

He ducked inside low and knelt with his back to the wall facing the window, pistol pointed in the two-handed grip. Three figures were silhouetted against the illuminated curtain with their arms in the air. "Pull the drapes," he said in both languages, his weapon still trained on the trio.

The figure on the left turned slowly and dragged back the curtain with one hand while keeping the other upright and visible. On the other side, the third person did likewise, before returning to face him.

In the strong daylight, he could see a middle-aged man, a woman in her mid-twenties and a young man a couple of years her junior standing in a row. There was fear on the faces of the first two, a defiant expression on the third. None presented any immediate threat. Wolff lowered his pistol a little.

"You live here?" The man nodded slowly. "What are your names?"

The three of them exchanged glances, but did not reply. "Your names," Wolff repeated more forcefully, lifting the pistol at them and pointing it directly. Eventually, the eldest man answered. "Arturs Bernstein," he said. "This is my daughter Urzula and my son Darius."

Wolff nodded and stood, letting the hand holding the pistol fall to his side.

"My name is Ako," he said. "I'm Hilda and Ludwig's son and I'm your nephew and cousin."

22

Wolff listened in silence as Arturs, Darius and Urzula told him their story. Arturs had not gone into his accountancy business in the city center since the Soviets had taken over the previous summer following the signing of the Nazi-Soviet non-aggression pact dividing up spheres of influence.

There was no point once the Bolsheviks banned private business. The rapid success of the Red Army invasion in June 1940 had come as a devastating blow to many in Latvia, who had hoped they could repeat the success of the Finns in holding off the Russians.

Arturs had never been among the optimists. After Molotov and Ribbentrop stunned the world with their unlikely deal in August 1939, he had removed important documents from his office and now kept them in a safe at the house.

He had also begun pickling vegetables from the garden out the back and storing them in the cellar, along with a stockpile of canned goods. It was this foresight which was sustaining the family now. "A Jew must always have a bolthole," Arturs said mournfully.

Tens of thousands of people, many of them Jews, had been deported to Siberia following the arrival of the Soviets. Confirming Kalejs' account, Arturs related how some senior communist figures had come out and requisitioned homes for themselves out in Kaiserwald.

However, the house Arturs had bought from his emigrating sister-in-law and her husband was one of the smaller in the neighborhood and had been passed over in favor of bigger ones.

Just to be on the safe side, they had smashed a few window panes and boarded up all openings from the inside. The family had not heard of the 'spontaneous' pogroms instigated by the Germans after they took over, as the house had no electricity and they went only in darkness to gather mushrooms. However, they were not surprised.

They had seen Kalejs and his cohorts driving around the area, looting homes. A few of them had made a half-hearted attempt to kick in the front door before leaving to seek richer pickings. But Arturs feared they would be back.

"They've been driving around more and more in the past couple of weeks, looking to scavenge what they can," he added. "We thought you were one of them. But now you're here, you can stop all that, can't you? Have you been assigned here by military intelligence?"

Wolff took a deep breath and sighed. "Not quite. I'm here to get you all out."

The family exchanged confused glances among themselves. "What do you mean 'get us out'? Get us out where?" Urzula spoke up for the first time.

Wolff held up his hands placatingly. "Just listen for a few minutes. Please."

He launched into his prepared argument. His promise to *Mammu*. Kristallnacht, the race laws and how things were getting progressively worse for every Jew under German rule. How, despite the flowers handed to arriving Wehrmacht troops, life would be just as bad as under the Soviets. If not worse.

There were more glances exchanged and Wolff could see that, as expected, his revelations were not going down well. This time it was Darius who responded. "But we know all this," he answered impatiently. "The Star of David, the curfews, all of it. We do have newspapers in this country, you understand? Or did, at least. We're not completely ignorant. Obviously, it will be difficult, especially seeing as he refuses to cut those off."

He made a vague swipe at where Arturs' *payot* hung from his temples, earning himself a glare from his father. Wolff sensed it was not the first time the subject had been raised.

"But we were raised Lutheran, not Jewish, so none of that will affect us," Darius continued. "He might have to stay out of sight until there is some order in place, but after that we can go out and work and buy food. At the very least, I can reopen the accountancy business again in my name.

"That wasn't possible under the communists. This is our home, Ako, you understand? Your father might have dragged you thousands of miles away to start a new life, but what are we going to do if we go abroad?

"This, all of this," he swept his hand expansively across the sitting room, "we would lose everything. Before the war, it would have been worth thousands. Who's going to buy it now? We'd be offered nothing. Those who left in 1939 got a pittance for their properties.

"No. We can't walk away from my father's life's work with nothing. Maybe when things settle down and there's some stability and money in the country, we can consider a move then." From the corner of his eye, Wolff saw Arturs shake his head unconsciously in response. "But not right now, we need to gather some money first," Darius concluded.

Wolff looked down at the floor. He had expected this and had kept his trump card in reserve. "You can't do any of that if you're lying in an unmarked mass grave," he said softly.

***

Wolff stood upstairs, watching the street through a crack in the curtains. It was quiet as the grave, but he knew that was only temporary. Kalejs and his fellow yobs had driven past twice more since he had been inside, slowing each time as they did to eyeball the house.

By themselves, they were not a problem, but reports of a German identifying himself as a lieutenant yet dressing in civilian clothes while checking out homes in Riga's wealthiest suburb might pique the interest of Stahlecker.

If there was one area where the Nazis liked to ensure they were rarely beaten, it was in the acquisition of spoils. The argument in the living room was still going, though less furiously now. At one stage, the shouting had gotten so loud, he had gone downstairs and asked them to keep their voices down lest they be heard from outside.

They had looked at him in fury then, the interloper bringing all this trouble into their lives. Still, he felt their suspicion of his motives had dissolved with his simple, unembellished descriptions of the murderous Special Task Forces and their horrific work.

He had not seen the evidence with his own eyes, but relayed the second-hand stories from colleagues who had heard of operations in Poland to round up Jews and take them to forested areas where large trenches had been dug. How the sound of multiple single gunshots had echoed all afternoon before falling silent with an hour's daylight left for some earth to be thrown on top of the corpses.

Any doubts over whether the same was planned for Latvia had been dispelled by the interaction with Kalejs. *Einsatzgruppe A* was already here and beginning its murderously efficient activities under Stahlecker.

The Bolsheviks' work in deporting some of the country's more prosperous Jews could only mean greater danger for the family - with the ostentatiously rich targets gone, attention would turn to others who might have lesser but still covetable wealth. Men like Arturs.

Wolff had also cut off Darius' argument about their Lutheran upbringing at source. In Germany, both siblings would be classified as first degree *Mischlingen*, or half breeds. Though their father was Jewish, their birth had preceded the introduction of the Nuremberg race laws in 1935.

As such, they would be afforded a degree of protection back in the Reich, even if Arturs would not. But different rules applied in the occupied east. Here, the children of Jews were considered

Jews and there was only one fate the Special Task Forces had in mind for them. Their mother's Baltic German ancestry would not save them.

The SS were already going through Latvian birth records with the aid of local collaborators. They would come looking for Arturs, and they would not be dissuaded as easily as the goons from the Arajs Kommando.

As they argued amongst themselves, the family had divided into three distinct camps, which at times formed temporary alliances of two on one and moments later switched to furious rows with each other all at once.

At one extreme stood Arturs, who was refusing point blank to even countenance leaving the country. Not only that, but he was gently, almost helplessly, insistent that he simply could not remove his *payot*, regardless of the price he might pay. The Torah forbade it, and that was that.

At the other end was Urzula, who had quickly grasped the impact of what Wolff had relayed and realized there was no point in being a property-owning corpse.

In between was Darius, who argued against both of them, contending that they could remain for an indeterminate length of time, but that Arturs would have to alter his appearance and find a hiding place away from the house, at least during daylight hours.

Worryingly, the young man had also expressed vague notions of joining some sort of resistance organization against the Nazis, even though he admitted he was not certain any such group even existed. His anger, though understandable, posed a threat to Wolff's plans.

It was Darius who had given voice to the suspicions shared by all three of them over what a German officer was doing helping a Jew and his two children to escape. It was clear they feared a trap, and Wolff could not blame them.

His identity was not in doubt. Apart from the details he had given them, he knew his mother's features shone out from his own. But from their perspective, there was every chance he had grown up to become the son of the short-tempered, embittered Ludwig rather than the child of the courageous yet gentle sister-in-law Arturs remembered so fondly.

Thus, Wolff was forced to delve into his past with his father and also address a series of questions about himself that he had never had to discuss with anyone since moving to Germany. What was he, after all? A Brazilian? A German? A Latvian?

He was all three, he insisted, something which was possible before Hitler and his hatemongers had taken power. Not anymore, Arturs had responded calmly. In war, one had to choose sides. Which one was he on?

Wolff opened his mouth to answer, but hesitated. The events of the past few days had made it abundantly clear to him who his allies and enemies were, but something still made him pause.

"I am on your side," he answered at last. "I know you are suspicious of me, despite the fact we are blood relatives. But I am not my father, and I am determined I will never be so. I can get you to safety. You will not have a lot of money and you will be leaving everything behind, true.

"But you will at least be alive, and if you stay here, it is only a matter of time before they come for you." It was this straightforward, unadorned speech which tipped the scales, though only just.

After the sun went down, he had joined in their humble supper of pickled vegetables. The following morning, he would take their photos and set off into the city to get them developed and affixed to the blank passports given to him by Canaris before he had left for Sofia and which he had somehow managed to preserve on his person throughout all of this.

He did not want to mention that to do so, he would use a camera invented by a Baltic German named Walter Zapp who had fled his homeland and handed over his ingenious device to the Nazi war machine. They were nervous enough of treachery from their supposed kin.

23

Wolff stood waiting for his turn at the desk, reflecting on the irony of the situation.

To prevent his uncle and cousins from being murdered in cold blood, he would need the assistance of the very people who would carry it out. He had been braced for trouble this morning. It would have been impossible to take Arturs' photo without removing his *payot*.

Ready for a fractious debate over their removal, Wolff was relieved to see Urzula simply produce a pair of scissors and lop off the curled sidelocks as her father sat silently, his eyes conveying his resentment at the situation.

It was as if the man had decided that during this 'temporary' move abroad, he could 'temporarily' set aside the religious rules which had governed his entire existence. Whatever mental mechanism he had applied, Wolff was extremely relieved he had concocted it.

With typical German efficiency, urban transport services had already been put back in action across Riga. After getting off the bus which he had taken in from Kaiserwald, he had asked a passing patrol for directions to the offices of the newly established Province General of Latvia.

Taking control after the fighting was done was an area in which Himmler and Heydrich had always specialized. As the army pushed further and further east, there was a power vacuum left behind the front lines. And who better to fill that vacuum than the SS, the backbone of the Reich Security Main Office?

At their new headquarters on Reimersa Street, they were already busy implementing the elements of the new regime which most concerned them. Tax collection, confiscating food and other raw materials to be sent back to the Reich and identifying land for new German settlers were all underway.

But the priority was to finish the job the Bolsheviks had started and render the Baltic states *Judenfrei*. Wolff had been guessing in his remarks about the SS going through birth records, but found it was indeed the case.

A dynamic new bureaucracy was already at work, assigning new civil status to local collaborators and 'ordinary' Latvians. It was also actively hunting Jews for *Abbeförderung*, or 'removal', yet another anodyne Nazi term coined to avoid uttering the unpleasant truth.

It was this bureaucracy that Wolff would have to surmount to get what he required. He could not risk going to the local Abwehr *Ast* as Canaris, or more likely Oster, might have guessed where he was now and issued orders for him to be detained on sight.

That process could be slowed significantly by going via the SS, though at the same time it was difficult to gauge how his letter from the admiral would be received here. The Abwehr was an army organization, and the SS did not take orders from the army.

Wolff entered the building and asked for the photographic section to develop the three shots from the Minox. He was directed up two flights of stairs and down a long, linoleum-floored corridor to the end where a bathroom had been converted into a makeshift laboratory.

The smell of the chemicals used to wash the prints filled the hallway as he walked down and turned into the office to one side of the darkroom. The minute he entered, he sensed this would be complicated.

His civilian attire had attracted little attention from the harassed-looking NCO at the front desk, but here he was greeted by a pudgy little man in his late thirties with the collar badge of an SS sergeant who looked him up and down disdainfully.

A typical *papiersoldat*, the clerical worker that Lothar dreamed of becoming, only with the added bonus of a uniform that kept him away from the fighting.

When Wolff introduced himself and his rank, the man shot to his feet and bellowed a Hitler salute. Before he realized what he was doing, Wolff replied in kind with the traditional army version, despite the fact he was not actually in uniform.

He noted the frown of disapproval he received in response.

Once more, he removed the letter from Canaris from his inside jacket pocket and adopted an imperious tone he felt would work best with the SS man as he handed it over unfolded for him to read.

"I am here on vital Reich business and require urgent use of your photographic laboratory facilities," he declared peremptorily. "I have some film here which I will need to be developed by the end of the day for collection."

The man refolded the letter, but made no attempt to hand it back. "Very well, sir, but as this is an SS facility rather than under army jurisdiction, I am afraid I must seek approval from my superior in this matter. May I show this to him quickly?"

Wolff steeled himself. He had no wish for the contents of his letter, which he was not even sure still remained in force, to be copied and relayed over the phone to Prinz Albrecht Strasse back in Berlin.

"No, you may not, Sergeant. Perhaps I have not made myself sufficiently clear. That is a letter from the head of the Abwehr, and I have been sent here by him personally on important business regarding the elimination of spies and terrorists.

"As such, I require the development of some material for urgent transport back to the Bendlerblock as soon as possible. I might add that this is a top secret matter and I will need to have a word with your technician before I leave to impress upon him the level of discretion required."

The sergeant's attitude changed drastically now. "That will not be necessary, sir. I shall develop it personally. I was a technician at AEG before the war, and I have experience with various types of film. Please rest assured that I will give it my fullest attention."

"Thank you..."

"Baumann, sir."

"Thank you, Baumann. I will make sure to mention your helpfulness if anyone asks how I managed in Riga."

"Thank you, sir." Baumann would know he was lying, of course, but the vague prospect of this actually occurring would provide extra incentive for him to keep his mouth shut.

He stood, this time giving a leisurely Hitler salute, and left the office. He was not sure whether Baumann would keep his word, but he had bigger things to worry about than the prissy little SS man.

After hours of argument with the family, a move to Switzerland had been agreed as a compromise. Wolff had told them he would secure enough money from his superiors for them to set themselves up in Zurich until they could get back on their feet.

However, this only provoked further Arturs' innate suspicion of the whole affair. Who were his superiors and why were they prepared to hand over such an amount of money? What were they getting out of this?

Wolff eventually lost his temper with the old man, explaining that he was placing himself at serious risk in order to fulfill his mother's wishes and once more emphasizing what he had seen of the Special Task Forces and their activities.

Afterwards, Arturs had gone off to begin arranging his belongings for travel, albeit with the petulant air of a sulking child. Wolff's latent anger with the family's intransigence meant he was preoccupied as he left SS headquarters.

He had entered as discreetly as he could, with his head down and the brim of his hat low over his face as a *Schlapphut* should. But as he left, deep in thought about what lay ahead, he spotted two men outside chatting in the sunshine and quickly turned away in shock.

One of the pair, he did not recognize. But the other was Stumpfegger, the SS captain he had attempted to strangle for executing a child just a few weeks beforehand. Stumpfegger had evidently been reassigned to Riga from frontline duties with Army Group North.

Wolff walked quickly down the street and into Esplanāde Park, where he moved behind a tree and observed Stumpfegger, who remained deep in conversation with the other officer. He had not been seen.

However, he would have to be extremely careful upon his return to the building. It was yet another complication he could have done without.

***

Back at the house, Arturs and Darius were finishing up packing their belongings. He had told them to limit themselves to one suitcase each, but was dismayed to find that Arturs had four times that amount and was insisting point blank on bringing his accounting ledgers with him.

Wolff's insistence that these would be of no use abroad cut no ice; instead Arturs went into a rant about his loyalty to his customers, to whom it was obvious he expected to return after a period abroad. Wolff let it go.

They had some time now before Wolff had to return for the passport images, but no immediately apparent way of filling it. Suitcases had been packed, and the family had clearly accepted the need to leave Latvia as a unit.

With nothing else to do, Wolff began asking Arturs about his parents. He was surprised to hear his uncle paint quite a complimentary picture of the couple. Ludwig and *Mammu* had been very much in love, Arturs said.

The Wolff family had been old money in Latvia, but had seen much of their wealth diminish with the breakup of their rural estates under land reforms by the new nationalist government in 1920, two years before his parents had set off for Brazil.

In contrast, *Mammu*'s family, who were merchants, had managed to retain most of their riches through the turbulent years of the Depression. The house in which the couple lived had been given to his mother by her parents, Arturs said, and this bothered Ludwig Wolff greatly.

"Your father is a proud man," his uncle said. "He wanted to show your mother he could become a success in his own right. She loved him and understood that. That's why she agreed to leave, even though she didn't want to. The real root of the problem lay with your paternal grandfather."

Wolff sat forward. He had never heard any of this before. "Ludwig's father was one of the leading supporters of the Baltic German militias who took on Latvian forces and lost after the Great War ended. He wasn't alone in this. Quite a few of the big *Baltendeutsche* landowners backed the Freikorps as a means of preserving their estates.

"The fighting was savage, Ako. No prisoners were taken on either side. And when the Freikorps lost, their supporters were always going to be targeted by the new administration. Most of the Wolff family land was out near Jelgava, about 40 miles south of here, and it was all confiscated.

"Your grandfather ordered your father to gather a few old Freikorps veterans to go out there and try to take it back. It was a hopeless cause, and they were lucky to escape with their lives, to be honest. When your father came back to Riga, your grandfather called him a coward and blamed him for ruining the family.

"It was after that your father started talking about going abroad. He told your mother they could go to Brazil and make their fortune before returning to buy back the old estates again to save the family honor. He said they would come back and build the biggest villa in Kaiserwald to show how well he had done."

Arturs looked at him sadly. "Unfortunately, it didn't quite work out for them like that. Life rarely does, alas."

They skirted around the subject of the cancer which had taken both *Mammu* and her sister. His uncle was philosophical about his wife's death, preferring to focus on the good times they had enjoyed together than dwell on the bad.

He told Wolff he had concentrated on his business after that, maintaining it secretly even following the Soviet occupation. His children were the most important thing in the world for him, and it was for their sake he had eventually agreed to leaving Latvia, he said.

By then, it was time for Wolff to travel back in to pick up the photographs from Baumann. On the bus into the city center once more, he reflected on the different approaches taken by Arturs and his father. Ludwig Wolff, forever with a point to prove, had dragged his wife halfway around the world in search of it, then wrenched his son from a happy, settled life when he felt anew that things had turned against him.

Embittered and resentful, he had eagerly embraced the Nazis and their convenient explanations for all German ills. He was not alone in swallowing such lies. Canaris and Oster had once been supporters of Hitler too. Wolff wondered how long it would take for his father to see the light. Or if he ever would.

Arriving, Wolff made his way carefully to Reimersa Street. Seeing Stumpfegger yesterday had been a massive shock, and he stood on the edge of Esplanāde Park observing the Province General headquarters for half an hour before deciding to risk going in, hat again pulled low over his face.

He only hoped Baumann would have done as agreed and there would be no further unpleasantness required, as Wolff was in no position to kick up a stink in an SS-run administration.

To his relief, the little clerk was remarkably civil and prompt in his issuing of the photos, which were certainly of sufficient quality for use as passport images. Ordinarily, these would be affixed to a *Reisepass* with a small metal binder ring in the corner, but he had no means of obtaining this here.

Glue would have to suffice until they reached Berlin, where he could place his cousins under the safety of Canaris' protection. As a precaution, Wolff asked for the negatives, which the bemused sergeant duly supplied. He wanted to leave as little trace here as possible.

He thanked Baumann and promised again to mention his cooperation to his superiors, before walking outside quickly with his head low and the manila envelope containing the images high and over his face.

Not until he was well down the street did he turn around to make sure he was not being followed before making his way to the bus stop for what he hoped was his final trip out to Kaiserwald.

The plan was to return to the city center with the family by bus before commandeering the nearest military vehicle to drive them out to the airfield. Once there, he would use his letter to guarantee himself and the three others a place on one of the daily connections which ferried senior Wehrmacht officers, SS figures and top civilian personnel between Berlin and its new *Reichskommissariat*.

The chatty private had informed him that one flight usually departed mid-morning, followed by a second late in the afternoon. With luck, they could catch the latter. Failing that, he would go for broke and demand a plane of their own to bring them to Germany, though the attention this might bring meant it would be a last resort.

He still had no way of knowing how actively Heydrich was seeking his arrest. If the man they called 'Himmler's brain' now had enough evidence to dislodge his old Kriegsmarine comrade in the constant game of oneupmanship, Wolff would be of secondary concern.

Disembarking, he made his way back to the house through the deserted leafy streets of Kaiserwald and gave the agreed knock. Darius opened the back door, and he slipped inside as a car made its way up the street again, which he assumed to be members of the Arajs Kommando making yet another pass through the area.

A few more hours and they could have the run of the house, as far as he was concerned. Darius led him to the sitting room, where Arturs and Urzula were waiting with their luggage. Both father and son were wearing their best suits, while Urzula had on a pretty summer dress and sensible shoes.

Wolff said simply, "Let's go", and they moved towards the back door for the final time. He opened it and reeled back in shock as an outstretched pistol forced him to retreat into the kitchen. Kalejs and his two companions from the green Ford-Vairog followed in behind as Stumpfegger, a triumphant smile now plastered across his face, surveyed the family and their luggage.

"So, Wolff. I believe you're a lieutenant now and providing passports for unknown parties to boot. You'll have to fill me in on how you escaped punishment battalion duty. I'm sure it's a fascinating story.

"Don't worry, I've got all evening."

24

Wolff sat with the others and watched as the two nameless goons went through the cousins' luggage. One had taken Darius' suitcase, and the other was taking visible pleasure in rifling through Urzula's, sharing oafish smirks with his comrade when he came across her underwear.

To Wolff's relief, neither had anything incriminating among their possessions, but it was what might be in the old man's baggage that worried him. Wolff had taken Urzula aside before heading off to get the photos developed and asked her to ensure her father did not pack anything which would give away their true identities.

Their passports were all under Felsko, the shared family name of their mothers and a safer option than Arturs' definitively Jewish alternative of Bernstein. Even this had provoked a storm of dissent from the old man, who demanded to know how they would be able to properly register themselves once in Switzerland.

Wolff had planned to inform them once they were en route that Brazil was a far safer destination, throwing in some false detail about how top secret plans were afoot among the Nazi leadership to invade its southern neighbor and appropriate the tons of gold kept within the country's famously discreet banks.

He was confident that he could persuade the family that a transatlantic move was the only option. Nowhere else on the continent was safe - Spain and Portugal were both under their own fascist regimes - and North Africa was not renowned for the welcome it offered Jews either.

Only in Brazil, whose anti-Nazi stance he had already heavily emphasized, could they expect to live in true freedom. Provided they could get past this current situation, of course.

Wolff could see the uncertainty in Stumpfegger's eyes as he tapped his pistol impatiently against the arm of the chair. The SS captain had confiscated the gun Wolff had been given in Budapest and had pushed it into his own empty holster.

The *finka* had been given to Kalejs, who was holding it reverentially, unaware that Stumpfegger would view retaining such an item as beneath him. Stumpfegger had bragged about how easy it had been to find him. Baumann had complained to anyone within earshot of the arrogant young Abwehr officer who did not even have a proper German name.

That had piqued Stumpfegger's curiosity when he heard about it and he had put out feelers to Kalejs and his yobs. When they confirmed that a Lieutenant Wolff matching Ako's description had shown considerable interest in this house, he had ordered them to keep it under surveillance. Sure enough, Wolff had shown up once more.

However, Wolff could see that the unfazed air he had adopted had unsettled Stumpfegger's intrinsic arrogance. The SS cared nothing for the Abwehr or interrupting whatever operations it might have running. But the prospect of a dressing down from Berlin based on a complaint by Canaris would seriously impact on Stumpfegger's career.

It was for this reason, Wolff suspected, that Stumpfegger had opted to take members of the Arajs Kommando along rather than other SS troops. The locals would do exactly what they were told and could be used as whipping boys in the event of any subsequent inquiry.

Wolff had so far been courteous towards Stumpfegger's superior rank and inferred pity over the looming consequences of the SS captain's actions. Everything would stand or fall on what might lie in the suitcases, which now lay open on the floor. Hence Stumpfegger's jitters.

Kalejs was going through Arturs' ledgers now, which appeared to contain nothing more than regular, tedious accounting records, judging by the growing distaste on Stumpfegger's face. Kalejs excitedly pointed out some names here and there, but having Jewish clients was not enough, and Stumpfegger knew it.

"I think it's time you explained yourself, Wolff," he said, picking a speck of something from the leg of his uniform trousers. "You see, I made some inquiries after you were taken away by the Secret Field Police. I wanted to make sure the army dunderheads would apply the proper punishment.

"I really should have shot you on the spot myself, but the paperwork..." He spread his hands in mock frustration. "I heard you had been sent back to your grubby little unit's headquarters in Brandenburg pending your court martial, and I became concerned about the delay in assigning you to the penal battalion.

"Then next I heard, you had simply vanished from the cells and nobody knew where. It was frustrating, but I put it to one side and concentrated on my work here. Now you pop up in Riga, as a lieutenant, no less, and flashing this letter from the Abwehr.

"Which at least answers the first part of my query, but not the second. What are you doing in Riga, and who are these people? I can see what their passports say, but I don't believe a word of it. The Abwehr has a reputation for cooperating with Jews, and if I find out that's the case here, well…" Stumpfegger smiled again.

"Fortunately, most of the property registration records were left intact when the *Bolos* retreated, so discovering who actually owns this house should be relatively straightforward." Wolff kept his face impassive, though inside his guts were churning.

"With respect, *Hauptsturmführer*, you have read the letter requesting full cooperation from any Reich officials towards the bearer. This is a top secret matter within military intelligence," Wolff put a heavy emphasis on the penultimate word.

"I am due in Berlin this evening, and if I am not there, questions will be asked. And unfortunately, I will have to explain that a captain of the SS," Wolff again emphasized Stumpfegger's rank, "decided to defy the authority of a full admiral due to his baseless suspicions."

Wolff let the threat hang in the air for a moment before adding: "Which sounds rather like grounds for your own court martial, *sir*." The remark, combined with the insolence of the sign-off, hit home and Wolff saw the fury rise in Stumpfegger's face. He grabbed his pistol from the armrest again and leaned forward. "You little shit, I…"

"Captain!" Stumpfegger's nascent rant was interrupted by an excited squawk from Kalejs, who was triumphantly waving something handed to him by one of the searchers.

Stumpfegger's expression switched instantly from fury to keen interest as he rose from his chair, Kalejs moving towards him excitedly with a book in his grasp. A knowing grin spread across Stumpfegger's face as he accepted the tome.

Though the book had no visible markings on its faded and worn cover, Wolff could see the faint outline of a five-pointed star on its spine. He closed his eyes to control the fury rising inside him at the old man's stupidity, cursing himself for not insisting on a check of their luggage.

Stumpfegger flicked through the pages in a leisurely, taunting manner before gently snapping it shut. He held it up as if poised to swear an oath and smirked at Wolff. "I think this is something that requires further investigation, don't you?"

Stumpfegger took one of the three passports from his breast pocket and opened it. "If, as this would indicate, Herr...*Felsko* is indeed a Jew, then he is required by Reichskommissariat regulations to wear a Star of David identifier.

"He is also forbidden to have one of these," Stumpfegger gestured at the ancient, dust-covered radio on a sideboard in the salon. "But we'll get back to that. In the meantime, I'm afraid all of you will have to accompany me down to Province General headquarters." He smiled at Wolff. "You know where that is, don't you, Lieutenant?"

Wolff tutted and rolled his eyes. He shoved his hands nonchalantly into his pockets to avoid Stumpfegger seeing them ball subconsciously into fists. He took a couple of casual steps toward where the luggage was spread out on the floor to give himself a moment.

There was a potential way out of this. Canaris had explained that the Abwehr was the one Reich body which was exempt from the Reich's ridiculous Aryanization laws. The admiral had managed to persuade Hitler to grudgingly allow this by pointing out that he might have to rely on intelligence from Jewish sources.

But Canaris had also revealed that this side deal with the Führer was not widely known and was retained by him as something of a trump card. Wolff could not afford a painstaking SS investigation into the background of Arturs and his children as part of a war of attrition by Heydrich against his old friend.

There had to be another way out of this. Stumpfegger was standing impatiently over Arturs, Darius and Urzula, who were still seated on the sofa beside Wolff's armchair. The trio knew they were in trouble, but as the exchanges had taken place entirely in rapid-fire German, they were unsure exactly what was going on.

Unlike *Mammu*, their mother had never spoken to them in anything other than Latvian.

"Get up," said Stumpfegger to his three new captives, beckoning with his pistol. The barrel of the weapon glinted in the light coming in the window. It had been carefully polished since Wolff last saw it, when it had been splattered with blood and brain matter.

Stumpfegger's gesture and tone left no room for doubt, but none of the three on the couch budged. Urzula was staring at Wolff with a pleading expression. Darius looked defiant, and Arturs simply resigned. Stumpfegger glared at them for a moment and then stood back and nodded at his own companions.

Kalejs' two underlings, taking their cue, moved past where Wolff was now standing. One grabbed Arturs, pulled him up from the sofa and roughly shoved him forward in the direction of the kitchen. The old man lost his balance and stumbled forward, tripping over one of the suitcases which still lay open on the floor and crashing heavily against the sideboard bearing the radio.

Kalejs chuckled, prompting the thug who had pushed Arturs to attempt a repeat performance with Urzula. Darius, who was sitting beside his sister, grabbed the man's arm and the pair grappled for a moment before the second tough also intervened, leading to a three-way struggle between them.

In the meantime, Urzula had knelt down to assist her dazed father. Stumpfegger, who had been watching it all with quiet amusement, turned and barked at Kalejs to go and help his comrades with Darius. Wolff's cousin was doing a solid job of tying up both men with his resistance.

Kalejs moved forward, unsheathing the *finka*. He grabbed Urzula by the hair, pulling her head back so that her throat was exposed. This would get her brother's attention. It meant Stumpfegger was distracted for a split second and as the SS captain turned his gaze back towards him, Wolff rose and took a step forward.

Then he kicked Stumpfegger firmly between the legs. The SS captain crumpled in a heap, and Wolff was on him in an instant. However, Stumpfegger still retained a firm hold on the Walther as Wolff sought to tear it from him. Kalejs turned, releasing Urzula from his grip.

He launched himself forward onto where Stumpfegger and Wolff were struggling for control of the weapon. Wolff grabbed Stumpfegger's wrist and twisted the gun towards the onrushing Kalejs. He pulled back on where Stumpfegger's index finger was inside the trigger guard.

The shot was deafeningly loud in the enclosed sitting room, and everyone froze in place. Kalejs seemed to halt in mid-lunge, looking down at the red stain spreading from the middle of his chest. Then he dropped to his knees and flopped forward, face down.

As Stumpfegger raised his head to stare in shock, Wolff turned the barrel of the gun round towards the SS man. It took a split second for Stumpfegger to realize what he was doing, but it was enough. All of Stumpfegger's cockiness vanished now as he fought frantically to stop his own weapon being used against him.

But Wolff's momentum and the angle of their tussle were against him. Stumpfegger's roar of combined anger and fear was cut short as the pistol bucked once more. The captain's head rocked backward before slumping onto his knees.

Wolff now removed the weapon fully from the dead man's hand and stood with it pointed at Kalejs' two companions, who stood back with their hands raised. "*Nē, nē!*" said the man who had shoved Arturs, before Wolff shot him in the head.

He then swung the pistol onto the other man, who looked as if he were about to burst into tears. Wolff fired twice more. He walked to where each man had fallen and checked for signs of life. Then he kicked Stumpfegger's corpse roughly to the floor and rooted through his tunic until he found both his all-important letter from Canaris and the three passports.

Luckily, none had suffered any damage in the firefight. Wolff stood and looked round at his cousins and uncle. Urzula was still kneeling on the floor, a protective arm around her father. Darius stood, mouth agape, beside the sofa, flanked by the two dead Latvian fascists.

"Well, now," Wolff said. "I think we'd probably better get a move on, don't you?"

***

If there was any upside to shooting Stumpfegger dead and setting off a city-wide manhunt, it was that it had convinced Wolff's cousins beyond doubt of his bona fides and eliminated the childish stubbornness of Arturs.

The old man made no objection as his luggage was quickly searched for any more potentially lethal material. There was not a word from him either when Wolff took the suitcases full of ledgers and placed them definitively under the stairs. Another side benefit of the killings was the issue of transport.

Stumpfegger had arrived at the house in a Kubelwagen, while Kalejs and his fellow thugs had driven there in the green Ford-Vairogs. Wolff moved the Ford round to the back of the house out of sight before they set off.

He had toyed with the idea of setting fire to the house to hide the bodies, but considered it more trouble than it was worth.

The smoke would be seen for several miles and would draw attention to the area and those who had been seen leaving it.

Subsequent investigations might turn up witnesses who recalled four people in civilian dress arriving at the airfield in an SS vehicle. Wolff was also convinced that Stumpfegger had not informed his superiors where he was going.

This was a personal mission, with the gathering of evidence secondary. Wolff also took Stumpfegger's *Ausweis*, though removing the special SS ID card would only slow identification of his remains by a matter of hours at most. The family had already cleared out the few family portraits from the house along with any other identifying material.

Wolff and Darius lugged all four bodies down to the cellar while Urzula had scrubbed the bloodstains from the floorboards as best she could. The dust sheets had absorbed most of the blood left on the settee, though some had still leaked through. It would have to suffice.

All going well, he and the cousins should be safely on a train heading for Switzerland by the time the alarm was raised. Wolff drove as sedately as he could towards the airfield, fighting the urge to accelerate and get there more quickly.

Throughout the entire journey, Darius sat beside him with Arturs and Urzula in the back. The confrontation at the house had stripped away any pretenses they were maintaining about their situation. They were leaving their homeland carrying just a fraction of their possessions, and it seemed unlikely they would ever return.

The SS plates on the Kubelwagen had seen them quickly waved across the pontoon bridge to the western side of Riga, but

Wolff decided to stop en route to the airfield and tore them off before throwing them into the Daugava along with Stumpfegger's *Ausweis*.

Any questions from a curious sentry at the airfield could be overcome with a simple wave of his Canaris letter, which he was planning to use to get all four of them on board a plane to Berlin anyway. The waiting at the airfield would be the worst part.

The departure times for the afternoon flight from Berlin were irregular and, until they were in the air, they would be forced to sit around while their imaginations played tricks on them. As it was, the delay provided further proof to the family of what had lain in store for them.

Prisoners in filthy civilian clothing toiled alongside emaciated-looking men in worn Red Army uniforms to rebuild the destroyed terminal building. Most of those in non-military clothing were stripped to their shirtsleeves in the summer heat, but some of the older figures still bore their jackets, all of which complied with the recently introduced laws requiring Jews in Ostland to wear a yellow Star of David.

Lest there be any doubt, a couple of the men also sported the *payot* of which Arturs had now been shorn. Wolff heard his uncle catch his breath and looked over to see him bow his head as Urzula clasped his hand fiercely and whispered into his ear.

"What is it?" he demanded.

"He recognizes some of the men," she jutted her chin out at the prisoners. Cursing his own stupidity, Wolff told them to stand up and herded them quickly further down the airfield.

The last thing he needed was one of the unfortunates spotting Arturs and drawing attention to them by attempting to secure some sort of lifeline. They moved down to where the blackened shell of a burnt-out hangar provided some shade from the unrelenting sun. The smell of aviation gasoline remained strong.

"This is the future here, Arturs," he said in a low voice. "I wasn't exaggerating. Your property confiscated, and you and your children worked to death here or somewhere else. And if that didn't kill you off..." Finishing the sentence was unnecessarily cruel. The old man was wiping his eyes as his daughter attempted to comfort him.

The sound of a distant but growing hum interrupted the conversation and, after a few seconds, a black dot appeared on the horizon. "That's it, that's the plane," Wolff said, as he stood up quickly. Though he had tried not to show it to the others, he had been living on his nerves since they had arrived there over an hour beforehand.

He had shown the Canaris letter to the laconic Luftwaffe captain in charge of Spilve, a Bavarian who seemed entirely disinterested in Wolff or whatever he was doing. The arriving flight was carrying medical supplies and booze for the golden pheasants at Reimersa Street, he declared, but no passengers.

The man had no information on travelers bound for Berlin either. "They either just turn up or radio us to have the plane held," he shrugged. The airman's remarks showed at least that he was not a Nazi true believer, though Wolff did not give much for his long-term chances if he was in the habit of repeating such phrases to complete strangers.

The aircraft was another Heinkel He 111 and its two pilots seemed in no mood to dally in Riga. Facilities at Spilve were basic at best and anyway, air crews were used to flying ten hours straight from raids on England the year before.

Once the plane had been unloaded, Wolff was beckoned forwarded by the Luftwaffe captain and given a form to sign bearing his own ID number and the bogus passport details of his uncle and cousins.

As Wolff signed, he noticed a distant dust cloud on the long straight road from the airfield, which ran alongside the Daugalva until it reached the city center. It looked like more than one vehicle was causing it. He thanked the Bavarian and asked a parting question, receiving a puzzled reply in response.

Satisfied, Wolff hurried the others through the rear hatch and into the aircraft's cramped interior. Like the other Heinkel, it had been stripped of its mid and rear guns, as well as the one located in the aircraft's belly, in order to provide more space.

Wolff pulled the door shut and gave the thumbs up to the pilot amid the deafening roar of the idling engines. The plane immediately began to turn around on the apron in front of the old control tower, pointing itself northward for takeoff along the main runway.

As it did so, Wolff could see some sort of commotion at the front gate, where a Kfz.1 jeep had pulled up, followed by a truck. His view was cut off then as the Heinkel straightened and began to taxi with increasing speed out towards the Baltic Sea.

The plane lifted from the runway, and Wolff watched the three faces around him blanch as it started to climb into the sky. He knew that feeling. As the pilot banked left to head on a westward course, Wolff looked down and could see infantry fanning out across the area.

Even at this distance, he could see a white speck on one side of their helmets. The shield with double lightning bolt insignia of the Waffen SS. The officer in charge, identifiable by the lighter gray of his crusher cap, walked swiftly over to where Wolff had parked Stumpfegger's Kubelwagen.

He watched the man peer inside the vehicle and then turn his face to the sky in the direction of the departing Heinkel.

25

Moments after takeoff, as the pilots concentrated on leveling out the plane, Wolff gestured for the others to be silent and rose to the half-crouch the confines of the fuselage allowed.

Checking to make sure the airmen were not paying attention, he moved as quickly as he could back to the radio beneath the unmanned defensive dorsal machine gun turret. Normally, a plane the size of the Heinkel would have a crew of up to seven.

As this was a transport flight, it had been stripped back to two pilots, one of whom acted as an auxiliary radio operator. The bemused Bavarian Luftwaffe captain had confirmed where the radio was located in the aircraft just before the door closed.

Wolff had potentially seconds to disable it before a call came through from the Riga-Spilve control tower ordering them to turn back. The protective metal casing around it was stamped FuG10 and he guessed it was a long wave version of the portable *Kleinfunkgeräte* devices used by the army in the field.

After a quick once over, he had decided against cutting the power cable which extended from it. If such obvious sabotage was noticed mid-flight, the pilots might insist on landing at the nearest airfield for a full ground check to ensure nothing else had been tampered with.

They had almost certainly used the radio to advise Riga-Spilve of their impending arrival, thus, their four new passengers might also end up being interrogated by the Luftwaffe military police.

Instead, Wolff had knelt and spotted a cluster of white wires visible in the miniscule gap between the bottom of the radio and its wall bracket. He inserted the blade of the *finka* and sawed and hacked at them until they were cut through.

A quick once-over confirmed there was no other wiring that he could slice apart without it being spotted, so he returned unobtrusively to where he had been sitting, smiling at the others who were looking at him anxiously. No explanations were needed.

Then he waited.

Almost two hours into the flight, the co-pilot rose from his seat, stretched and made his way back down the gangway between the folded-up legs of his four passengers. Wolff guessed he was planning to contact Gatow, Adolf Hitler's favored airfield in the west of Berlin, ahead of their planned landing there.

Only Wolff had ensured he would not be able to do that. Or at least he hoped so.

Even though Wolff had lifted the receiver to make sure the machine was dead, he still held his breath as he watched the co-pilot repeatedly attempt to raise Gatow before giving up in frustration. As expected, the man checked the power cable, but could find nothing wrong.

With a peeved look on his face, he made his way back up to his colleague to inform him that they now had no means of contacting their destination. An irritated exchange took place between the pair, and both turned and stared suspiciously at their passengers.

Arturs and the others bowed their heads demurely, as civilians might when dealing with military men, but Wolff looked back at them with a convincing display of puzzlement. When his expression shifted to anger at their rudeness, they turned away. It was, as ever, all about the body language.

Wolff waited a few more beats before making his way up and perching on both men's shoulders. "Lieutenant Wolff, Abwehr," he said. "Is there some sort of problem?" The two pilots looked at each other before the senior man replied, still looking forward.

The shame at having to admit a technical problem to some desk monkey from Berlin was overwhelmingly apparent. "There's an issue with the radio."

"I see." Wolff put as much disappointment and disapproval into the two words as possible. "Well, that *is* inconvenient. You see, there's been a change of plan, gentlemen. I was unable to tell you before for reasons of operational security. We cannot land at Gatow. We have to fly onwards to Brandenburg-Briest."

The airfield near Wolff's training base at Lake Quenz, west of Berlin, was the only one he knew intimately enough to be sure would have relatively lax security. At the start of the war, Brandenburg-Briest had been the launchpad for bombing raids on the Poles and the initial stages of Barbarossa.

Now though, it was too far away from the lines to be used as anything other than a flight instructor school and a testing ground for the nearby Arcado aircraft factory. The senior pilot stiffened in his seat, but did not look backwards.

"I'm afraid that's quite impossible, Lieutenant," he said, his voice tight. "Our radio has suddenly stopped working, and we will have to land immediately at Gatow to ensure everything else on board is as it should be." It was abundantly clear neither man regarded the malfunctioning radio and Wolff's abrupt demand for a change of destination as a coincidence.

Wolff knew instinctively what was required here. On infiltration missions, each situation had been different. It had been necessary at times to cow suspicious Ivan defenders through the implied threat of severe consequences. At others, to appeal to their humanity by posing as retreating forces bearing badly wounded comrades.

This man had been embarrassed in front of a member of another Reich agency and a junior colleague. Wolff needed to offer him a way out of the situation to prevent him digging his heels in. One which would allow him to emerge with a universally acknowledged victory.

And for men of the Luftwaffe, that meant putting one over on the 'sea rats' of the Kriegsmarine. The two organizations had been at each other's throats for years, with the navy demanding control of its own aviation wing and the air force refusing to cede such power. The rivalry made the relationship between the SS and the army look positively fraternal.

A member of his unit whose brother was an aerial gunner had once told him how relations between the navy and air force were so atrocious, Admiral Raeder had concealed details of a Kriegsmarine early warning attack system from his Luftwaffe counterpart Hermann Göring for years - and then tried to hamper Luftwaffe efforts to develop their own once the secret emerged.

Wolff leaned in conspiratorially. "See those two men in the back?" Both pilots turned their heads towards Arturs and Darius, who stared back at them uncertainly. "They might not look like much, but they were working on an advanced radar system for the Russians.

"Canaris wants to hand them over to his old Kriegsmarine buddies for interrogation. But there's a Luftwaffe radar fellow waiting at Brandenburg-Briest who's going to have first crack at them." There was another look between the pilots, and Wolff knew he had struck gold.

The lead pilot squinted back again at Arturs, who looked for all the world like the accountant he was, and Darius, who was barely old enough to shave properly. "We'll let you off at Brandenburg, but we're taking straight off again and going back to Gatow once we fix the radio. And if there's any grief over it, you'll be the one carrying the can."

Wolff smiled. "Actually no, gentlemen." He pulled out Canaris' letter and unfolded it so they could read its contents. "As you can see, it'll be the admiral who'll cop any flak." The two pilots grinned. This was sounding better and better.

The Heinkel landed at Brandenburg-Briest without incident after they performed a couple of flypasts while waggling the wings at the control tower, which Wolff assumed was a universal Luftwaffe signal of distress.

While the pilots went off to find a radio technician, Wolff hurried Arturs, Darius and Urzula off the plane and used Canaris' letter again to commandeer a Horch 901 field car he saw parked beside the control tower. He needed to take a short trip to the

Brandenburger training school at Lake Quenz, he told a dubious Luftwaffe NCO.

The ruse could help send his pursuers off on yet another wild goose chase. In fact, he planned to cover the 80km or so to Berlin, where he would need the help of Oster. The quicker he got going, the less chance there was of SS roadblocks being thrown up to stop him.

***

"How exactly did you fuck this up, Wolff?"

Wolff had expected Oster to be angry. After all, not only was he being actively sought by the SS, he had also brought three Latvian Jewish and half-Jewish refugees directly to the colonel's smart apartment home in Charlottenburg.

However, Oster did not appear overly concerned about that and merely grunted when Wolff informed him he had shot dead Stumpfegger and his local stooges in Riga.

Instead, the colonel's preoccupation seemed to be entirely with what had happened in Sofia and the subsequent chase across Yugoslavia. He insisted upon discussing this in his kitchen before he would even touch the issue of what to do with the three strangers in his salon.

It irritated Wolff, who felt the colonel already had the most important details. After all, it was abundantly clear that whatever chance there had been of securing a peace with the Soviets was now gone thanks to the SD's intervention. Still, Oster went over things again and again, interrogating Wolff from different angles on each event.

Had he seen either of the SD men hanging around Riunione?

What exactly had the Russian told him at the hotel?

Was the diary the only thing the SD had taken from the dead Ivan, or was there anything else?

It soon became clear to Wolff that the cross-examination had as much to do with checking and rechecking his own version of events as anything to do with the SD. He bit his tongue and gave as complete answers as he could, hoping Oster would soon be satisfied so that they could move on to what was, for him, a far more pressing issue.

The fate of the three people waiting outside. Before that, though, he needed to find out what had happened to the NKVD diary. Had the Abwehr managed to intercept Udolph or was the evidence now in Heydrich's possession?

Oster regarded him for a second. "We do not believe that what Heydrich has will be sufficient evidence to bring to Hitler," he said eventually. "The Pig is the ultimate judge in these things. Only if he is satisfied will Heydrich be able to move.

"As I've told you before, there is a reason why Hitler has set up so many organizations with overlapping responsibilities. He wants us fighting amongst ourselves rather than attempting to overthrow him." He sighed. "Unfortunately, more often than not, we oblige him."

"So I'm in the clear then?"

Oster nodded in affirmation. Wolff could hardly believe it. He had watched the Heinkel disappear off into the distance in

Budapest with the fatalism of a man whose death sentence had just been pronounced.

Everything he had done since then had been governed by the principle that he was living on borrowed time. He had shot Stumpfegger and his three goons because he felt he had no other option, but was now learning he had put himself and the cousins in greater danger than was required.

The overwhelming emotion coursing through him was not the relief he would have expected, but indignation. He pushed his swelling fury away. It was not Oster's fault, and he needed to concentrate.

The priority was to get the three people outside in the salon to Switzerland and - if he could convince them - onwards to Brazil. He had thought of joining them, of returning to the land where he grew up and would be safe, but he could not abandon Ludwig to his fate under the loathsome *Sippenhaft* laws of collective familial responsibility.

Even if he could somehow make it across the country to Hamburg, there was zero chance of his father agreeing to come with them. No, the old man would die in Germany, that was certain. The only question was whether it would be in that damp apartment in Ottensen or in a concentration camp.

But there was something else holding him back too, he knew. A more promising future for both of them dangled tantalizingly by Canaris and Oster. Something better for Germany. For Wolff, for Ludwig, for Arturs, Darius and Urzula and for Lothar.

Something in which he felt he had a stake and for which it was worth continuing to fight. He shook his head and refocused on the problem at hand. They needed to get Arturs, Darius and

Urzula out of Berlin as quickly as possible, but for that, new documents would be required, he told Oster.

The SS would by now have details of the passports in the name of Felsko presented at the airfield in Riga. New IDs would be needed before they could be moved again. Moreover, Wolff had yet to come up with a credible excuse as to why he had been driving the Kubelwagen of a murdered SS officer who had previously reported him for assault and insubordination.

He was unsure how he might come up with one either. He was relying on dealing with all that later.

"The Abwehr has some properties unknown to the SD here where we can stash them while we develop new passports," Oster said, acknowledging Wolff's concerns for the first time after an hour and a half spent grilling him on Sofia, Yugoslavia and Budapest.

"I presume they can be relied on to stay there and not venture out onto the street, drawing attention to themselves?" Wolff nodded. Of that there was no doubt. Whatever obstinacy had been initially displayed by Arturs and Darius back in Riga was now long gone, replaced by fear and unstinting compliance.

They would do what they were told in a strange city, terrified of the consequences if they did not. "How long will the passports take?" he asked.

"A day or two," Oster answered airily. "Much will depend on if the right people are on duty or not, and I don't know that offhand. Heydrich still has his spies within our organization, and we have to ensure they know nothing about this."

Wolff pursed his lips. He instinctively felt his cousins and uncle to be in far greater danger here in the belly of the beast, even though he knew the opposite was probably the case.

"Someone will need to go and buy their train tickets to Zurich too," he said. "It's best if it's not me in case they're watching for me. Once they're in Switzerland, I can arrange for them to fly onwards to Lisbon and take the boat to South America."

"Actually, it's best if they don't take the train at all," Oster replied. He waited for a second, appearing to enjoy the look of alarm on Wolff's face. "That train will stop at every major city between here and the border, giving the SS the chance to get on and check identification."

"Even if you seat them separately, they may be looking for three non-Germans and they'll probably have a description from the Luftwaffe captain in Riga. It's too risky. They'll have to take a commercial flight instead. There's one Swissair connection to Zurich per day. It does make a refueling stop in Stuttgart, but that can't be helped."

Wolff did not know whether to be relieved at Oster's suggestion or irritated at him for the roundabout way he had delivered it. Instead, he tried to channel his annoyance into something productive. He leaned forward to show Oster how serious he was.

"Colonel, whatever else happens, you have to promise me that you'll get them out. I don't care about myself, but this was my last pledge to my dying mother. If they're caught, they'll be sent to a camp and I'm not sure they'll survive. I'm asking you as a gentleman to guarantee this to me."

For the first time since their meeting several days ago, Oster looked him straight in the eye with an entirely transparent expression. "You have my word as a German officer, Wolff".

The sensation of a burden lifting from his shoulders was almost dizzying and Wolff felt the need to lean against the countertop. But Oster was not one to dwell on sentimental matters. "As for what happens to you now, well, my boy, that is an entirely different story altogether."

"I do have an idea how you can come out of this in one piece. But tomorrow you're going to have to come to me and explain everything to Old Whitehead."

26

After a night spent with his uncle and cousins in an Abwehr safe house down some obscure west Berlin side street, Wolff walked to a corner of the Kurfürstendamm and was picked up by Oster and his personal driver.

Oster assured him he would have someone drive the field car 'borrowed' at Brandenburg-Briest back to the airfield and dump it nearby to avoid unnecessary Luftwaffe inquiries into its whereabouts. Wolff had argued briefly against accompanying Oster to the office to brief Canaris the following morning.

He saw it as utterly needless and another example of the colonel's apparent addiction to needless risk-taking. However, Oster had been adamant, and Wolff had been too exhausted from the tension of the day to oppose him any further.

Despite sleeping nearly twelve hours, he was still bone weary as they drove along the famous old avenue and past the Tiergarten towards Abwehr headquarters along the Landwehr Canal. Berlin was green and radiant in the summer sunshine.

There was no hint of the war of extermination being carried out on the dusty plains of lands thousands of miles from here. How shocked would the well-dressed men and women he saw walking along the streets be if they knew what their sons were doing in the name of the Fatherland?

Or perhaps they secretly already did, but were happy to ignore it as long as it happened in Ostland. Oster told his driver to pull around the back of the Bendlerblock and led Wolff in a side door and up through a labyrinthine series of staircases and corridors.

Eventually, he recognized the gloomy hallway they were striding down as the one leading to Canaris' office. Oster, who was a few steps ahead of Wolff, knocked once and entered without hesitating for a reply. Wolff followed him in the door to hear Canaris tell the colonel that "we" had been waiting for "you two gentlemen".

He was already inside when he saw with a start who the "we" were. Sitting opposite the admiral were two men with the double lightning flashes of the SS on their collar tabs, accompanied by the diamond-shaped sleeve patch and yellow blouse indicating they were members of the SD.

One of them, grinning broadly, was Udolph. The other was a slight man with boyish, almost effeminate features and a smile which did not reach his stare. Wolff's eyes went to Oster, who was taking his seat, but there was no assistance in the blank look he received in reply.

Had the colonel betrayed him?

"Come in, Wolff," Canaris said gravely. "This is Lieutenant Colonel Walter Schellenberg and Captain Udolph of the *Sicherheitsdienst*. I ran into them outside as I was returning from riding this morning with General Heydrich."

Schellenberg. The hero of the Venlo ambush and Heydrich's right hand man.

"There is a small matter they wish to clear up that you may be able to assist with." Wolff's heart stopped as he spotted the 'small matter' to which Canaris was presumably referring. What looked very much like the blue NKVD diary described by Kuznetzov back at the Red Star hotel in Sofia lay in front of Schellenberg on the admiral's desk.

Judging by his promotion from major, Schellenberg's prestige within the SD had only increased since his daring exploits two years beforehand. It was also amply clear that the SD pair's arrival at the Bendlerblock this morning was no accident.

What was uncertain was whether the move by Schellenberg, a man given to audacity, had received Heydrich's approval in advance. As they sat in Canaris' office, the admiral stroking the wire-haired dachshund in his lap, Wolff sensed not.

Heydrich was known to be a man who rewarded initiative. Schellenberg would likely be seeking that bounty. The Iron Cross which hung from his uniform breast pocket proved his form in that regard. But how had Schellenberg apparently known Wolff would be in the Bendlerblock this morning?

Was he keeping the building under surveillance for Oster's car, or was there something more sinister afoot? It was Oster, after all, who had assured him with a nod that he was "in the clear". Was this another of these ridiculous intelligence games in which the form of words used were open to various interpretations?

Or just a straightforward double cross?

There was no clue in Oster's face, which was inscrutable apart from his customary half-smirk. Nor was anything visible in the expression of Schellenberg, who was studying him with cold, gray eyes. Wolff took a second to examine him in turn. It was not what he would have expected.

Far from a stereotypical hulking Aryan warrior, Schellenberg appeared pale and almost too small for the uniform cap which sat on the desk in front of him. The only hint of any potential ruthlessness within his slim frame came in the form of a dueling scar on the right side of his mouth.

Even this appeared entirely incongruous with his overall demeanor. Perhaps it was just such an impression which had lured the men from British intelligence into a false sense of security. In any case, if muscle was required, the burly Udolph appeared more than willing to provide it again.

So they sat, Canaris and Oster on one side of the desk, Schellenberg and his pet thug on the other. Wolff was directed to a chair over by the window, very much on the periphery physically and in every other sense. The layout was like that of a courtroom trial, and what the blue hardback notebook between the other four contained would serve as evidence for the prosecution.

"It is with the utmost regret that I have to bring this to your attention, Admiral," Schellenberg was saying. In another of those infinite paradoxes that pervaded the Third Reich, Wolff had a sense that the SD man was not lying. "Obviously I thought I should discreetly take it to you first," Schellenberg continued, "so that we might best figure out how to handle it."

Schellenberg had a notebook of his own out now, apparently containing a translation of Ilyin's diary. "As you will see, Admiral, the Bolshevik spy made extensive notes of his meeting with the traitor." The offhand flick of the wrist with which

Schellenberg gestured towards Wolff reinforced his status as a helpless bystander in what was unfolding.

Schellenberg read from his own notebook in a quiet, matter-of-fact tone. "There are details of the proposed peace negotiations, the nature of the settlement and where it would be agreed. The Bolsheviks seemed to believe that a senior Reich official would agree to meet them in Stockholm to continue the discussions."

Schellenberg went on and on, calmly and accurately summarizing the extent of Wolff's interactions with the NKVD, which Ilyin seemed to have so faithfully documented. Throughout it all, the blue copybook lay untouched on the desk in front of him.

Nor did he once turn his head towards Wolff, signaling almost distastefully with his free hand instead when required. It was as if to interact with either more than the minimum required would contaminate the purity of the SD man's national socialism, the one absolute in these discussions from which there could be no public deviation.

As a piece of theater, it was remarkable, and Wolff had to marvel at Schellenberg's approach. He had placed responsibility for the entire affair upon Wolff's shoulders, but the unspoken question of how a mere recently-elevated lieutenant could take it upon himself to negotiate a secret peace with Soviet intelligence hung heavily in the air.

A lieutenant promoted by Canaris, moreover, having been taken from the cells where he was awaiting court martial on accusations of attempting to strangle an SS captain. An SS captain who, by remarkable coincidence, had been found murdered along with three Latvian auxiliaries at a house in Riga, after an upstanding civil servant who had taken a home nearby reported hearing shots from inside.

The captain's vehicle had later been abandoned at the city's main airfield by a man identifying himself as Wolff in the company of three individuals of questionable origin. It seemed Wolff had also previously requested the development of three passport images at Reichskommissariat Ostland the day beforehand, and then taken away the negatives to ensure no record remained.

It was all quite irregular, Schellenberg explained. The house in Kaiserwald was still being searched, he added, but property records indicated it had belonged to a Jew named Bernstein before the Soviets had occupied the Baltic states in June 1940. All in all, it was pretty incriminating.

And it left Canaris with two unpalatable choices: back his man and potentially go down with him or profess shock at the extent of Wolff's evil treachery and be tainted by association. The admiral absorbed the information wordlessly, leaning back in his chair with one arm resting in his lap and the other absently stroking his dachshund's head.

"May I?" he asked eventually, stretching out his hand. Schellenberg nodded to Udolph, who picked up the diary and leaned across the desk to pass it to Canaris. "And the translation?" This time, Schellenberg himself rose slightly from his seat to hand his own notebook over.

Canaris flicked through the blue NKVD book for a few seconds before looking over towards where Wolff was sitting for the first time since the meeting had begun. "Lieutenant," he said, "would you come here please?" Wolff obeyed and Canaris, via

Oster, passed him both items, further confirming his status as an untouchable for the protagonists of this discussion.

"Would you compare both of these and ensure you are satisfied that the translation is correct. You can use the desk over there in the corner. Take your time, by all means." Wolff looked the admiral in the eye as he accepted the two tomes, searching for some sort of cue as to what he might do, but received nothing.

Instead, Canaris blinked and turned back to Schellenberg. Oster did not even look at him. Wolff brought both books over to where Canaris had indicated and sat down to begin leafing through them, while Schellenberg and the admiral fell into polite chit chat.

He quickly rifled through the Soviet notebook and found to his dismay that Ilyin had compiled thorough notes of their discussion, all written in a neat Cyrillic hand.

"The contact, who uses the name Schreiber, is young but typically arrogant in the bourgeois capitalist fashion....the fascist offer appears to be genuine, they are clearly aware of the terrible mistake they have made....there may be potential here to allow the Nazis to decapitate themselves from the inside..."

Ilyin had attempted to cover himself against potential accusations of defeatism from his own side by stuffing his analysis with appropriately patriotic Sovietisms, but it was still as damning as it could get from Wolff's point of view.

Between this and Stumpfegger's death, it seemed as though Canaris and Oster would indeed have no choice but to offer him up as a sacrificial lamb. And what of Arturs, Urzula and Darius? Would they too go the same way?

If Canaris was making the decisions, Wolff had confidence that the right thing would be done. But for Oster, the viability of his sacred mission would trump all else. He cast his mind back to their first meeting just a few short days earlier.

There are no half measures.

The admiral is too squeamish.

Was this his deputy's way of moving the old man aside? Oster had given his word as a German officer and had seemed sincere, but Wolff had learned the hard way how the intelligence game was played. He was unsure what would happen now.

Schellenberg might insist on arresting him and taking him away to Prinz Albrecht Strasse for interrogation. There, the case - and Wolff - would be further broken down between the constituent parts of the Reich Security Main Office.

The polite, almost effete Schellenberg would withdraw, and the men of the Gestapo with the rolled-up shirtsleeves would take center stage. Perhaps aided enthusiastically by Captain Udolph. Or Canaris could pull rank and inform the SD man that the Abwehr would deal with its own turncoat.

Either way, it was the end for him. He was a pawn in the delicate, high-stakes game of chess between the admiral and Heydrich. And everyone knew what happened to pawns. As he closed the books and stood to return them to Canaris's desk, he took a moment to compose himself.

Though his fate was sealed, he felt strangely calm. It might be better this way, he reflected. Whether he died here or in combat made little difference, but at least he had fulfilled his pledge to *Mammu*. A lump formed in his throat as he thought of what awaited his father, but there was nothing he could do about that either.

The old man had made his choice. Such options had not been open to Arturs, Darius and Urzula. Or Anna.

He handed both notebooks back to Oster and cleared his throat, standing upright to attention in a way he had not done since joining the Brandenburgers. "I can confirm the accuracy of the translations, Admiral." He braced himself for more and was surprised when Canaris gently ordered him to resume his seat by the window.

Schellenberg was looking at the admiral expectantly, but there was a tinge of regret rather than victory on his face. He really did like the old man. Beside Schellenberg, Udolph was like a barely restrained Rottweiler, awaiting the command to jump up and march Wolff to their car outside.

Canaris cleared his throat. "Well, Colonel, I can confirm that your agent is correct. Lieutenant Wolff did indeed meet with two members of the NKVD in Sofia." Wolff's jaw dropped open in astonishment. Canaris was going to bat for him.

27

Even Schellenberg looked shocked at this unexpected turn of events. Beside him, the slightest grin appeared on Udolph's face.

"But there was a context to the lieutenant's meeting with the Russians." Schellenberg adopted a polite, almost pitying smile. There was no chance of Canaris talking his way out of this one. Udolph now bore an almost contemptuous victory sneer.

With a sorrowful look, Canaris opened a drawer and took something out before turning to Oster. "May I?"

Oster handed him something, also out of sight behind the desk. Canaris picked up the blue NKVD notebook, opened it flat at its middle pages in front of him and tossed some sort of clear liquid onto the pages. Just as quickly, he flicked open the metal case of the lighter which had appeared in his other hand and worked the flint wheel.

A plume of blue flame burst instantly from the diary before subsiding just as quickly. There was a startled squawk of protest from Udolph, who jumped to his feet and made to snatch the notebook away. He was prevented from doing so only by Oster, who rose himself and harshly ordered the man to sit back down again.

After a few seconds, Canaris, eyes still on Schellenberg, turned the notebook around so that it was facing the two SD officers. Of the pair, only Udolph leaned forward to see what was upon it. Schellenberg barely glanced downwards, before returning to meet Canaris's stare. The triumphant look was gone, replaced by one of cold fury.

"Those are the transmission frequencies and codes for a one-time pad given to NKVD agent Ilyin, real name Kirill Igorevich Morozov, for use in communicating with us upon Wolff's return from Bulgaria," Canaris said softly.

"As you are no doubt aware - and as Captain Udolph clearly isn't - they were written in ink which remains invisible until treated with the correct solution and heat is applied. Codes supplied by Lieutenant Wolff, I might add, in the cafe in which they met in Sofia.

"Morozov also held the rank of lieutenant in the NKVD. He was a Georgian, and had come up through the ranks with Beria. Morozov had remained a trusted figure even through the wave of paranoia set off by Stalin's purges. Moreover, his twin brother was also in the NKVD and was in charge of monitoring Red Army units in the Caucuses, where Army Group South hopes to secure the oil fields around Baku."

Canaris sat back and laced his fingers across his chest with a mournful sigh. "The Führer has been demanding for some time that the Abwehr develop more agents in Moscow, but the distance, the harsh regime implemented by Stalin and the lack of opportunity made that quite difficult," he said.

"We used to run agents from the legation there, but that's no longer possible for obvious reasons. It meant we have nobody on the inside within the USSR telling us what Stalin's long-term plans are. Information which would save the Wehrmacht quite a bit of time and resources, not to mention lives.

"Morozov was set to become our first major success in that area," Canaris clucked his tongue regretfully and glanced down at the diary on the desk as if blaming it for the debacle with which he had been forced to deal, before looking back up at Schellenberg.

"And your man killed him."

The silence hung excruciatingly in the air for a moment before Oster cleared his throat. "Admiral, perhaps at this point given we are discussing top secret matters, all those without the required clearance should leave the room," he suggested, staring pointedly at Udolph.

The heavyset captain opened his mouth to protest, but was silenced by a furious glance and a jerk of the head from Schellenberg. Udolph got to his feet, straightened his uniform tunic and performed a textbook and unnecessarily loud Hitler salute, before striding from the room. Nobody bothered to respond.

Schellenberg was staring at Canaris now, a mixture of astonishment and respect in his eyes. It was clear he did not believe a word of what he had been told, but equally obvious that his trump card had just gone up in smoke.

"And the death of SS Captain Stumpfegger in Riga?" he asked lightly, clinging to his last hope of rescuing the situation. Canaris picked something from his own tunic and rubbed his fingers together to drop it on the floor. He looked up at Schellenberg almost absentmindedly.

"I'm afraid I have no information on that," he replied blankly. "As you are aware, under the terms of my agreement with Obergruppenführer Heydrich, the Abwehr has responsibility for external matters only. Ostland and the other new territories fall under the SD."

He straightened. "Lieutenant Wolff here was in dire need of transport to the airfield in order to catch the last flight of the day to Berlin. He saw the Kubelwagen parked in the city center with the keys in the ignition, used his initiative and took it. He informs me there were no SS plates on the vehicle when he came across it.

"I can assure you that no offense was intended to our brothers in the Schutzstaffel, but it was a matter of some urgency. As for the unfortunate Captain Stumpfegger, I can only imagine his murder was the work of partisans.

"It may well be that there are Bolshevik spies within this Latvian fascist group which is being used by the new administration and they removed the vehicle's registration to aid their escape. Perhaps that is something the Reich Security Main Office can look into," Canaris concluded drily.

He stared at Schellenberg, and Wolff could see in the admiral's eyes the challenge to the SD man to play his last remaining card. Wolff hoped Schellenberg would not, though after Canaris's scintillating destruction of the SD case, he was almost looking forward to the *coup de grâce*.

It would be useful to know whether the SD had ascertained that the owner of the house in Kaiserwald, Arturs Bernstein, was the widower of a woman named Felsko. Though if they had not already done so, it would probably be uncovered in the future. However, it was apparent that Schellenberg knew when to quit.

He rose to his feet, lifting his uniform cap from the desk in front of him. "Well, I am certainly glad that we were able to get to the bottom of this, Wilhelm," he said affably.

"Indeed, Walter," Canaris replied. "I'm relieved that you had the good sense to discreetly take it to me first." He paused for a second, before adding, "So that we might best figure out how to handle it."

Schellenberg blinked in surprise at hearing his own words from only a few minutes earlier quoted back at him. For the first time since Wolff had entered the room, Oster turned to look at him, the glint of amusement in his eye almost prompting Wolff to burst into nervous laughter.

"I shall see you in the Grunewald forest to go riding on Sunday?" Canaris was smiling genially at Schellenberg.

"Same spot as every week," Schellenberg replied pleasantly.

"Colonel," he nodded to Oster, before swiveling to where Wolff was rising shakily to his feet. He was still reeling at how he had gone from a firing squad to being in the clear in the space of ten minutes.

"Lieutenant," Schellenberg said, and half-turned to leave before pausing. "You seem to be a rising star within the intelligence community. I'm sure our paths will cross again in the future." Wolff nodded back, unsure of what else to do as Schellenberg walked from the office.

Canaris watched as the SD man exited through the door before turning to face Wolff with his eyebrows raised. Wolff opened his hands without saying anything, the questions apparent in his eyes. Instead of answering them, Canaris said: "You need to be very careful there, Wolff. You've made a very dangerous adversary.

"A man so ambitious that he has previously kidnapped and now killed enemy agents on neutral soil to get ahead. Schellenberg has seen how Heydrich rose up the ranks by exploiting Hitler's obsession that the British were behind Georg Elser's bomb in Munich. Sofia was his attempt to gain Heydrich's approval in similar fashion.

"He has been humiliated here, and he is capable of doing quite literally anything to redeem himself. Anything, Wolff."

Wolff nodded dumbly. The dangers posed by Schellenberg, real though they might be, were the last thing on his mind right now. "But how…"

It was Oster who answered, the supercilious smile back on his face. "Your flight from Budapest to Riga, Wolff. How was it? Did you enjoy a little nap en route?" Wolff stared back at him. "The coffee."

"Yes, the coffee. I'm told you seemed quite aggrieved when you realized Udolph was being placated with such a fine beverage. So much so that you insisted on having some yourself." Wolff lowered his head in embarrassment. He felt tremendously foolish, a *naif* in a world of savants. He looked at Oster.

"So the codes were written in while he was out cold?"

Oster shared another of his conspiratorial glances with Canaris. "The original plan was to swap the notebook for another one, but we could not be sure that Udolph hadn't photographed the pages as a precaution. Unfortunately, the SD has access to the Minox too."

Wolff stared at him uncomprehendingly. "But how could you have swapped…" He looked down at the distinctive blue cover before looking back at Oster and Canaris again.

"Oh, that." This time it was Canaris who answered. He grinned at Oster before turning back to Wolff. "Standard NKVD issue," he said as he opened a drawer and took out two more identical notebooks and held them up. "The beauty of communism. They all have to use the same ones.

"We confiscated dozens of them when we entered Minsk. The Ivans were in such a panic to get away, they didn't even bother to burn the place." Suddenly, the import of how narrow Wolff's escape had been struck him, and he sat down almost involuntarily. He felt indebted to Canaris, even if it was he who had forced Wolff into carrying out the mission in the first place.

But this was it. This was what he had been searching for. His place in the Reich, except without the requirement of ignoring the evils of Nazism. Now, he would confront them. And, God willing, bring an end to them.

With the faultless prescience that had become his hallmark, Canaris said: "So, Wolff. You are one of us now." A statement, not a question. He held out his hand, and Wolff grasped it.

"Yes, Admiral. You saved my life there." Wolff was anxious to show he was not ungrateful for what he had just witnessed. "I'm sorry things didn't work out in Sofia. I underestimated just how low the SD are prepared to go in this war. It will not happen again, I assure you."

Canaris sighed and he sat down heavily in his own chair. "I blame myself, Wolff. I thought we had successfully isolated Heydrich's spies in here and but once more it has been shown that we were not careful enough. And now it is Germany who will pay for our errors.

"Our sources within the Bulgarian government tell us Stamenov initially tried to avoid being drawn into this matter. Firstly, because he was afraid of it blowing up in his government's face and secondly, he could see what any rational analysis of the situation would conclude.

"That we will never fully overcome the Russians and, without a negotiated peace, this war is bound to end in disaster, just as it did for Napoleon. We might have sent off Schellenberg with his tail between his legs there, but Heydrich has still managed to ruin any discussions before they had even started.

"Just as he succeeded in doing with the British through the kidnapping in Venlo. They have refused to engage with us meaningfully since, and now this..." He spread his arms wide mournfully.

"This, I fear, was our last opportunity. We are doomed, Wolff. It is only a matter of how long before the end arrives."

28

Wolff sat in the virtually empty departures lounge at Berlin's Tempelhof airport staring at the floor.

He should have been on a high after his narrow escape the previous day and the fact he had implemented his promise to *Mammu*, but Canaris's closing comments had left him deflated. Aiding the escape of his uncle and cousins had once more placed his own situation in sharp relief.

He had abandoned a life he loved out of loyalty to his father and found himself in a society he despised. It was still possible for him to flee, as his new status within the Abwehr would allow him to contrive a reason to visit a neutral country from which he could escape to Brazil.

However, the fate of Ludwig Wolff was no longer the only anchor preventing that. Wolff had placed his life on the line for Germany in the east dozens of times in the past few months, but only now did he feel that he was truly fighting for her.

It seemed strange to feel a sense of duty towards a place which his ancestors had left hundreds of years beforehand, not to mention discordant with the humility which is the inherent trait of Brazilians. Yet he felt obliged to stay and aid the effort to overthrow Hitler, even if he had only discovered its existence less than a week ago.

For the first time in his life, he had an honorable long-term goal towards which he could strive other than the pledge to rescue his uncle and cousins. Canaris's analysis about what lay ahead if they did not succeed was entirely logical. Wolff had witnessed first hand the fatalistic servility of Red Army soldiers who threw themselves desperately at German guns, seemingly ambivalent as to the consequences.

The initially positive attitude of locals in Ukraine, White Russia and the Baltics would be further undermined when Hitler's settlers arrived, intent on claiming their *lebensraum*. The best the invaders would ever be able to hope for was a shaky peace along a lengthy and impossible to defend frontier, the fear of an eventual mass Soviet counterattack interminable.

Arturs and Darius seemed to share his despondency as they sat glumly waiting for the one daily flight to Zurich. Wolff had been genuinely awed by the size of Templehof, which Oster had informed them was the world's biggest airport as he dropped them off.

The terminal was laid out in a T-shape, the departure gates forming the stroke at the top in a concave curve. The hall which represented the stem was almost half a mile long and completely empty as they crossed it, footsteps echoing from the bare limestone surfaces.

Hermann Göring had intended Tempelhof to be an introduction for visitors to the irresistible power of national socialism. Certainly, it had played its part in intimidating the family into silence. Even the normally indefatigable Urzula had succumbed to the general melancholy.

One part of Wolff sympathized with their plight. Despite the upheaval of the last few years, the family had always been able to cling to the certainty of belonging. Now, even that had been ripped from them. But he also felt resentment at their refusal to grasp the new reality in which they lived.

He could accept that it was difficult to believe the horrific truth about the Einsatzgruppen, the Special Task Forces, but that was what had awaited them. Arturs would have been executed, and Darius and Urzula would probably have suffered the same fate when they tried to save him.

Their property would be confiscated under the giant kleptocracy that was the Third Reich. Were it not for the arrival of Stumpfegger and his Arajs Kommando goons, he might still be trying to coax them to leave Riga. He had also risked his own life and that of his father to save them, but had not received a shred of gratitude in return.

He dismissed the thoughts from his mind, lest they might sour his last few hours with his relatives. He would be accompanying the trio as far as Stuttgart in case of any further attempted SD interference. Once the plane had refueled there, they would continue the rest of their journey alone and after that, he might never see them again.

He wanted their parting to be on good terms, for them to realize how important they had been to *Mammu*, and as a result, to him. In a way, they were his last means of keeping his connection with his mother alive.

As if sensing his need for that bond, Urzula began to quietly ask him more about life in Brazil. He had given a brief outline back at the house in Riga, but his explanation had been constrained by the overt hostility of Arturs and Darius and their precarious situation. Now, with only the flight to wait for, Wolff went into greater depth.

He told her of growing up in Porto Alegre, of the German community there. He told her of the city's great natural port along the Guiaba River and the smell of coffee and the hessian sacks used to transport it which pervaded his father's warehouse.

The beautiful summers and mild winters of the Brazilian south, the neo-colonial architecture cheek by jowl with more functional buildings and the simple cheerfulness of the ordinary Brazilian, in spite of the humble circumstances in which many of them lived.

At first, Darius glared at his sister accusingly, as if she were betraying the memory of the homeland she had only just fled. But soon his natural curiosity drew him so thoroughly into the conversation that even Arturs began to pay keen attention.

Wolff kept expecting his uncle to interject with protests about how they would only be in Switzerland until events in Riga had settled down. One of Arturs' most vociferous objections to abandoning Latvia was that it would also mean relinquishing the home that he and his late wife had made with so much love. But none came, and Wolff's irritation with the old man softened.

He was the nephew Arturs had never known who had come into their lives to simultaneously save them from a horrible death and tear them from everything they had ever held dear. It would take time for him to adjust. So absorbed had they all become in this hopeful discussion of their future that Wolff lost track of time until Darius suddenly asked whether the flight to Zurich would be boarding soon.

He checked his watch and noticed it was ten minutes after the scheduled take-off. The Douglas DC-2 was sitting out on the apron, its pilot visible inside the cockpit, but no other signs of preparing for departure. "Perhaps there's some bad weather over the Alps," Wolff suggested.

He instantly regretted his choice of words as Arturs visibly blanched and clutched his suitcase tighter to his chest. They fell into silence then, Wolff's deliberately hagiographic descriptions of Brazil drying up as the minutes ticked by and they all fed off each others' quiet nervousness.

There was nobody around for Wolff to query the delay with, and he did not want to leave the family alone to investigate further. There was only one other passenger awaiting the flight in the cavernous and otherwise deserted building, an expensively-suited businessman Wolff judged to be a Swiss banker. They were the only people really doing business with the Reich these days.

The gate at which they were waiting was on the left hand side of the semi-circle. After 40 minutes, Wolff spotted a middle-aged man in Luftwaffe uniform walking slowly down the corridor from the direction of the control tower and guessed he was one of the controllers going off shift.

He approached the man, who had an exhausted look on his face and was smoking incessantly. "Excuse me, my companions and I are waiting to board the flight to Zurich and it seems to have been delayed. Do you know what's going on?"

The controller looked at him curiously, doubtless wondering what such a young man in civilian clothing was doing away from the front. Eventually, he seemed to accept that the quickest way to get rid of the obstacle preventing him from going home was to answer. "Yes, we were told to hold it."

"Do you know why?"

This time the response came from the back of the controller's shrugging shoulders as he tired of the impediment in his way and continued to shuffle onwards. "Some bigwig, perhaps. Who knows?"

Wolff returned to the family, who looked at him with fearful expectancy. Conversations with uniformed men rarely resulted in anything positive in their experience. "Some bigwig is running late and has ordered the plane to be held for him," he repeated with a confident bonhomie he did not feel.

Arturs looked at him with an expression of almost pathetic gratitude mixed with pleading. *Don't let it all fall apart now.*

Wolff was attempting to resurrect the conversation about Brazil when he was silenced by the sound of the swing doors at the terminal entrance opening and crashing closed again. It was swiftly followed by the cacophony of several sets of footsteps making their way down the lengthy hall towards them.

Though the steps were not in time with each other, the smart and swift military rhythm rang loud and clear: they came from legs shod in jackboots. All three looked at Wolff simultaneously.

"This will be our bigwig now. About time, eh?" Wolff said, again attempting to lighten the mood. Nobody smiled. Instead, they remained rigidly in place, listening to the footfall grow ever nearer. At once frighteningly quick and agonizingly drawn out.

After what seemed an age, the advancing party finally turned the corner onto the curved wing of the departure gates. Wolff froze. At its head was Walter Schellenberg, striding confidently towards them, the taller figure of Udolph at his side.

Both men were flanked on either side by two burly Waffen SS privates, MP38 submachine guns slung around their necks. Behind the foursome came another figure, who was blocked from view. There was an ugly, triumphant smile on Udolph's face and, as the military men parted to let the person trailing behind catch up, Wolff discovered why.

There, clad in the shabby excuse for his best suit and with his golden party badge pinned to the lapel, was Ludwig Wolff.

There was a gasp from Arturs, who seemed to physically shrink into his seat. He had not let go of his suitcase since they arrived in the airport, but now he was almost attempting to hide behind it. Their quarry in sight, Schellenberg slowed a little as he covered the last few yards between them.

Wolff could hear Urzula urgently whispering questions to her father in Latvian, but not a word came from Arturs in return. From the corner of his eye, Wolff could also see Darius turning his head rapidly between the newcomers, his father and Wolff, attempting to decipher exactly what was happening.

Wolff straightened himself, spread his feet and stood forbiddingly in front of the family. Futile or not, he resolved that he would have to be physically removed before he would allow them to be arrested and taken away.

"Lieutenant," Schellenberg said pleasantly.

"Colonel," Wolff replied, his stance still as aggressive as he could make it. Schellenberg smiled sadly, as if apologizing for what Wolff was going to force him to do. In contrast, Udolph looked to be relishing what was about to happen.

"I'm afraid some irregularities have emerged in the matter concerning your charges here, and they will have to come with me." Wolff understood now why Schellenberg had not pushed the matter in front of Canaris the previous day.

Somehow, perhaps through an intensive overnight trawl of birth records in Riga, the SD had uncovered the link between him and his uncle and cousins. His father had been sent for in order to identify them.

Though Ludwig could not meet his eye, the shock and shame on his face led Wolff to believe he had not been informed in advance of what was required from him. He could imagine what was going through Wolff Senior's mind right now.

Judging by the way he was dressed, he had been on blackout patrol with his colleagues in the SA when they had found him. Wolff could picture the simultaneous bafflement and pride that he was being collected by the car sent by some important Reich official for a mysterious purpose.

The glances of curiosity and envy from the others who went out with him every night wearing those ridiculous armbands. How his father would have been looking forward to sating, or perhaps prolonging, the intrigue upon his return.

The SD would have told him nothing, of course, other than some vague nonsense about an important duty for the Führer. And Ludwig Wolff would have been vain enough and so desperate to belong, he would have gone along wholeheartedly.

Now here he stood in front of the son he had disowned a few short days beforehand and the Jewish brother-in-law he had turned his back on two decades ago. A man whose religion he had learned to despise in the interim.

"Well, Herr Wolff?"

Schellenberg knew without needing to be told that he had finally hit pay dirt in a way not even Canaris could overturn. It was clear as daylight that Ludwig Wolff recognized the man sitting in front of him and vice versa. All that was required was the official identification.

"Herr Wolff?"

Schellenberg's prompt was a little more forceful now. He was not a sadist and wanted this over with quickly. Ludwig Wolff's eyes at last met those of his son, and Wolff could see the regret in them.

Wolff stared back, calm but unyielding. He saw something flicker in his father's expression and the beaten down man in the worn-out suit straightened almost imperceptibly.

"Answer the colonel!" Udolph snapped, pushing his face into that of Ludwig, so that the old man took an involuntary step backwards.

"Yes," his father said quietly.

A thin smile appeared on Schellenberg's face. Ludwig Wolff cleared his throat. "I can confirm that this man," he pointed an index finger at Wolff, "is my son. But I do not recognize the others."

The smile instantly vanished from Schellenberg's mouth. He glared at Ludwig. "Are you sure, Herr Wolff? Take a good look again and ensure you are certain. I would remind you of the penalties for lying to a Reich official. Stand up!"

Arturs, responding too slowly to Schellenberg's bark, was roughly pulled to his feet by the two SS privates.

"Are you saying that this man is not your brother-in-law, Herr Arturs Bernstein?" Now it was Schellenberg's turn to invade Ludwig Wolff's personal space, but this time the old man did not budge. Ignoring Schellenberg, he looked grimly at Arturs, who himself appeared on the verge of collapse.

"Yes, Colonel," Ludwig responded, an undertone of sulky, embittered defiance entering his voice now. "I have never seen this man before in my life."

The fury in Schellenberg's expression was terrifying, but once more the innate German requirement for proper procedure and documentation came to the fore. Given what had already transpired, the rules would have to be obeyed here.

Wolff understood now that if the SD man had felt frustrated at having his prize snatched from his grasp at the last moment by a worthy adversary like Canaris, he would be incandescent at being denied once more by the stubbornness of an old man.

The only saving grace for Ludwig Wolff was that there was not much more they could do to him. He already lived in one of the worst areas of Hamburg, held a menial factory job and volunteered for night-time duty nobody else wanted.

But his faint hopes of advancing further in Third Reich society would die here and now, and Wolff could see in his father's face that he knew it beyond doubt. Schellenberg was too intelligent to have informed his superiors about the ace up his sleeve until it had been successfully played.

Otherwise, the hitherto pathetically loyal old Nazi might soon find himself in a concentration camp on some fabricated political charge. Ludwig Wolff would not have the satisfaction of explaining that afternoon's events to his SA colleagues. He would be forced to deflect their queries, and there would be no reveling in their curiosity.

Wolff attempted to wordlessly convey his own contrition at his father being dragged into this situation, but the old man simply nodded at him and said: "Stay safe, Ako."

He shuffled backwards then, eyes on the floor. There was a last piercing stare from Schellenberg and Wolff was reminded of Canaris's warning, before the SD man turned on his heel and strode back out the way he had come.

Udolph, a disbelieving look on his face, hurried after him, followed by the two SS privates marching on the double and lastly Ludwig Wolff, half-jogging in an attempt to keep up. How he would make his way back to Hamburg now was anyone's guess, but that was not the priority here.

Once the entire party had rounded the corner and were audibly headed for the grandiose exit, Arturs finally collapsed into a trembling heap on his seat.

Urzula gently consoled her father while Darius stared incredulously at his cousin, whose own eyes were still firmly fixed on the spot where his father had disappeared from view.

"You too, Papa," he whispered.

THE END

Real events behind the story

The events described in this novel are fiction, but they are something which possibly could have become reality. The peace offer from Stalin mentioned in the opening pages did actually take place as described, according to Pavel Sudoplatov's memoirs.

Historians are divided as to whether Sudoplatov, who rose to become a lieutenant general in the KGB, is telling the truth, and there is no evidence that Ambassador Stamenov ever passed on the information to Berlin.

Bulgaria was walking the tightrope outlined on these pages and may simply have wanted to stay out of the matter. If Stamenov did, it was quickly discounted, which is hardly surprising given the euphoria among the Nazi leadership following the early successes of Operation Barbarossa.

As someone with a long fascination for World War II, I have also striven to keep the contents of this historical fiction as factually accurate as possible elsewhere.

There was a Brandenburger division under Abwehr control, which carried out operations as described. It was made up of multilingual, ethnically German troops who had either grown up or lived abroad in locations as diverse as Palestine, Brazil and South Africa.

There was also a Brazilian Nazi movement which was rapidly crushed by a fearful dictator Getulio Vargas, who feared fifth columnists within the country's sizable German immigrant community.

And, last but by no means least, Admiral Wilhelm Canaris and Colonel Hans Oster, were among the leaders of the much-criticized German organization known as *Der Widerstand* (I refer to it throughout by its title in German, as its literal translation 'the Resistance' is usually more associated with organizations such as the French *Maquis*).

Canaris's and Oster's roles within that movement were broadly as outlined here, albeit with some poetic license. Ako Wolff represents the view of the majority of German General Staff officers during World War II, according to what the captured Abwehr officer Major Richard Ernst Heinrich Wurmann told MI5.

Unlike most of these senior figures however, Wolff is prepared to act upon it.

Owen Conlon,
June 2024

P.S. If you've enjoyed this book, I would be very grateful if you could leave a review (as long or as short as you like) on its sales page. It could make a huge difference to the book's success. Thanks a million.

Continue reading for a preview of the second book in this series, *Operation Second Chance*.

Acknowledgements

The author would like to thank his family, friends and partner for their support in writing this book.
Any errors of fact, history or geography are purely the fault of the author.

ABOUT THE AUTHOR

Owen Conlon has been a journalist for over 20 years. He started his career with the now-defunct radio news network INN, spent some time in Spain working as a freelance journalist and is currently Irish deputy group news editor at Reach plc, which owns the The Star and Irish Mirror newspapers in Dublin, Ireland. He speaks Spanish, Portuguese and French and lives in Dublin with his partner.

Also by Owen Conlon

Fiction
Operation Second Chance
Project Desert Fox

Non-fiction (with Stephen Breen)
The Cartel
The Hitmen

PREVIEW

If you have enjoyed *The Honorable Traitor*, don't miss the next thrilling installment in the adventures of Ako Wolff, *Operation Second Chance*.

Read on for a free sample of its first two chapters.

1

January 1942,
Gatchina, south of Leningrad, Soviet Union

"Strip," Lieutenant Ako Wolff told the man.

He had done this every time and, like the others, this man gawped back at him.

At first, he had attempted to explain himself, but now he just issued the order. It was for their own good, after all. And he was not particularly bothered by hurting this one's feelings.

"Take off your clothes!" he said again, more forcefully this time.

Slowly and unsurely, Agent A-701 began to disrobe. His reluctance was understandable. Aside from the humiliation, it was twenty degrees below freezing in the street and probably not a whole lot warmer inside the empty former machinery factory in which they stood.

Even with his own heavy woolen greatcoat Wolff could feel the chill seeping into his bones. He wanted to get this over with, so he could get back into the heated office the *Abwehr* had commandeered here in the town.

The town itself was nothing special, yet had a chequered history which summed up Russia's turbulent past. The last tsar, Nicholas II, had grown up at the royal palace on its outskirts. After the 1917 revolution, it had been renamed in honor of Trotsky.

When he became a non-person under Stalin, it had been given the title Krasnogvardeysk, or Red Guard City. Its latest liberators were calling it Lindemannstadt, after a general who was part of Army Group North. Meanwhile, the SS were liberating its palace of anything they could carry.

Wolff privately referred to the place as Gatchina in his own small, futile gesture of defiance. He studied the man's frame as he took off his Red Army uniform. Lean, like most people in this part of the world right now, but not especially scrawny.

Major Redwitz, Wolff's superior here in the east, had suggested the man be parachuted into Leningrad to monitor the situation on the ground.

Wolff had ignored that. The man was simply not emaciated enough for someone surviving the now four-month-old siege of the city on a diet of captured rats, jelly from boiled leather belts and bread bulked with pine sawdust.

A-701 would never have passed for a *blokadnik*. He would have been spotted instantly by the dreaded NKVD and taken in for interrogation.

The man was down to his underwear now. Wolff nodded in approval. No silly jewelry, at least. The previous September, they had sent three Russian emigrés equipped with radios behind Soviet lines to spy on their own countrymen.

Wolff had later discovered the three had entered public baths wearing small gold Orthodox crosses around their necks. They had been arrested, interrogated and shot. He winced at the memory. That was in the old days and the NKVD had gotten a lot smarter since.

This one's shorts were the correct sort, at least. Soviet-manufactured, with the fly buttons covered. SMERSH, the newly-created NKVD unit whose name was an acronym for 'Death to Spies', would check. So Wolff had to too.

This war had turned underpants into a life or death matter.

But he could not stop there. "Those too." The agent frowned at him, alarmed. Wolff sighed. He did not have time for this. "Take them off! Now!"

Slowly, the man lowered his woolen underpants to the floor and stood there with his palms shielding his privates, wary. Wolff looked down. The insides of the garment were filthy. He was not handling that. "Hold them up."

The man bent and hooked his thumbs into waistband, holding them forth for inspection. No identifying tags. Good. Less for SMERSH to work with. He looked down at the man's genitalia, prompting an instinctive, defensive squirm.

"Hold still, for God's sake."

Uncircumcised. Also good. There no shortage of anti-Semites in the NKVD either. He would have expected that from this one though, given some of the disgusting rhetoric he had spouted about *Zhydi* earlier on.

The man's hatred of Jews and covert Orthodox faith was ostensibly the reason why he had volunteered to work as a German spy behind Soviet lines, even though he was Russian.

Though really, you could never tell in this war. People did things for the strangest motives. Wolff had given up trying to analyze them.

A-701 stood there shivering in the sub-zero temperatures for a few seconds, while Wolff walked around him for one last inspection. Satisfied at last, he nodded. "Okay, put your clothes back on."

This time, there was no hesitation in carrying out the order.

Wolff walked to the window while the man dressed himself. Leningrad was less than 50 miles away, and, in the distance, he could see a Stuka plunging into another of its steep dives in preparation to release its bomb load.

He could imagine those underneath looking up and hearing the "trumpets of Jericho", the screaming air-driven sirens purposely fitted to the wings to inspire terror in civilians and defending troops.

Or perhaps they would welcome death as a release. They would, if they knew what the Nazis had planned for them.

Redwitz spoke neither Russian nor Latvian and relied on Wolff a good deal as his eyes and ears around Riga. He also needed him to interrogate and brief those, like this man, who volunteered to be sent back behind Soviet lines to spy for the Abwehr, as German military intelligence was known.

As such, he let Wolff in on a lot more than he should.

Such as Hitler's order to let those trapped inside Leningrad between the *Wehrmacht* and the Finns starve to death. Under no circumstances was Field Marshal von Leeb to accept capitulation and the burden of feeding three million civilians.

No, they were to be allowed to die of hunger. Hitler had even had his scientists estimate how long it would take if the Axis prevented more food being brought in. A matter of weeks, supposedly. Afterwards, their city - complete with its numerous beautiful palaces, cathedrals and canals - would be razed to the ground and the territory offered to Hitler's Finnish allies.

"Ready, sir."

The voice from close behind Wolff made him jump and he turned sharply. He had allowed himself to drift off into his thoughts, which could have been fatal. Granted, the man was not armed.

He would only be handed his Soviet-made Nagant revolver and ammunition just before he leapt from the plane. Russians were simply not trusted with weapons in *Reich*-held territory.

Too many fanatical Red Army troops had pretended to lay down their rifles in the early days of Operation Barbarossa only to whip out sidearms and begin firing again in a suicidal gesture of defiance when German soldiers approached to take them prisoner.

Wolff began a final double check of this man's documentation. If that did not match up, then A-701 would not even get the chance to display that he had Soviet-made underwear on.

NKVD patrols scoured the zone behind the frontline into which the man would be parachuted, checking for spies, deserters, saboteurs and anyone else they took a dislike to.

Anyone in that area had to carry between five and 10 different documents, including leave orders, a military identification book, a pay book and military orders.

All of these could be and were forged by Abwehr 'cobblers', as the agency called its paperwork specialists, so the Russians had begun paying special attention to the minutiae of such material.

As Wolff examined the papers, A-701 began babbling again. Wolff had forgotten the man's real name. Mikhail something.

"...will not let you down, sir. I hate the Bolsheviks as much as you do, most Russians do. They promised us everything and gave us nothing..."

Wolff's eyes flicked between A-701 and a last once-over of the documentation. The man's claimed motivation, that his parents had been *kulaks* - relatively wealthy peasants who had lost everything to enforced collective farms - seemed real enough.

He was either a world-class actor or he genuinely did despise the communists. That, Wolff did not have a problem with. It was his other utterances. He checked the A-701's forged military orders and tutted silently to himself.

Wolff had been asking for weeks for the cobblers back in Riga to abrade down the edges of their rubber stamps so that they would resemble the well-worn ones used by Soviet officials. Overly-crisp seals were a giveaway of forgeries.

This one had been issued with a somewhat eroded stamp, but it still looked too defined to Wolff's eyes. There was nothing he could do about that now.

"...I just wish I had been allowed to take part in some of the executions, but they only seem to let Balts and Ukrainians join the Special Task Forces. Even to take part in bringing those wretched kikes out to the forests, that would almost have been enough..."

Wolff stared at the man now, making no attempt to hide his distaste. Like the others, A-701 had undergone six weeks of training at the Abwehr spy school on the outskirts of Riga after first being photographed shooting a fellow Red Army POW in the head as a test.

Wolff's own Front Reconnaissance Detachment, as these spy insertion units were called, was only one of dozens up and down the 1,800 mile-long eastern frontline. Their operations were generally unsuccessful, either because the NKVD was too alert or because their agents panicked and turned themselves in.

Assessments from Berlin were that only 40 percent of missions on the eastern front resulted in any degree of intelligence provided. But Redwitz had confided in Wolff that the real rate was 20 percent.

The rest were either caught by the NKVD and executed or forced to engage in radio playbacks feeding false information back to their German handlers. When the Abwehr eventually twigged the game, the captured agents would then be shot.

It would not particularly bother Wolff if this happened to the anti-Semitic A-701. Even the man's cryptonym was depressing. The Abwehr had used handles consisting of a letter and three numbers for its *V-men*, or trusted informants, since the outbreak of the war.

The first one Wolff had dealt with had been A-459. That had been four months beforehand. Now they were at A-701, with no discernible product improvement. So many lives wasted on missions resulting in little appreciable gain.

It was a metaphor for this war in general.

He brought A-701 outside and they got into a *Kübelwagen*, the frontline staff car's canvas roof sagging under all the snow which had fallen upon it earlier.

Wolff considered using his hands to shovel it off, lest the weight of it tear the material, but then realized he did not care. He got in and started the engine. There was not much he cared about out here.

Most of his actions here on the front line were pointless. Designed to gain a slight advance in one area, only to be beaten back in another. As futile as Operation Barbarossa itself.

Even if the invasion of the Soviet Union had reached its planned objective of the 'A-A Line' - a new Greater Germany boundary stretching from Arctic Archangel to semi-arid Astrakhan on the Caspian Sea - the Germans would simply have faced the same problems on the far side of Moscow.

Relentless, periodic attacks from an implacable enemy along a theoretical 1,300 mile border, with Aryan colonists, the Nazis' so-called 'defensive peasants', providing a bulwark against the Slav hordes.

They passed the short drive to the airfield in silence and Wolff could sense the tension growing in the man beside him. As might be expected from someone who was due to jump out of a plane at 500 feet and land without injury.

Without any training.

At night.

Wolff had argued over the stupidity of this with Redwitz, but had been overruled. Time-consuming parachute training was not to be wasted on men who had less than a 20 percent chance of mission success.

Which paradoxically contributed to their low success rate in the first place. But, no. Slav V-men were disposable as far as the Reich was concerned.

A-701 would be given the same pep talk as the others. Told that a practice jump would have only made him more nervous. That he would be fine if he followed the instructions.

Feet together and knees bent as you come into land, though it was difficult to actually see the ground on a moonless night. Tuck your elbows in and roll over to the side, so that first the calves, then the thighs and then the backside hit the ground, cushioning the fall.

A piece of cake. And then the clincher. That first jumps were usually "lucky". Wolff hated delivering that particular trite phrase, mainly because they always believed it. They wanted to, needed to believe it.

They were at the airfield now. Four of the hangars had been rebuilt, but the six others remained as the retreating Russians had left them, dynamited, with their roofs twisted and bowing drunkenly to the ground.

It would be dark in an hour. A-701 would have to wait until then to set off and try to succeed against the odds.

Wolff decided to bring him inside, introduce him to the crew and remind them not to hand him the loaded Nagant until the second before he was to jump. And then only while holding a sidearm of their own.

With some of the V-men, he had stayed until the Junkers Ju-52 took off. Not with this one. He had no intention of listening to any more of A-701's praise for work of the *Einsatzgruppen*, the so-called Special Task Forces, in the forests.

OWEN CONLON

Thousands of men, women and children were being slaughtered on a weekly basis. It was happening everywhere. Just before Christmas, over 25,000 had been marched several miles from the Riga ghetto to the woods at Rumbula and shot at the edge of giant pits.

Wolff was angry enough at the instruction from Abwehr HQ in Berlin not to interfere with such matters. More specifically, orders from Abwehr chief Admiral Wilhelm Canaris, the man who had inducted him into *der Widerstand*, the German resistance against Hitler.

Do not participate, but do not interfere either. Somehow, he had expected more from Canaris, a German patriot who always found a way to frustrate Nazi orders.

He understood the logic. The murders were being carried out on the orders of Himmler, the head of the SS and one of the most powerful men in the Reich after Hitler.

Attempts to stop them would have been doomed to failure and might only draw attention to Canaris's anti-Nazi scheming.

But all the same, Wolff felt it was a lot easier to issue such instructions thousands of miles away in Berlin than it was to obey them where the massacres were occurring. He seethed at his own inability to do anything other than to pretend it was not happening.

One of the reasons Wolff disliked visiting this particular town was that Einsatzgruppe A, the murder battalion for the Baltics and northwestern Russia, had chosen it as its forward base.

This evening, he would return to the office, perhaps have a game of cards with the others and spend another uncomfortable

night on the camp bed. And then he would await contact from
A-701.

He was jumping without a radio, with instructions to contact
another V-man who had gone with one and who had vanished.

Wolff snorted. This one's chances were probably even lower
than 20 percent. He got out of the Kubelwagen, making his way
inside.

"*Leutnant!* We have been waiting for you."

The sergeant in charge of the Luftwaffe ground crew. Reasonably polite, but not overly friendly. They had not spoken beyond
the necessary up till this point and Wolff was slightly alarmed at
the man's tone.

If the sergeant was trying to tell him that the jump could not
go ahead tonight for whatever reason, he would not be happy.
Not happy at all. He did not want to babysit this one all evening.

Instead, the sergeant said: "We have been radioed by Riga. You
are to get on a plane to Berlin.

"Immediately."

2

Tempelhof airport, Berlin

Major General Hans Oster was waiting for Wolff when he arrived. Tempelhof was the city's main civilian airport, but was primarily used for military purposes these days. Along with everything else in Germany.

They had been obliged to fly there as it was one of the few facilities near the city center with facilities for night landings. The order to leave immediately for Berlin rather than wait for the morning had unsettled Wolff.

Seeing Oster waiting for him put him even further on his guard. The perpetually acerbic former cavalry officer, who had been promoted from colonel since Wolff last saw him, was not there to make Wolff feel welcome.

That much was obvious from the fact that he did not bother to get out of his chauffeured Opel Kadett, coupled with the terse nod Wolff received through the thick fug of the interior generated by Oster's incessant chain-smoking.

They drove off in silence and Wolff waited until they had cleared the armed guards at the gate before speaking up. The driver was the same one Oster had always used and Wolff knew the man was reliable.

"What's this all about, sir?"

"I don't know, Lieutenant. I was hoping you could tell me."

Oster wore his usual blithe expression, but Wolff could hear the undertone of frustration in his voice. Wolff considered that for a moment. Whatever it was, Canaris's right-hand man in the Abwehr and fellow anti-Hitler conspirator, was this clueless about it too.

Oster was looking out the window. Berlin was entirely in darkness. Blackouts had been mandatory ever since the first RAF bombing raids in August 1940, despite the boasts by Luftwaffe chief Hermann Göring that not a single Allied plane would ever fly over Germany.

"He's been keeping it all very secretive," Oster said finally. The pique in his voice was palpable. "I got the impression he was still waiting to receive it when he gave the order for you to come back from the front earlier today."

"The last thing came from outside and worked its way up the chain, so there was no reason not to share the information. But this seems to have come from inside the Reich. He has told me nothing."

The 'last thing', as Oster so nonchalantly termed it, had started the previous August with Wolff being summoned from a cell where he awaited court martial for attempting to strangle an SS officer who had shot a Latvian child in front of him.

It had almost ended with Wolff on the traitor's guillotine at Plötzensee prison.

Canaris and Oster had sent him to Sofia to negotiate a secret peace deal with the Soviets. They believed such an agreement would finally convince the ever-wavering army generals to overthrow Hitler.

However, things had gone disastrously wrong when the *Sicherheitsdienst*, the SS intelligence agency known to all as the SD, had gotten wind.

Perhaps that was behind Canaris's caution - and Oster's glumness. The admiral's insistence on secrecy to prevent further leaks was understandable. But the exclusion of his rabidly anti-Nazi deputy clearly rankled.

"How has he been anyway?" Wolff asked, attempting to lighten the mood somewhat.

Canaris had ultimately saved him from the SD's clutches through a stroke of genius. As a result, Wolff felt great affection for the veteran naval officer, though Canaris's command to not interfere with the Einsatzgruppen atrocities had strained his feelings somewhat.

"That's the remarkable thing, Wolff," Oster replied.

"He was quite down after Sofia went sideways, kept saying it had been our last chance. That only got worse when the Gestapo arrested one of our guys in Prague last October and he had to sort it all out."

Oster paused as he lit a fresh cigarette and wrapped his greatcoat tighter around himself against the frigid conditions inside the car.

"I'll tell you about that another time. Fellow called Thümmel. Quite a messy one. Anyway, poor Old Whitehead was even more down in the dumps after the Russians pushed us back for the first time outside Moscow just before Christmas.

"There is all sorts of finger-pointing going on at command meetings. Stalin has brought forward Siberian reserve troops which we didn't know about and it's being painted as an Abwehr intelligence failure. Which, I suppose, it is.

"And then of course, war was declared on the *Amis* the day after Pearl Harbour. Mind you, that kind of stupidity would depress anyone. The admiral was spending a lot of time visiting our people in the south of Spain.

"Said he was there checking on them monitoring shipping channels, but I think he just wanted to get away from it all. I basically had to take over everything here. But whatever it is he received lately has rejuvenated him.

"It's like he's got his spark back. He won't say why, though." Wolff again noted the peevishness in Oster's tone. But more than that, for the first time, Oster was addressing him almost as an equal. This really was brand new territory.

The general looked at him. "So if he does ask you about how things are in the east, don't lay it on thick, eh?"

They drove into the courtyard of the Bendlerblock, as Abwehr HQ was known, and entered the building through the stem at the center of its H-shaped architecture. The heat inside was stifling and Wolff took off his greatcoat as they made their way up to Canaris's office in the rickety old elevator.

The lift stopped on the fourth floor and Wolff trailed the general down the narrow corridor. They entered the office to find Canaris standing in front of a Magnetophon sitting on the edge of his desk.

Wolff had seen one of the new recording devices at a captured radio station in Riga, where it was used to broadcast Nazi propaganda and audio of Hitler's speeches to the locals. It was almost as big as a small cow.

"Ah, good," Canaris turned. "Welcome, Wolff. Hans, perhaps you can help me with this?"

Oster frowned surreptitiously at Wolff and went to assist his superior in fitting the massive, chest-sized tape reels to the device. Canaris meanwhile smiled and gestured to one of the two chairs in front of his battleship-sized *escritoire* before turning back to the machine.

Wolff sat down. The adjoining perch was evidently meant for Oster. The contrast with Wolff's first visit here the previous summer could not have been greater. Back then Oster had been part of a united front with Canaris on the other side of the desk.

Wolff had learned to take nothing for granted since entering the intelligence world, even the utterances of his anti-Nazi colleagues in der Widerstand. But the set up and Oster's overall behavior lent credence to his claims that he was entirely in the dark on this one.

Oster finished hooking up the tape reels and both he and Canaris took their seats. Canaris leaned over and was on the point of pressing play on the Magnetophon when he hesitated and looked at Oster.

"You're sure you've hooked all this up properly?" he asked. "This is rather important, Hans."

"I believe so, Wilhelm. But I'm not an expert. If you wish, I can have one of the technicians come and have a look at it." Canaris grinned at the impertinence of the response. Both men knew that whatever was on the tape, nobody outside this room would be invited in to listen.

Canaris pressed a button and the tape began playing with a low hiss.

"Good afternoon, gentlemen, and thank you for coming. We are here today to work out a means of dealing with the Jewish question in Europe. Last July, Reichsmarschall Göring appointed me in charge of finding a solution to that problem.

"By the time this meeting ends, we should have found that final solution.

"The most important thing is that there will be centralized control in the handling of this final solution, irrespective of geographical boundaries".

The voice was thin and nasal and Wolff frowned as he tried to recognize it. It sounded at once boyish and prissy, yet spiteful and commanding. "Heydrich", Canaris said quietly.

Reinhard Heydrich.

The power-hungry chief of the head of the Reich Security Main Office, the umbrella organization in charge of the SD, the Gestapo and the ordinary *Kriminalpolizei*. Who was constantly trying to undermine and weaken Canaris and the Abwehr as a whole.

And who was also - paradoxically - the admiral's regular riding companion.

The audio went on and on, with Heydrich detailing statistics around Jewish population levels across Europe. He said "evacuations" to the east had been approved now that Jews were forbidden to emigrate from Germany. "Small-scale deportations" had already taken place.

Wolff had heard of this. Jews being forcibly moved from one area of the occupied territories to others. For slave labor, he supposed. As far as he knew, the Einsatzgruppen massacres were restricted to the Baltic states and Ukraine.

On the tape now, there were occasional interjections from other voices, but only briefly, and to ask questions which Heydrich either answered impatiently or overrode altogether. Canaris detailed the names of the others as they spoke.

Heinrich Müller, aka 'Gestapo' Müller, chief of the notorious secret police. Rudolf Lange, SD commander in Riga. Otto Hoffmann, head of the SS Race and Settlement Office. It was hard to tell how many were present in total, but Wolff got the sense that it was more than a dozen.

He could not help but look across at Hans Oster, who caught the movement and returned the glance via side eye. It was abundantly clear now why Canaris had been so secretive about all of this.

Somehow, he had managed to bug a top level meeting attended by some of the most powerful Nazis in the Reich.

The audio had now degenerated into a long and repulsive discussion about "half-Jews" and "Jews in privileged mixed marriages". Wolff shuddered involuntarily. They were talking about people like his Latvian cousins, Urzula and Darius, and their Jewish father, Arturs.

Wolff had rescued all three from the clutches of the SS the previous summer, though it had almost cost him his life.

"Gentlemen, gentlemen." Heydrich's raised voice saw the others fall silent on the recording. There was no doubt who was in

charge of this meeting, wherever it had taken place. *"I feel we are getting away from the main point of today's discussions.*

"The very useful Nuremberg Laws can be used to specify who qualifies for evacuation to avoid these tiresome interventions on behalf of this Jew and that Jew. For particular issues, such as Jews who fought for the Kaiser in the last war, we have set up a special holding camp in Theresienstadt, which is around 40 miles north of Prague.

"This will be portrayed as a model ghetto, where such individuals can settle and live out their retirement. However, these will be a minority of cases. Where there are no such obstructions, Jews will be put to work in the east under appropriate leadership as part of the final solution.

"There, they shall work their way eastwards, constructing roads. The vast majority will be eliminated by natural causes. Those elements which endure will have to be dealt with appropriately to avoid, as the experience of history confirms, the germ cell of a new Jewish revival."

Wolff's lips curled back from his teeth. As he had suspected, the enslavement of an entire people to achieve Nazism's preposterous, impossible goal. Beside him, Oster was stroking his throat and grimacing.

Only Canaris appeared unaffected by it all. Calm. Patient.

As if the most important part was still to come.

There was the sound of Heydrich bringing the meeting to a conclusion, followed by the general hubbub of individual, inane discussions. Eventually, the audio fell silent altogether and the only noise was the slight hiss as the reels wound round and round.

The seconds became a minute and then another. Oster leaned over to press stop.

"No, no, Hans." Canaris shook his head apologetically.

Oster looked at Wolff again, uncertainty in his eyes. He settled back in his seat and the tape continued to emit its barely audible static.

Then suddenly, the recordings started again. There was more background chat, but of a lower level and with fewer individuals taking part. Heydrich could be heard asking people if they wanted a cognac.

It all seemed much more convivial, more informal than before. And with less echo. The previous discussion sounded like it had taken place in some sort of boardroom. This, as if it were in a salon, with carpets, curtains and soft furnishings absorbing the reverberations.

Canaris cleared his throat.

"What you are about to hear, gentlemen, was recorded a couple of weeks ago at a villa in Wannsee, just beyond the Grunewald forest where Reinhard Heydrich and I go riding every weekend. It is being referred to within senior Nazi circles as the Wannsee Protocol.

"And I think you are going to have trouble believing your ears."

Purchase *Operation Second Chance* on Amazon, Kobo, Google or wherever you purchase your books

Printed in Dunstable, United Kingdom

70094184R00211